Sleepytime

A Mercy Johnson Novel

Reita Pendry

Reita Pendry

July, 2012

DEDICATION

To Sam
1945-2012

ACKNOWLEDGMENTS

Thanks to Buffy Holt, for editing and formatting the manuscript for publication, to Tim Holt for cover design, to Mary Margaret Myers and Gail Gerebenics for reading the manuscript and offering thoughtful suggestions, and to Penny Marshall and Gail Gerebenics for comments on cover design. Thanks to Don Carroll, Laura Joyce and Faith Bushnaq for reading earlier versions of the manuscript.

OTHER BOOKS BY REITA PENDRY

China White (A Mercy Johnson Novel)

Sleepytime

A Mercy Johnson Novel

Chapter One

"Stay put, LeBlanc!" the voice commanded. Theodore "Sleepy" LeBlanc came groggily to, as a rough hand shook his big shoulder hard. He heard a voice calling, but he couldn't focus his attention quickly enough to respond. His long body curled into an "S" on the seat. The sun bounced off the tinted window of the prison bus, leaving a film of warmth against his shoulder and the side of his face. He wanted to slip back into the place where the warmth was all he knew, but he forced his eyes open, and tried to sit up. A hand held him firmly in his seat.

Sleepy used all his energy to fix his eyes on the face that belonged to the hand.

"Lieutenant?" he finally managed to say.

"Who the devil you think it is, LeBlanc? The Sandman?"

"What's wrong?" Sleepy asked, beginning to understand that there was some emergency, or Lieutenant Randall would not be on board his work bus. "What's going on?"

"Like you don't know," the Lieutenant growled. "Listen, LeBlanc. Somebody killed Harkness. Somebody let all the other prisoners go. So how is it you didn't hear the rifle shot or see who shot Harkness or see what happened with your crew?"

Sleepy rubbed his eyes hard, hoping to rub some sense into his head, hoping to clear some fog away so that what he was hearing would turn out to be a dream. The crew boss dead? That couldn't be. He was alive and cursing when Sleepy went back onto the bus. The crew gone? Not possible. The crew boss had a rifle. He had two men under him, and both carried rifles. Where were they?

"What about Strafe and Pockets?" Sleepy was still too numbed by sleep to realize that he had used the prison nicknames for the crew boss's helpers.

"Knocked out, as if you didn't know. Looks like somebody

slipped something into their coffee. We'll get the lab reports before long. Then we'll know what you and your buddies did to *Jones* and *Helms*." The lieutenant emphasized their proper names, and Sleepy took his point—inmates were not to take liberties with the names of officers.

Sleepy slumped back against the seat. "Lieutenant, I've been here on the bus since right after we got out here today. Crew boss didn't make me cut the weeds, because he didn't trust me with the scythe. He said I was like the walking dead, and he didn't want me with a weapon that could hurt somebody, or myself."

"Huh!" the lieutenant snorted. "From what I hear of ol' Harkness, he wouldn't give a rat's patoot for you, or any other inmate. Why you think somebody wanted him dead? Probably 'cause he was the meanest hombre ever worked this crew. And you're trying to tell me he let you sleep so you wouldn't hurt yourself or some other con!"

The lieutenant's face had turned a dangerous red, and his hand curled into a fist, just inches from Sleepy's face.

Sleepy forced himself to remain calm. "No, sir, I don't think it was out of any concern for me, or the other inmates. He said he didn't want an accident on his record, didn't want to look like he couldn't manage his crew, didn't want the paperwork. When he told me to get back on the bus, I took it as his way of making things easy on himself, not on me."

The lieutenant paused. If he gave Sleepy's explanation any weight, he didn't let on. But he relaxed his hand, moving it to his belt, and stepped a couple feet back from Sleepy.

"Get up and hold out your hands," he grunted.

When Sleepy complied, the lieutenant placed the handcuffs on him, leaving just enough play so the cuffs didn't cut into Sleepy's flesh.

"Get off," he said, as he pushed Sleepy toward the front of the bus.

Sleepy stepped outside, and into what looked like a cop convention. The area was swarming with officers. Sleepy recognized the uniforms worn by the Sheriff's Department, the local police, and the Highway Patrol. He could see cars from those agencies, as well as an unmarked grey sedan like the ones favored by the FBI. Somewhere in the mix he suspected there would be cars belonging to the State Bureau of Investigation. To add to the chaos, two ambulances and a fire truck were near the bus, flashing lights emitting reds and blues and whites. Line them up right, and they'd look like the flag, Sleepy thought. Then he spotted the hearse from Walkup's Funeral Services, its back doors open and a plastic body bag resting inside its hatch. Next to the hearse was the blue van with white lettering reading "Office of the Medical Examiner."

Right then, Sleepy was glad for the lieutenant's escort. The sight of the body bag made him light-headed and his stomach queasy. He didn't want to lose his breakfast on the lieutenant's spit-polished shoes. The lieutenant held Sleepy's arm and steered him toward a cluster of officers standing underneath an oak tree. The tree was old, and its height and fullness sheltered the gathering. A man in a grey pin-striped suit was perched on the protruding roots, clipboard on his lap. The lieutenant moved Sleepy to the man, who had to crane his neck to take in the length of him.

The lieutenant barked at Sleepy, "Sit down!" then addressed the man. "Okay agent Nash, here's the con from the bus."

The lieutenant stepped back a few paces and leaned against the trunk of the tree.

Sleepy eased to the ground awkwardly, trying not to topple for lack of bracing from hands and arms. Nash waited for Sleepy to sit, then looked hard at him, and back to his clipboard. "LeBlanc," he muttered, as if reading aloud. "B & E, felony." He stopped, waiting for confirmation.

Sleepy said, "Theodore LeBlanc" and paused, but then to avoid causing himself trouble, added "Sir."

"What kind of name is that?" Nash snorted. "The-o-dope, sounds to me like." He slapped his knee at his joke. Sleepy said nothing. He was used to the corruptions of inmates' names that prison guards could think up. He didn't much like the name himself, tell the truth. But his mother had given it to him, that he knew from the aunt and uncle who raised him, and since it was all he had from her, he kept it.

"So, The-oh, you want to tell me what happened here?"

"You can call me Sleepy if you want, sir. All the guards and cons do."

"So, The-oh," Nash repeated, "you want to tell me what happened here?" This time, he stared directly at Sleepy, and held his pen over his clipboard dramatically, waiting.

Sleepy looked back at him, lowering his voice slightly. "I don't know what happened, sir. I was asleep."

Nash smacked the clipboard on the tree root, and the noise caused the lieutenant and the other officers to turn to Nash, worried expressions on their faces. Sleepy did not move. Nervous officers with fire power was not a winning combination for him. He saw some resting their hands on their guns. Nash caught Sleepy's glance to the gathering of officers a few steps behind him, and laughed.

"Thought I'd wake you up with that one, The-oh. Now that I got your attention, let me explain something to you. We got us a dead prison guard here. We got us two other guards, looks like somebody slipped them a mickey. We got a work crew—nine men—run off somewhere. We got no leads, 'cept this big dumb guy we found on the prison bus. He thinks he can get over on us, claiming he was asleep. But we ain't buying it. You see, the guard was shot with a rifle. Thing sounds like a tank when it goes off. Even assuming our witness was asleep when the shooting happened, the shot had to wake him. He had to see what happened next. No living human being who ain't deaf as a post could sleep through that sound. So, Mr. Witness, you better get to talking, and talking fast, or we gonna have to indict you for murder, just 'cause ain't nobody else 'round here to indict. You get the picture?"

Sleepy looked at Nash, and repeated what he had said earlier, more slowly this time. "Sir, I was asleep. I didn't see or hear anything. I did not wake up 'til the lieutenant shook me awake, when he came onto the bus." Sleepy knew not to look to the lieutenant for confirmation, if it meant he had to take Sleepy's side against the agent. But the lieutenant did not contradict him, which he appreciated.

Nash looked at the lieutenant and smiled. The way his lips curled, it was more a sneer than any sign of warmth or humor. "What we got here is a failure to communicate!" Then he laughed. "Best damn Newman movie ever made, you ask me, Newman at his best, his very best. . . .unless, you count Hud, that is." Nash looked at Sleepy for a long minute. "Cool Hand Luke, you ain't, boy. So what's the story? What happened here? You know it'll go a lot better on you if you tell us now. You play games, trying to fool us, that's gonna cost you. DA'll ask for no bail. Or maybe the feds will prosecute, and hold you under the bail statute—nobody charged with murder gets out, under the federal statute. Think about that, boy. You just making a heap of hurt for yourself, stalling with the officer here."

Sleepy expected Nash to take out a toothpick, and start to chomp on it, so good was his 'good ol' boy' routine. If Nash noticed that his Brooklyn accent stripped the routine of its authenticity, he didn't let on.

Patiently, but aiming for a tone of respect, Sleepy repeated himself: "I was asleep. The crew boss always lets me sleep, because he says I'm dangerous with a scythe in my hand. I have a sleep disorder. I fall asleep at all the wrong times. I can't stay awake, no matter what I try.

Harkness saw me fall asleep standing up, several times. He didn't want to risk me hurting myself or one of the cons, 'cause then he'd have a bunch of paperwork to do. He might lose the guard post and have to go back inside. He was trying to protect his job, so he let me back on the bus. I didn't hear any shot. I was asleep 'til the lieutenant shook me awake."

Nash did not acknowledge Sleepy's response. Instead, he wrung his hands together and flung them apart, in a 'I wash my hands of this' gesture. Then he made a show of standing up, shaking his hands and legs in some parody of the old Hokey Pokey routine Sleepy learned in grade school. He lifted each of his feet, clad in snakeskin boots just slightly darker than his charcoal grey suit, and faked wiping them on the grass. "Bullcrap's too deep in here for me," he said. He turned and walked away, nodding to the lieutenant.

The lieutenant came over to Sleepy. This time he helped him maneuver himself into an upright position. "Come on, LeBlanc. I'm taking you to the hole. He wants to talk to you again, he can go through the warden."

It was no surprise to Sleepy that he was headed for the hole. He would be in disciplinary segregation as long as the investigation into the shooting and escape went on. Then, if charges were actually filed against him, he'd stay there until his trial. What surprised him was that the lieutenant showed some annoyance at Nash.

His puzzlement must have been obvious, because the lieutenant said, "Look, LeBlanc, here's the deal. I don't like you, or any other con. You got nothing coming, far as I'm concerned. But I can't stand that scumbag Nash. Thinks he's hot spit, and thinks we're a bunch of dumb crackers. Ever since they started this Violent Crimes Task Force, he's been lording it over the locals. Whenever there's a crime that could be remotely connected to drugs, the FBI horns in, holding press conferences and acting like the locals are only good for handing out parking tickets. I guess he's here because a prison guard was killed and a bunch of inmates escaped, and since half of them are serving sentences for drug crimes, he's claiming it must be about drugs. I can't see any other way the FBI has jurisdiction over this crime. Word is, Nash's bucking for regional director. He needs a high-profile bust right about now. He's liable to try to get that big title from busting you for murder. If you know anything about what happened out there today, you'd best tell it. Ain't no reason for you to do down, just to protect some bunch of murdering cowards. They run off and left you, don't forget. You don't owe them nothing. You'd best look out for number one."

"Thanks, lieutenant," Sleepy said quietly. The lieutenant helped Sleepy into the back of a prison van, and secured him into a seat, fastening the ankle chains to the seat in front of him, and one handcuff to his seat. They didn't speak during the ride back to the prison or as the lieutenant dropped Sleepy off at Receiving and Discharge to be processed into the prison.

Sleepy sat on the concrete slab outside the R & D office. Because he was now under investigation for a serious crime, he had to wear handcuffs even inside the prison complex, whenever he was moved from one unit to another. From now on, he couldn't move about inside the complex without an escort. He closed his eyes, and rested his head against the wall behind the concrete bench.

Suddenly, he felt the bench move with the weight of another body. He opened his eyes, and recognized a prisoner sitting next to him. The man kept his eyes down, toward the floor. His lips barely moved. He glanced quickly at the monitoring camera that was mounted on the opposite wall in the R & D area, then said, in a near whisper, "Keep your mouth shut, plowboy. We know where your peoples live."

Before Sleepy could react, the man was up and gone. It's started, Sleepy thought. He was the only man left on the bus when the cops arrived. He was the one they would pressure for information. The bus crew knew that, and they were afraid he would cave. They'd do what they could to make sure that didn't happen.

Chapter Two

Nash rested his feet on the warden's desk, his boots gleaming in the brightly-lit room. Sleepy sat in a straight-back chair. His height made him top heavy in the small chair, so he leaned forward and propped his long arms on his knees. Even bent nearly double, he could still look Nash in the face.

Nash shifted in the warden's chair. "Okay, The-oh, ready to go?"

Sleepy did not respond to the question. Nash's face set in a hard stare. If Nash was trying to unnerve Sleepy with his look, he would be disappointed. Sleepy had been locked up over a year. He was familiar with all manner of posturing by inmates. Some tried to take his canteen by intimidation. Some tried to start a fight, so they would have an excuse to gang-jump him. Some just wanted to try him because he was big, to boost their own reputations among their fellow inmates. Sleepy just looked levelly at Nash, without any emotion. Nash was the first to look away.

When Nash spoke, Sleepy noticed he had abandoned his fake redneck accent. Must be because there are no locals here to impress, Sleepy thought.

"Okay, The-oh, you don't want to talk to me. Then I'll talk to you. Let me set the scene for you. You're cleaning the shoulders of the interstate highway for all of nineteen cents an hour, the sun is hotter than a furnace, and Harkness is cursing you all because the job's not perfect, or you took too long when you stepped back to take a leak, or somebody waved at a blond in a convertible when she slowed to stare at the crew. So you and your buddies decide to get rid of him. It's no secret that everybody on the crew hated him. And probably for good reason, from what I'm hearing. One of you drugs the two gun guards. Somebody on the crew grabs Harkness's gun, the others overpower him, one of the crew shoots him, everybody gets away. Probably had their girlfriends pick them up. Dumb broads. Playing Bonnie and Clyde."

Nash paused to take a breath. "How'm I doing so far, LeBlanc?"

Sleepy spoke quietly, but he looked squarely at Nash. "I wouldn't know, sir."

"Oh, right, The-oh," Nash emphasized the "oh" even more this time. "You don't know, because you were asleep, is that right?" Disdain for Sleepy's statement dripped from each word.

In spite of Nash's sarcasm, Sleepy stayed calm. "Sir, I have a sleep disorder. I fall asleep when I don't mean to. It's not something I'm making up. Check my records, and see for yourself."

Nash threw his feet off the desk and shot backwards, causing his chair to slam the wall behind it. He exploded out of the chair like a crazed jack-in-the-box. "Because I'm not stupid, LeBlanc, that's why I didn't check it. Do I look stupid to you?" Nash was yelling now, and his face was splotched a deep red.

Sleepy looked at his large hands, cuffed and resting idly in his lap. He was afraid to look at Nash, for fear he'd laugh at the obviously-practiced "bad cop" routine.

Suddenly the warden burst through the office door. "What's the problem?" he asked, his voice a mix of irritation and alarm. Sleepy didn't move.

Nash seemed to be calming himself with effort. "Nothing, warden, everything's fine. I just knocked the chair over, trying to put my feet up."

The warden's irritation was now visible. "Put your feet on your own desk, Nash," he said, without smiling. "You feds can afford all the furniture you want. That desk has to last me 'til I retire, and unfortunately, that won't be for another five years. Five years, three months and twelve days, to be exact. So mind the furniture, if you please."

The warden turned to Sleepy. "And LeBlanc, sit up and talk to this man. The sooner you tell him what he wants to know, the sooner I'll have my office back."

Sleepy nodded. "I'm trying to tell him what I *know*, sir."

The warden eyed Sleepy, then looked at Nash. "How much

longer you gonna be, agent?"

"Not much longer. I think LeBlanc is about to appreciate the seriousness of his situation. I'm sure that will help his memory."

The warden grunted as he closed the office door. Nash settled back into the chair, resting his feet on the edge of the desk. "I solve this case, I'll buy the cretin a new desk," he muttered.

He began quietly. "Listen, LeBlanc, maybe we got off on the wrong foot here. I know you're in deep doo-doo. Your gang ran off and left you. The plan was probably that you would all take off, but somehow you didn't make it. So you climbed back on the bus, knowing that you'd pulled this sleepytime routine on these dumb locals, and knowing it had worked so far. I mean, I can appreciate your situation. You ain't trying to take the fall for these other guys, but you're the only one didn't get away. So, what are your options? You can sit on the bus, wait for the cops, tell them what happened, maybe get yourself a death sentence. Murder of a guard is about as serious as it gets, you know that. And even if the State wants to give you a break, let you plead to life without parole, you know they're gonna catch your buddies eventually. They're cons, for Christ's sake. They got no place to go. What, they gonna fly to Mexico and hide out in some small town where the natives don't watch 'America's Most Wanted'? I don't think so. No, they gonna do what cons always do. They gonna go crawl into bed with their girlfriends, maybe stop by to see their mamas first, eat a good home-cooked meal. Evening news is gonna come on. Neighbors gonna see 'em, call the cops. Nobody wants an escaped murderer in his neighborhood. Then they all coming back in here. They're gonna hear right quick that LeBlanc give 'em up. Then you're dead, regardless of what the State offers you. LWOP don't seem so sweet, you gotta watch out for some maniac with a shiv all day long, every day. Can't shower. Can't sit down in the dining hall. Can't work out on the rec yard. Life in solitary confinement is the only way to stay alive, and even that ain't no sure thing.

"I see how it might have looked to you, LeBlanc. So you said, 'Let me see can I fake it and claim I slept through the whole episode and don't know a thing.' Does that sound about right, LeBlanc?" Nash interrupted his monologue to look closely at

Sleepy.

Sleepy stared at Nash, eyes wide and motionless. His body was very still. His hands still rested in his lap. His mouth was open slightly, but he said nothing.

Nash seemed puzzled that Sleepy was not responding, but he continued his sales pitch.

"Listen, LeBlanc, I know the situation looks bad to you. Rock and a hard place, you're probably thinking. But here's the deal. I can get you into the prisoner's Witness Protection Program. The Bureau of Prisons uses it to protect their snitch witnesses. They got whole prisons of nothing but snitches, and in good places, too. Florida, California. Guys live good. T.V., weight rooms, programs they don't have in the regular joints. I've sent lots of guys to these cushy protection joints. All you got to do is be straight with me, tell me what happened, tell me who planned the break-out, who did the shooting, where these clowns are headed. You help me with the round-up, and we'll get you out of here. We'll put you in a snitch prison where you'll be safe. Then, you go to trial, tell the jury what you tell me, help us put these creeps away forever, we get you out of the joint, into regular Witness Protection. Put you in a new town, give you a new name, foolproof papers, a job, some money to live on. You can make a new start. You won't live grand, but you'll live."

Sleepy heard the "I can help you" speech, but it seemed to come from a long way away. His breath was coming softly now, and he slumped even further into his chair, his long body collapsing in on itself. He began to tilt slightly in the chair. Sleepy's eyes were still open, but he could not focus. He felt the straight-back chair start to move, and as it did, it made a screeching sound on the floor. He gave way to the overwhelming urge to relax. He was asleep before he hit the linoleum floor.

Chapter Three

Nash was pacing the hallway, waiting for the warden. When he called the command center from the warden's phone, he was told the center would page the warden. The medics arrived within two minutes, and wrestled LeBlanc onto a stretcher. It had been nearly ten minutes and the warden was not here yet. Where the devil was he? Nash looked through the partially open door to the warden's office.

Finally the warden rounded the corner of the hallway and headed for Nash. "What's the big emergency, agent?"

Nash was so furious, he didn't even notice the slight. "Dumb con. Sucker thinks he can con me. Thinks he can run this sleepytime scam on me, like he's been doing here since he came in. Well, I'm not falling for it. I want his records. I want all his records, and I want them now."

The warden's indignation was obvious. "Look, agent, I ain't on your payroll, okay? You better learn how to talk to me, or you can take your federal rear end right out of here. I run this joint. You don't run squat. Got it." He was speaking in a low tone. But his anger was palpable. His body was rigid, his face a dark shade of red, and his voice cracked. He spat out the words.

Nash realized he had committed the cardinal sin for an agent—needlessly antagonizing the locals. He hated to do it, but he knew he had to eat crow.

"Sorry, warden, I'm out of bounds. You have every right to be upset with me. That fool LeBlanc got me so upset, I lost it for a minute. I meant to say that I need your help."

Nash's placating words and tone must have done the trick, because the warden settled down. "That's more like it, agent. What is it that you need?"

"I need LeBlanc's records. He came in about a year ago, somebody said. I want to see everything you all have learned about him in that time. I need to study him like a bug under a microscope, see what makes him tick. I need to find a way to get to him. If I don't, we got some problems when it comes to prosecuting the people on the bus for anything but escape. They can all claim somebody else shot Harkness, and they might find a jury stupid enough to indulge the possibility. Then that 'reasonable doubt' crap some idiots in long black robes made up will rear up and bite us."

Nash hoped that by including the warden in his plan, making him feel part of the prosecution team, he could mend fences and get his full cooperation.

"You're welcome to his records, Nash. That's not a problem. I've been in corrections all my adult life. I've seen lots of cons try to fake it for one reason or another. You watch LeBlanc long enough, you'll see what I mean. I don't think anybody, con or not, is smart enough to pull off these sleep sessions without ever messing up, giving himself away. We've yelled at him, banged loud objects near his ear, shook him hard enough to shake his teeth out, picked him up and wheeled him from the yard to his cell, all the way across the prison complex. Nothing brings him out of it. When it's over, it's over. Until then, there's nothing you can do to bring him around."

Nash thought that was a bunch of baloney, but he kept his opinions to himself. He needed the records, and if he pushed the warden again, he not only wouldn't get the records, he might well get pulled from the case if the warden complained to his superiors. Nash reverted to his hostage negotiation training. Don't antagonize, appear to compromise.

"You may be right, warden. I'd just like to go over the records, if it's alright with you."

The warden and Nash had reached the door to the warden's office. The warden went to his desk and picked up the phone. "Get me Prison Records."

After a short pause, the warden ordered, "Bring me LeBlanc's file, Carter. I need it yesterday."

Nash forced himself to say "Thank you." The warden nodded.

"I'll just sit out here in your waiting room, and read through this file. When I'm done with it, I'll give it back to your secretary."

"Be sure you do," the warden warned. "Those files can't ever leave this institution. Security, you know."

Nash nodded and found a chair in the small vestibule that passed for a waiting room.

While he was waiting for the file, a young officer rushed into the vestibule, hat in hand, and rasped at the secretary, "I got to see the warden!" He must have run from a distance, he was so breathless. The secretary looked hard at him, but picked up the phone immediately and dialed her boss. "Warden, Officer Crest is here to see you. It must be urgent, he's in such an all-fired hurry." She smiled reassuringly at the young officer, and told him to go on in.

A few minutes later, the warden emerged, his arm draped across the young officer's shoulders. "Thanks, Crest, you were right to let me know as soon as you could. Now get back to your post." He dismissed the young officer with a smile.

The Warden came over to Nash's chair. "Good news, agent." He waited 'til Nash looked up from the report he was writing. "They caught Hammer. Hastings, I mean. Charles Otis Hastings. Meanest S.O.B. this side of Hell. Runs things in here, or so he thinks. He was on the bus, and you can bet your paycheck he led the escape. He wouldn't allow anyone else to be in the lead. Crest just told me. Said he heard it on the news just now. Said Hammer's old lady turned him in. Hadn't been home twenty-four hours before he beat the stuffing out of her. She must have got used to living normal, 'cause she was on the phone in a New York second, calling 911. Hammer thought she was faking, cops said. He stuck around, and lo and behold, we have him back among the fold. Great news, huh?"

"Sure is," Nash agreed. His mind was racing. The news couldn't be better, he thought. If LeBlanc thought he had trouble when Nash was asking him questions, wait 'til this "Hammer" guy got to him. Nash rubbed his hands with delight. We'll squeeze him from both sides, now, he thought. He'll crack. Pretty soon, he'll be begging to see me. Begging me to put him in Witness Protection. All I got to do now is wait.

As Nash was leaving the vestibule, an idea began to take shape.

What if he could speed up the clash between Hastings and LeBlanc? If Hastings was back in custody, he must be wondering what happened to his dream of freedom. Maybe I'll fill in the blanks for him, Nash thought. He went back to the warden's office. "Warden, how long before Hastings will be available for an interview?"

The warden frowned. "I guess you'll want to use my office for that interview, too."

"If you please," Nash said, forcing himself to smile. "I'd like a brief chat with him now, and I'll do a more in-depth interview when he's had time to settle in, get used to being in the hole again."

The warden snorted. "Hastings lives in the hole. He just takes the occasional vacation out to population, to check on the dimwits he calls his crew. It's almost like he can't survive in population. Most of the stuff he gets busted for is not even that bad. He just can't abide by rules. Anybody's rules. If he didn't make 'em, why bother with 'em? He smokes when he's not supposed to, throws his butts where he's not supposed to, spits on the floor, refuses work details, calls the officers 'Hack.' He's really a study in anti-social behavior. The truth is, we have more problems with Hastings when he's in the hole, than when he's out. From segregation, he manages to get in touch with his various flunkies and tell them what dirty work he wants done. Then some guy's head gets smashed on the rec yard, or somebody's cell gets feces thrown in it, or some guard gets piss thrown on him while he's checking the blocks. Hastings just lies back on his bunk, and waits to get word of the chaos he set in motion. You'd better interview him in the seg unit, where there's ready backup."

Nash tried not to sound accusing when he said, "I wondered why somebody like this Hastings got on the road crew in the first place. I thought the road crew was screened, no long-term guys, no guys with a history of violence."

"We are supposed to do just that," the warden said. "And technically, Hastings probably qualified, though I'm going to find out who put him on a road crew, and see that the proper procedures were followed. And if they were, this experience means we better re-evaluate the procedures. Hastings is serving an eight-year bit for a drug offense. There was no major trafficking involved. He's never been convicted of a violent crime. He doesn't do violent crime. He sends his henchmen to break the kneecaps. It's hard to prove that when the henchmen will take the fall, if they get caught, rather than tell on Hastings. We know about him, but we don't have proof that would stand up in court. So he earns privileges, like anybody else."

"What is it that you know?" Nash liked to be prepared for his confrontations with cons. If he was going to have to play rough, he wanted to be equipped.

"This guy is special. He does not care about consequences. What can we do to him, that hasn't already been done, is his view. He was raised by a crack whore who rented him out when she needed money. If you want to see a blueprint for how to create a sociopath, read his file. Now, he has one simple rule. Whatever he wants, he will take. If there's resistance from any quarter, he'll destroy it. Don't play with him. I don't need the fallout."

Nash did not argue. "Warden, I appreciate the information. I'll take your advice, and see him down in the seg unit, in that little interview room right underneath the guard bubble. If that's alright," he added.

The warden picked up the phone at his secretary's desk. "Get me segregation. This is Warden Watts. Who's in charge of the unit? Fine. Let me speak with her."

"Officer Carlyle, this is Warden Watts. I've got an FBI agent here, wants to speak with Hastings. Is he checked in yet? Good. I'm sending the agent down to the interview room there. Keep an eye out. You know how Hastings is. Yeah, thanks."

The warden turned to Nash. "Okay, you can go on down. He's back in his cell in seg. Carlyle will bring him to the interview room. He'll be in handcuffs and leg chains. Leave him like that. Do not remove his restraints. That's my orders."

Nash wanted to ask the warden where he got the moxie to order a federal agent around, but he swallowed it. This was his prison, he was in charge. Nash would have to take his orders and act like he liked them.

Nash was surprised when the guard brought Hastings to the interview room. Nash had expected to see a large man, someone with physical presence. Instead, he saw a guy who was entirely ordinary in appearance. Hastings was medium height, medium build, had lank brownish hair cut above his ears, brown eyes, a slightly pock-marked complexion the color of light sandpaper. If Nash witnessed a crime, and Hastings was the perpetrator, he'd have a hard time giving the cops an adequate description. Nothing about the guy stood out.

Hastings was dressed in grey prison garb, and was wearing the plastic shoes which marked him as a segregation resident. People in seg were not allowed to wear the prison work boots that were regulation for prisoners in open population. One of his hands was cuffed and attached to a ring in the wall next to the interview table, restricting Hastings's sphere of motion. He wore leg chains around his ankles. Because he was inside the prison complex, he was not in a belly chain. He appeared so mild-mannered, Nash was about to wonder whether the cuffs and leg irons were overkill.

All that changed when Nash spoke to Hastings. "Hello, Hastings. I'm Nash, FBI. I'm investigating the escape from the prison bus, and the murder of Officer Harkness. I'd like to speak with you about that incident. Before I do, I need to read you your rights."

The transformation in Hastings was instantaneous. He bolted from his chair, straining at the cuff which was attached to the wall. Nash forced himself not to move backward, assuring himself that he was well beyond Hastings's reach. Hastings's tanned complexion turned a deep red, and the veins at his temples pulsated. He didn't raise his voice, but he dropped the range to a low growl. He spat the words at Nash.

"I ain't got no rights. I'm a con. What planet they beam you in from? You can forget that Miranda bull. That's for if somebody wants to talk, you got to warn them first that it could hurt them. No need to warn me. I got nothing to say." Then he yelled, "Hack, get me out of here!"

Nash tried to calm him.

"Look, Hastings, you don't have to talk to me. You know your rights, I know your rights. But you could listen for a minute. That wouldn't hurt you. Let me at least run down what I'm interested in.

I think the information I have for you is something you'll want to hear."

Hastings bellowed, "Hack! Get me out of here!" Then he turned to Nash and growled, "What could some G-man tell me that I'd want to hear?"

Nash didn't bother to take offense. He pulled his FBI shield from his jacket pocket and placed it on the table between them. While Hastings was deciding whether to inspect it, he launched into his spiel.

"Look, Hastings, there's something you need to know. When indictments start coming down in this case, people are going to be looking at a lot of time. Maybe even federal time. You'd be surprised what the prospect of life in prison without parole, or even the death penalty, can do to loyalty. There's a good chance one of your buddies will break rank when the numbers start adding up. We only need one. Once one turns, the others will get on the band wagon. Even if your crew hangs tough, we got a witness who was on the bus. Right now he's claiming he was asleep and didn't see anything. What are the odds he'll stick with that story when he's waking up in a cold sweat, thinking about the needle? You want to play the odds, or you want to talk to me, give me your version, see if I can help you?"

"I don't need your help, G-man. I ain't done nothing, nobody saw me do nothing, can't nobody prove I did nothing. All they got on me is some low-rent escape charge. So what, they give me another five, and box car it? I can do it standing on my head. So get out my face, man. Call that hack in here, take me back to my cell. You don't, I'm gonna scream brutality all the way to the governor's office."

Before Nash could get to the door to knock on it, Hastings was yelling. "Hack, hack, open this door now!"

The guard who was stationed outside the door was in the cell in a second. "What's up?"

She eyed Hastings, checking to make sure all the cuffs were holding and that he could not attack.

"I got nothing to say to the G-man here," Hastings said. "Get me back to my house, now." Hastings stood up, and turned his back to Nash. Nash stepped back as the guard uncuffed Hastings from the wall, secured the cuffs around both his wrists and took him by one arm. The guard was large and looked like she worked out. It was unlikely Hastings would try her, especially in cuffs and leg irons.

Even so, Nash stood outside Hastings's range. "You better think about it, Hastings. You're not going to get another offer from me. You can get word to me through the officers here. They know how to reach me. It's your funeral, as they say."

Hastings's face twisted. "May be a funeral. Won't be mine." He stepped through the door and into the hallway, his body as tense as a wild cat stalking prey. Nash knew he'd never call. But this chat might shake something loose. That was how Nash would solve this case. Somebody had to talk. Otherwise, a bunch of cold-blooded murderers would end up doing five extra years apiece for escape. Harkness was a S.O.B., but he deserved better than that. And Nash deserved to head the regional office. Two worthy goals, he thought. Both attainable, if he worked smart.

When he was outside the prison complex, he reached for his cell phone. The number for his favorite news reporter was already programmed. She wasn't in, but he left a message. "Call me. I've got information about the escape." He knew that would whet her appetite. She had already scooped the other stations about Harkness's murder and the escapes, because Nash had called her the minute he got the call. She had tried to get into the prison to interview Sleepy, and would try again now that Hammer was back. Warden Watts was still "assessing the situation," and "would get back to her," bureaucratese for "no way, no how." So Nash was an invaluable pipeline for her. When she was reporting details about the case that were not publicly available, Nash would be "a well-placed source within the investigation." When she recounted information that was not confidential, she portrayed him as the agent in charge, the brains behind the investigation. The favorable publicity put him one step closer to his goal.

Chapter Four

Sleepy's cell in solitary confinement was small and without any of his usual comforts—his books, his writings, his pet rat Be-Bop. The cell had a steel slab with a thin mattress for a bed, a toilet, a small sink with cold water. No sheet or pillow for the bed, one rough blanket. No hot water, no radio. The only window was a small glass slit high above the bed. It was an improvement over the old days Sleepy had read about, when the "hole" was true to its name—a 7 x 7 concrete box with a hole in the center of the floor for body wastes. Sleepy had been in segregation two times in his prison term—once for being out of bounds, talking to his best friend, Rosie, a minute too long before returning to his cell for count, and once for fighting when one of Hammer's crew smacked him for no reason. Each time, he did fifteen days, saw the review board, and was back in general population. Escape was different. He might do the rest of his time in solitary. He'd miss Rosie, and Be-Bop, but in other respects, it wouldn't matter. He'd sleep in solitary just as soundly as anywhere else. He worried about Be-Bop, but he figured his property was pretty safe. He doubted anyone would want the history books he had ordered with his prison wages, and no one would be interested in his writings. The songs he wrote were not worth anything to anybody but him.

One of the guards had slipped Sleepy a newspaper. The guard didn't believe that Sleepy had helped Hammer escape, or been part of the shooting and assaults on the other guards. He knew Sleepy couldn't stay awake. He'd seen him fall asleep standing up. The guard wouldn't buck the powers that be, but when he could help Sleepy in small ways, he would. The newspaper was gold to Sleepy. It would occupy him for a day, in between naps. And it gave him corners, and borders and other empty spaces to use for kites—small messages inmates in segregation slipped to inmates in general population. He just hoped his pencil would hold out long enough for him to get settled in down here.

Sleepy pulled the newspaper from underneath his mattress. His hiding place would not be good enough, if the guards searched his cell, but it worked for everyday intrusions like bringing his food tray. If he got caught with the paper, he would get a write-up and a few additional days in segregation. His worry was that the administration might trace the newspaper to the guard who brought it. Sleepy might not be able to cover for him, so the best thing was to make sure the paper never got spotted.

Sleepy opened the paper and took in his breath. The headlines were at least two inches high. "VIOLENT CONVICTS ON LOOSE!" Underneath, in smaller type, "Why are convicted felons on road crew?" The article quoted a highly placed source within the investigation. Probably that jerk Nash, Sleepy thought. The article blasted the prison administration for allowing convicts with a propensity for violence to be on the road crew, and named several of the escapees as examples. Curiously, Hammer was not one of the names. Sleepy wondered about that, since Hammer was known throughout the prison as a very dangerous man. He felt bad for the warden, who had always been decent to him. Watts was no bleeding heart, but he listened to reason. He made decisions that he thought were fair, and then he stuck by them. Sleepy wondered what would happen to him. He liked the fact that Watts did not make excuses for the men being on the road crew. All he said was, "We have extensive review procedures to assure that men placed on work crews do not pose safety threats. If the procedures were not followed in this case, we will take the appropriate action. What the media is overlooking is that this is a first for us. We have used road crews for over ten years, since state legislation restored inmate rights to work outside the prison for extra wages, and we have never had one incident. I would match our safety record against that of any other penal institution in the country. We will continue our investigation in this case, and when we have additional information, we will inform the public." Watts had read the prepared statement at a news conference, and then answered questions. From the articles in the paper, it seemed he had done a very good job of diffusing the outrage expressed at the escapes.

In the section reporting mostly local news, Sleepy noticed an article about Harkness's wife. He was surprised to see how young she looked in the picture which ran with the article. Harkness had to be fifty, but his wife looked like she was still in her twenties. The reporter spoke with her at her home, where she was surrounded by relatives and friends. She said what a good man her husband was, that everyone who knew him loved him, that he was her best friend. The reporter described her as "overcome by grief," but noted that local court records showed at least two cases where she had charged Harkness with spousal abuse.

From what Sleepy knew of Harkness, the spousal abuse seemed more likely than the portrait of the man loved by all. When he was through the local news, and about to open the Sports page, he heard a noise outside his cell door. He got up, and put his ear against the door. The hallway was quiet. But he smelled something. Something acrid. What was it? It smelled like smoke. He knew the prison was a non-smoking facility. Some people sneaked smokes occasionally, but the seg time was stiff, and it wasn't really worth it to any but the most die-hard nicotine addicts.

Suddenly Sleepy saw something white wafting underneath his door. It was smoke. Something was on fire, and it was near his cell. The fear gripped him. He was terrified of fire, but especially when he was locked up, and had no way to run from it. He knew he could be dead before any guards got to him. He banged on his cell door as loudly as he could. He took off his shoe, and used it to pound the door. The plastic shower shoe made slapping noises, but it was not even as loud as Sleepy could hit with his fists. He abandoned the shoe, and pounded the door alternately with his fists, scraping his knuckles in the process. Sweat was drenching his shirt. He took the shirt off, and put it over his face, to use as a mask. With his other hand, he kept up the pounding on the door.

After what seemed like a decade, his door opened. The corridor outside his cell was filled with a thick white smoke. He could barely see the guard who opened the door. The guard wore a gas mask, and gave Sleepy a wet towel. "Here, LeBlanc. Put this over your face and keep it there. Breathe through the towel. Hold onto my belt and walk right behind me. I've called in the alarm, so the fire

22

crew will be on its way down here. We just need to get you out to the atrium."

Sleepy's eyes ran with tears, and he coughed deep lung-busting coughs. He grabbed the guard's belt and held on. The atrium was the common area at the center of the cellblock, where all the corridors intersected. The control bubble was in the atrium. From the bubble, officers controlled all movement in the cellblocks, mechanically opening and closing doors. Guards also had keys to open all the doors, in case of an electrical malfunction. In this old building, electrical failures were common.

The fire must be confined to his corridor, Sleepy thought. If it had been elsewhere in the unit, he doubted the guard would be taking him to the atrium for shelter. With a heaviness in his being, he knew the details. The fire was for his cell. Somebody had set a fire, to burn him. Or at least to scare him. The war was on. Sleepy against the crew. He'd have to get the word out that he was asleep on the bus when Harkness was killed, that he didn't see anything. If he wanted to stay alive, he had to make them believe him. Today he was rescued. Apparently no one working the unit on today's shift was on the crew's payroll. Next time he might not be so lucky.

Chapter Five

The housing unit officers used heavy-duty fans to evacuate the smoke from the corridor and from Sleepy's cell. After a few hours, he was allowed to go back. He was still shaken, but felt better being back where he was. He could have switched cells, but he figured, why bother? Hammer's network was good. They would find him, and he would be no safer in a new house than he was here. Better to try to deal with the problem head-on. He wanted to get a kite to Rosie. He knew the guy in the kitchen who handled the trays for the segregation unit. He'd ball up a kite in his milk carton, hoping the guy would check it. Since passing kites that way was a regular thing, the kid would probably know to check the carton and pass on the note.

He fished out the note he had found in his uniform pocket. Sleepy read the kite again. "Birds nesting, missing one. Watch." He knew the kite came from Rosie. The message was in the pocket of the uniform the guard brought him when he got the rare shower he was entitled to in the hole. Rosie worked in the laundry. He would know when the escapees got caught. Sleepy was surprised the crew was rounded up so quickly. He wondered who the missing bird was. Either one of the road crew was smart enough to leave the country, or something had happened to him.

From a tiny slit in the sole of his shoe, he removed a pencil stub. He examined the point and was pleased to find it intact. Pencils and paper were among the supplies inmates in population could purchase from the canteen. In the hole, where anything that could be used as a weapon or to contact other inmates was contraband, pencils and paper were guarded like gold. Sleepy didn't know when he would get another newspaper, so he had to economize. He tore off a small corner piece and wrote, "Feed Be-Bop."

Rosie hated rats, and wouldn't have anything to do with the pet at first. When Sleepy first saw Rosie react to the idea of the pet rat, he couldn't help but laugh. Rosie weighed over two hundred and seventy-five pounds, all of it muscle. He was a Golden Gloves champion heavyweight in his earlier days. When he got too old to contend with the youngsters in the ring, he got a job as a bouncer at a tony gentlemen's club downtown in the state capitol. He did so well there, he was about to start his own security firm, when a set-up landed him here. He was not afraid of the Devil himself, except when that little Be-Bop showed up. Then he acted like an army of terrorists was after him.

No matter how much Rosie hated the idea of the rat, he would make sure Sleepy had what he needed. Sleepy would do the same for Rosie. If Sleepy wanted his rat fed, Rosie would feed the rat, somehow.

Sleepy drained all the milk from his carton, and used his shirt tail to wipe it clean. He put the note in the corner, and closed the carton.

Sleepy knew that if he was in solitary, the men who were caught would be, too. Sleepy couldn't see them, because the cellblock was arranged to prevent contact between inmates in that unit, and to give the guards in the control bubble in the center of the unit a way to control the movements of the inmates and prevent trouble. But Hammer and his group would find a way around the rules, that Sleepy knew. Before long he'd hear from them again, one way or another.

When the electronic doors to the unit opened, Sleepy barely noticed. The clanging and whining of the old mechanism rarely even entered his conscious mind, so long had he heard it and learned to ignore it. He was surprised when a guard came to his cell door, and rattled it. "LeBlanc!" the guard called loudly. Before Sleepy could rise off the bunk and get to the cell door, the guard called his name again and opened the door. He could get a write-up for not answering up as soon as his name was called.

The guard looked hard at him. "LeBlanc, put out your hands." Sleepy held his hands out to the guard, who placed plastic security cuffs on his hands, tightening them just a fraction shy of hurting. "Step back," the guard ordered.

The officer turned Sleepy around and pointed him toward the

hallway. He took Sleepy by his bound wrists, and steered him down the narrow corridor, first locking the door to his cell.

"Where am I going?" Sleepy asked.

"Where I take you," the guard replied.

Okay, Sleepy thought, he's new, and has something to prove. No need to make a fuss.

A few turns down hallways just like the one outside Sleepy's cell ended in a brightly lit area underneath the bubble. "The atrium" was a euphemism. If the sun ever shone into it, Sleepy never saw it. Since segregation was a lockdown unit, there were no inmates in the area, no one sweeping or mopping, no one walking about. Maintenance was done on a strict schedule, and the guards accompanied the trusties who did the cleaning, to prevent unauthorized contact between the trusties and the inmates in the hole. Sleepy looked up at the bubble. He couldn't recognize any faces through the smoked glass.

There was a park bench bolted to the floor outside a doorway. The guard directed Sleepy to the bench, then motioned for him to sit. The guard knocked on the door. Sleepy was not happy to see Nash open the door, lean out, and call his name. "So, The-oh, wha's up, my man?"

Sleepy sat still on the bench. Nash said to the guard, "It's okay. Leave him with me. And uncuff him."

The guard looked like he wanted to question Nash, but he did not. He took a device from his belt ring and unlocked the plastic cuffs. "He's all yours," he said to Nash. The meaning was clear— you asked for him to be uncuffed, if he hurts you, it's on your head, not mine.

"Come on in, The-oh," Nash invited. Sleepy got up and followed Nash into the tiny cubicle he was using as a temporary office. Sleepy sat on the chair beside the desk, even though it brought him into too-close contact with Nash.

Nash remained standing. He looked at Sleepy and said, "Hammer's back."

Sleepy did not react. So Hammer's not the missing bird, he thought. The thought surprised him. He figured the cops and FBI would get all the crew sooner or later. Hammer would be later, he thought. He wondered what happened. Nash must have sensed his curiosity, because he explained.

"Hammer beat up his girlfriend. She called the cops. It's a new day out there, The-oh. Women don't like getting beat on. They got all these help lines and crisis lines. Woman just got to pick up the phone, dial 911, and say 'Help,' and the cavalry is on the way."

Sleepy thought, from Nash's tone, that he might be a wife beater himself.

"But that ain't all. We got all the crew now, except Watson. Watson must have decided he'd rather be dead than back in the joint. Dumbass drew down on the cops when they had his house surrounded. They shot up the house and Watson in it. Riddled him full of holes, cops said. I didn't see it.

But guess where they found your buddies? Most of them were laying up with their girlfriends. 'Cept Robinson. He was at the DMV! Idiot tried to get his drivers license. It expired while he was locked up!" Nash was gloating. Sleepy wanted to laugh, too, but he wouldn't give Nash the satisfaction. It was pretty dumb, he had to admit. Why Robinson needed a driver's license, he couldn't guess. All he ever drove were getaway cars.

Nash emphasized his point. "Hammer will probably think you're talking to us. Who else could we get information from? You're the only one on the crew who didn't escape. Hammer will figure you'll be busy trying to save yourself, so you won't care about him. He'll try to shut you up, you know that. He and his boys will be coming at you from every side."

Sleepy didn't respond. What could he say to that? Of course he knew it. Did Nash know about the fire? If he did, he didn't let on. Sleepy couldn't think of a better way for Hammer to announce his intentions.

Nash waited, like he was giving Sleepy time to digest the news. Sleepy played along, appearing to think about his situation. Then Nash said, "He's gonna start pressing you, The-oh. You know that. Hammer will get his boys back together down here in segregation, and they'll all start pressing you. You're gonna be in a world of trouble then. You'll want to speak with me. You'll need my help. You know it's gonna go down that way, so why don't you just save yourself some worry, and talk to me?"

Sleepy stood up. "It's lunchtime. I don't want to miss lunch. Can you get me back to my house now?"

Nash looked irritated. "You'll pay for this, LeBlanc. You'll be a sitting duck for Hammer and his crew. I don't care if they kill you. You're so hardheaded, you go ahead and deal with them. I'll be waiting to pick up the pieces. If there are any."

Nash handed Sleepy a newspaper. It was yesterday's edition. Sleepy was hoping he could get the follow-up to the first day of coverage of the escape. He looked at Nash. Nash said, "Go ahead, take it. Read it. I think you'll find the story about you pretty interesting."

Nash's sneer got on Sleepy's nerves. But he wanted to know what the paper said about him. His aunt and uncle would probably read it. Brenda might even read it, if she got the time. He didn't want them to think he was in trouble again.

The article listed the background of each of the escapees, and Sleepy. He knew most of what he read about the escapees— juvenile delinquents, graduating to more serious crimes, none presently serving sentences for crimes of violence, but some with violent histories. He scanned their articles. When he got to the article about him, he read it quickly. He had only one conviction, the breaking and entering he was serving time for now. The story made him seem like a nut case. Caught in the department store dressing room, asleep on the floor. Surrounded by men's clothes, all still with the store's tags. Represented by one of the city's best criminal defense attorneys. Didn't testify. Convicted after two days of jury deliberations. It was all true, as far as it went.

He looked up to find Nash looking at him. "So, The-oh, what do you think Hammer will do when he reads about that wimpy charge? He'll probably laugh himself silly. Makes you look like some nerd, or some nut case. Either way, that will spell "W - E - A – K" to the Hammer. You better think about my offer. I can help you."

Sleepy handed Nash the paper. "Thanks, sir. I appreciate your letting me read the news."

When it was clear he had nothing more to say, Nash turned

angrily to the door, and opened it. "Officer!" he called out. When the guard came to the room, he pointed to Sleepy. "Take him out of here," he said. The guard looked pissed to be ordered around by Nash, but he motioned to Sleepy to step out of the room. As Sleepy was leaving, Nash said, "Remember, The-oh, call me anytime. And hope it's not too late when you do."

Chapter Six

Rosie undid the wadded-up note from Sleepy. Another kite already. Not good news. Sleepy's first kite, asking Rosie to take care of his pet rat, just got to Rosie late yesterday. Now, a more urgent message. "Call for help." It was not like Sleepy to involve anybody from the outside in his situation. Rosie knew that meant things were heating up. He'd read that Hammer was back in the prison. He could guess that the heat came from Hammer or one of his loyal idiot band.

Rosie read the note and put it in his pocket. Luckily, he was just minutes from finishing his shift in the laundry. When his shift ended, he clocked out and headed for the phone bank outside his cellblock. When he first got to the prison, some of the young toughs tried to tell him he had to pay them to use the phones. Rosie did not like violence, but he knew he was not going to pay extortion money for phone privileges. The toughs needed a lesson in civility and he took on the obligation of teacher. When the word spread that his quick jab could send even a big man to his knees, the toughs stayed away from Rosie. Today none of them were at the phone bank.

Rosie selected the phone that was most likely to be working, and dialed a Washington, D.C. number. He was relieved when he heard his cousin's voice.

"Sam Lester. Mercy Johnson and Associates."

"Sam, it's Rosie. How you be, cuz?"

"Rosie! Man, it's good to hear your voice. You know I tried to come down there to see you. Peoples said no go. They didn't want some ex-con visiting in their prison. Ain't they supposed to let you see your family, man?"

"Yeah, supposed to," Rosie said. "But you know how it go. Get a good case manager, things done by the book. Get a hard case, then it's 'What book?' Got me one of those, unfortunately."

"You doing all right, though? Nothing's wrong?"

Rosie was touched to hear the concern in Sam's voice. "Nah, man, not with me. But I got a friend with a big problem. I wondered if you could talk to Ms. Mercy about it. My friend ain't got much money, but his peoples got a little."

"Money is always important, but Mercy isn't driven by money. If she thinks the case has merit, she will work with the client about payments."

Rosie's heart felt lighter. "Sam, man, you don't know what that means. This guy is a real friend. If I can keep something bad from happening to him, I'll do it."

"Tell me about him."

Rosie told Sam about Sleepy's case and what brought him to prison. Then he related the prison break, the guard's death, and the FBI's interest in Sleepy. He also told Sam about Hammer and how he was putting the squeeze on Sleepy.

"Rosie, let me get this information to Mercy. Then I'll let you know whether she can help your friend. Can you try calling me back in a couple days?"

"Have to be next week, Sam. We get one phone call a week."

"Okay, next week it is. And Rosie, this time I'm in a position to help. You know I would have helped you, if I could have. You doing time for something you didn't do. I know it, you know it. I already been thinking can I do something about that. We'll see about your friend, then I'm gonna see about you."

"Thanks, Sam. I didn't ask you for help when my case was going down, 'cause I knew you couldn't do nothing. But I'd be grateful for anything you could do now, working for Ms. Mercy and having your own life on track."

"Talk to you next week, then," Sam said.

Rosie put down the phone, and nodded to the guy in line behind him. He'd kept the call to ten minutes, as he was required to do. If he'd gone over, the guy would be hot by now. But Rosie wasn't one to hunt for trouble. In this place, trouble hunted for you. Like Sleepy. Never bothered nobody, and look where he was. Caught in the cross-hairs. Rosie had to do what he could to help his friend. Sam didn't say he would do something if he didn't mean to do it.

Sleepytime

Rosie felt better than he had since Sleepy got hauled into this mess.

Chapter Seven

The Washington law office of Mercy Johnson and Associates was on Fifth Street, N.W., within walking distance to the District of Columbia Superior Court on Indiana Avenue, and the United States District Court on Constitution Avenue. Mercy represented clients in both courts. The office was not fancy. Its proximity to the courts was its most convenient feature. Her clients could get to her office by bus or subway, her staff could avoid heavy parking fees by using public transportation, and she could walk to both courts. She could also walk to work from her home in the Shaw neighborhood near Carter University. If the weather was bad, she was a quick subway ride away from the office.

Mercy was putting away her laptop and packing up to go home when Sam stuck his head in the door. "Can I talk to you for a minute?"

"Sure, Sam, what's up?"

"Just got a call from my cousin, Rosie. Remember, I told you about him? Doing time for some nonsense the governor's aide down there set up, to get even for Rosie tossing him out of a bar when he manhandled one of the dancers."

"Yes, I remember it now. How's he doing?"

"He's okay for now. But he's got this friend who's in trouble and he asked if we could help. His friend is locked up on a first degree burglary. He has some kind of sleeping sickness. He fell asleep in a department store, and because he had a bunch of clothes in the dressing room with him, he got charged. It was after hours when the cops found him asleep there. Got a felony sentence, ten years, I think it was."

"Hmmm, sleeping sickness? Do you mean narcolepsy?"

"Yeah, that sounds right. Rosie couldn't really remember the name of the disorder, but I think narcolepsy is a sleep disorder."

"It is, indeed. And in some cases, it can be very disabling. Sleep comes over the person, and they are unable to resist. They sleep in odd places. They are almost trance-like, if the disease is bad enough."

"Yeah, that sounds like what happened to Rosie's friend. Anyway, he's in a real mess now. He was on the prison bus when some men on the work crew shot the guard and got away. The FBI is looking at him for the murder and the escape. He told the authorities that he was asleep on the bus and didn't know what happened, but the FBI agent won't let it alone. To add to his troubles, the escaped prisoners have been caught and are back in the prison. One of them is putting the screws to Rosie's friend, to make sure he don't talk."

Mercy sat down at her desk, abandoning the packing up. "What is the name of Rosie's friend?"

"You can't guess? It's Sleepy. Sleepy LeBlanc. His real name is Theodore LeBlanc, Rosie said."

"Does he have a family? Are they still helping him?"

"You mean, how will we get paid?"

"Yeah, that, and what are they going to tell the FBI when they are approached, as they will be, about the incident on the bus?"

"Rosie said his peoples could pay something, but he didn't tell me any more about them."

"Well, Walter's family is from down that way. He's still got an aunt, and some cousins down there. I guess we could ride down there and I could talk to Mr. LeBlanc. Walter needs to get out of the house anyway."

Walter, Mercy's husband of twenty-five years, was recovering from surgery to replace a defective heart valve. Mercy was still in the nursemaid role. Sam felt sorry for Walter, knowing that Mercy would watch every bite he ate, every thing he tried to do, hound him about his pills, and generally be in mother-hen overdrive. But he wouldn't say that to his boss. What he said instead was, "Yeah, I bet he'd like a little ride down the country."

"Where is LeBlanc in prison?"

"Southern part of the state, near the mountains. Place called Walton Correctional Institute, a medium security facility. Want me to pull up his information so you can make an appointment to see him?"

"Yeah, and I'll tell you tomorrow what day Walter and I can go. I have to make sure he doesn't have any doctor appointments, and that he feels like making the trip. We will probably have to stay overnight, and I need to make sure his doctor is good with that."

Sam suppressed a groan. Lord, this woman was predictable when it came to taking care of her family. Mercy's mother, ninety plus, lived with Walter and Mercy, and she was as fit as the average seventy year old. Even Walter's cat got special treatment, though Mercy described herself as "not a cat person."

"Okay. I told Rosie to call me when he could. He said it would be next week. I'll let him know that you can see LeBlanc, and we will take it from there."

"That's good. I don't want to promise anything. I'm hoping the family can pay us a little something. If not, we will see if LeBlanc will sign a contract to pay when he's released. That may be the best we can do."

"Ever feel like we're bartering services for chickens and eggs, like in the old days?"

"Nope. Don't eat chicken, eggs don't pay the rent."

"Speaking of which..."

"Oh, Lord, Sam, did I forget again? Here, let me write you a check right now. Hard as you work, you shouldn't have to wait on your paycheck. I guess my mind is on other things these days. Now that Walter's heart issues are resolved, I can breathe again. I'll do better in the future."

"You worry about Walter, and about these cases we're working on. I'll remind you if you're forgetting anything important."

Mercy went back to packing her briefcase. Sam went back to his office. He wrote a quick note to Rosie and readied it for tomorrow's mail. It would ease Rosie's mind and that way, he wouldn't have to wait 'til next week to hear the good news. The odds just changed to Sleepy LeBlanc's favor.

Sam knew that when Mercy said she would help a client, she would not rest until she had done everything she could to improve his lot. Sometimes that was negotiating a favorable plea agreement. Sometimes it was convincing a jury that the government's case against the client wasn't strong enough to support a verdict of guilty. Sometimes it meant marshaling facts for sentencing to mitigate the client's wrongdoing or at least explain it. Sam liked how she worked.

He had been an investigator in Mercy's office for nearly two years. She represented him years ago, when she was an attorney with the public defender's office. She promised Sam a job when he came home, on two conditions. Remain clean and sober. Attend AA meetings at least once a week. He didn't argue with her on either score. She was right to set the conditions, and she was right that AA was his best hope of staying away from drugs or alcohol.

Sam had given his word, and he had kept it. Now he was the chief investigator in Mercy's one-woman firm. Since leaving the public defender service, Mercy had built a solid practice. She kept the office going. Kept the rent paid in their modest office building. Their office was near metro stops on the green and red lines, so Sam didn't need a car to get back and forth to work. When he needed one in an investigation, he borrowed Mercy's car, or she rented him one to use. The other investigator she used was going to law school, so she only worked part-time. Sam and Walter's cousin, who was the office receptionist, were the only full-time staff except for Mercy.

To call Mercy full-time was not quite accurate. The woman was a work horse. Her first priority was always her family, but her work ran a very close second. Sam had no idea what Rosie's friend had done, or why he was in the mess Rosie described. But he knew if Sleepy had Mercy on his side, he could at least count on the system giving him a fair shot. Mercy would cajole and maneuver and connive, if she needed to, to be sure of that.

Chapter Eight

Mercy and Walter took half a day to drive to the foothills in the southwest part of the state. They meandered, as Walter called it, stopping here and there to take pictures of the fall landscape, enjoying a roadside picnic lunch Mama insisted on packing. Mercy realized that being out in the country was bracing for Walter. He seemed livelier than he had since the surgery.

"Are you glad you came with me?" she asked.

"Of course. You know I'm always glad to be with you. Except when you're on the verge of going to jail, that is. Then I might wish I was home in my bed, with the covers over my head."

Mercy laughed. "You aren't ever going to forget that episode, are you?"

"What episode?" The twinkle in his eye was one of the many things Mercy loved about her husband. A couple years ago she got in a showdown with a pig-headed judge, and the judge held her in contempt. Walter was in court that day and nearly stroked out. He still liked to tease her about it.

Mercy changed the subject. "Walter, have you heard from Toby? I know he's working hard on the Task Force, but I wish he'd keep in closer touch. You know I worry."

"I know you do, baby. But he's grown now. We have to let go a little bit. I suspect Sergeant Banks has him tied up in some big drug investigation, and he's afraid to talk to us about it. You know most of what he does is top secret."

"Yeah, but I worry. He still hasn't said anything about Helen. Do you think he ever hears from her?"

"Lord, I hope not. That woman was trouble, for sure. Running off with millions of dollars worth of heroin, days after her father was carried up to his Maker. What kind of woman would be planning a heroin heist while her father was being waked and cremated?"

"A scheming one, which is why I wish I knew more about what was going on with Toby. When we get back, he's coming to dinner. Mama can fix him all his favorites. You know that boy can't turn down Mama's cooking. And she can get him talking, too. You know how she is."

"Boy, do I." Walter busied himself with his food then, ignoring Mercy's look. She knew he didn't mean anything bad about Mama. He loved her like his own mother. But she could be a bit nosy. Or more accurately, she could outperform any intelligence operative when it came to prying information out of one of her own and relaying that information when she felt it was appropriate.

Mercy let Walter finish his meal without interruption, but she couldn't help feeling uneasy. Toby, Walter's nephew, was like a son to Walter and Mercy. They never got around to having children, and by the time they made a place in their lives for a baby, they were past the prime child rearing age. They decided to content themselves with loving Toby, who treated them like parents, especially after Walter's brother died. Toby worked for the Metropolitan Police Department. He was assigned to the Narcotics Task Force, a consortium of officers and federal agents under the direction of Sergeant William Banks of the Narcotics Branch of MPD. Two years ago Toby got involved in a heroin operation that led to his shooting. Mercy had ramped up worrying about him after that. The operation involved a woman, Helen, the daughter of the businessman who smuggled the heroin into the country. When Toby's Task Force recovered the heroin, Helen stole it. She fled and was still on the run. Mercy had a suspicion, one she did not want to give voice to, that Toby was still hurting about Helen's betrayal. She knew Toby and that hurt made him vulnerable. She was more watchful as a result.

The plan to get Mama involved made her feel better. Even if Toby was just working so hard he couldn't take the time to stay in touch, he needed his family. She would remind him of that, with some good home-cooking and family time.

Walter finished his lunch and packed up the recycling and trash. Mercy put the recycling in the car and the trash in a receptacle by the side of the table. "Let's go on to the motel. You need to rest this afternoon. I will go to the prison while you take a nap. Then we'll find some place to get dinner, and get to bed early. Tomorrow we can drive back to D.C. through the mountains. The scenery and fresh air will do you a world of good."

"Mercy, stop fretting about me. I am doing very well, according to the cardiologist. All my tests are good. Thank goodness the valve replacement could be done without open heart surgery, or you would have taken me on full-time and given up the practice of law."

Mercy hugged him tightly before helping him into the car. "Walter Johnson, you are full time. I can't stand it when you are sick. I worry so much, my hair has turned grey."

Walter must have known there was no diplomatic response to that, since Mercy's salt-and-pepper hair, which she wore in short twists, was the same color it had been for at least the last five years. So he just got into the car and let her shut the door.

When she was buckled in, he said, "Listen, take your time at the prison. Don't rush back for dinner. I'm happy with a long nap and a sandwich later. We can probably carry in something."

Mercy gave him a look, but kept her thoughts to herself. He could eat a sandwich, if that's what he wanted. She was going for some home cooking. It wouldn't rival Mama's, but out here in these mountains, she knew she could get some cornbread and beans, some fried okra, and maybe even some stewed cabbage. That she would not pass up.

Chapter Nine

Mercy spotted the prison as soon as she turned onto the state road from the highway. The parcel of land on which the prison sat spread over several acres. Concertina wire fences surrounded several large red brick structures. The wire was three levels deep, forming three squares, each level separated by small grassy plots. At the four corners of the outer square, towers stood several stories high. She knew the towers would include armed guards who watched the perimeter for breaches of security. Mercy turned into the prison gates and pulled up to the squawk box on the pole at the parking entrance. She announced that she had a 2:00 p.m. appointment for a legal visit with Theodore LeBlanc. She was directed to a parking slot, and told to leave her cell phone and any other electronic devices in the car. She wondered if that included her laptop, but since she was fine with a legal pad and pen, she didn't ask.

She approached the administration building, following signs marked "Visitors." At the building, she rang for admission. A steel door whirred, and moved on its track. It opened into a vestibule, with a glass-enclosed area where two guards were seated. A metal detector was between her and the exit door. One of the guards asked to see her identification and she presented her drivers license and District of Columbia bar card. The guard eyed the card, then asked, "Where is your state bar card?"

Mercy had anticipated the question. "I don't have one. I am entitled to visit a prisoner, so long as I am a member of any state or the District of Columbia bar. Your website makes that clear. Even if it did not, that would be the rule. If I accept representation of this prisoner, I will take steps to associate a local lawyer. Right now, I'm exploring that possibility."

Mercy spoke quietly and calmly. No need to start a fight, if she did not need to. The guard said, "Just a minute," and went to one of the phones on the desk behind him. He spoke for a few minutes, then came back. "Warden said it's okay. That means it's okay." Mercy got the point. He wasn't taking her word for it. Fine, so long as he let her in.

The guard returned her credentials and nodded at the steel exit door. "Through that door, down the steps, across the quad, through the main entrance."

Mercy followed the directions and was shown to the visiting hall. She looked up from her legal pad when she heard LeBlanc's name called. A tall man, at least six feet eight inches, was making his way toward the glass-enclosed room where Mercy was waiting. He nodded to several other prisoners who were visiting with family and friends in the common area outside the legal visiting room. He opened the door to the room and looked at Mercy.

"Hello, Mr. LeBlanc, please come in and have a seat."

LeBlanc settled himself in the chair across from Mercy, but he did not look comfortable. His height meant that his knees were almost to his chest

"I don't think they designed that chair with you in mind," Mercy said, smiling and extending her hand.

"No ma'am, I don't reckon they did." LeBlanc smiled, too, and when he did, his angular face softened. He was a handsome man, Mercy noticed, with short blond hair and blue-green eyes in a tanned face. He looked fit, and except for very large hands, his physique seemed to go with his height. He rested his hands in his lap and waited for Mercy to speak.

"Your friend Rosie called us about your case, Mr. LeBlanc. He is concerned about you. Rosie is a cousin to my investigator, Sam Lester. I am here to see if there is a way we can help you."

LeBlanc sighed. "I think you could help me, Ms. Johnson. But my family doesn't have a lot of money. I don't know how they could pay you for your help. I don't want to ask my aunt and uncle. They raised me, and they would want to help. But they are up in years. Uncle Samuel is not well. Aunt Ruth is a retired school teacher. They stood by me when I got locked up, but I can't ask them to do anything more. My ex-wife Brenda—she would try to help, but she doesn't make much."

Mercy could see pride warring with some other emotion, maybe fear, as LeBlanc spoke.

"Mr. LeBlanc, let's not talk about the money right now. First, let me see what is going on with you, and whether my firm can be of help. If we can help you, then we can talk about payment. It may be that there is nothing we can do, in which case I will tell you that, and you will not owe me anything for today's visit. Does that work for you?"

LeBlanc smiled again. "Yes, ma'am, it sure does. Where do you want me to start?"

"You can start with dropping the ma'am. You can just call me Mercy. And I will call you Theodore, if that is okay."

"Sure. That's my true name."

"Then Theodore it is. Tell me first what brought you here, then we'll get to more current events."

LeBlanc related the story of his arrest in the department store, his trial, the big-city lawyer his family hired, and his prison sentence. Mercy noticed that he did not seem to be complaining about anything. He gave a coherent narrative, devoid of any anger or finger-pointing.

"Let's explore this sleep problem you have. How long have you had the problem?"

He told her that the sleep thing started in his childhood. At first it was just that he couldn't stay awake after lunch, then he couldn't stay awake in the evenings, then it progressed to falling asleep at his desk, on the playground, on the school bus. Kids dubbed him "Sleepy" and made fun of him. He knew he couldn't control the sleepiness, but the adults around him were frustrated by it. As he grew up, he tried everything, taking naps, going to bed early, going to bed late, caffeine, no caffeine, sugar, no sugar. If he read about a remedy, he tried it. Once he and Brenda got together, she was always searching for help. It probably worried her more than it did him. But nothing worked. One minute he was awake and functioning, the next he was dead asleep. That was all he knew about it.

"Okay, now tell me about the incident on the prison bus." Again, LeBlanc's account was straightforward and complete. "I used to fall asleep when I was working on the road crew. Harkness had seen me do it plenty of times. Finally, he said he couldn't risk that I'd get hurt, or hurt somebody. I figured he didn't want to do the paperwork, or that it would look bad for him if something happened. I knew he didn't give a damn about me or the other inmates. He hated us. But he didn't want to look bad, and lose that cushy job. So he told me I could sleep on the bus. That's what I did. When I started feeling the least bit sleepy, I'd just get on the bus and go to sleep."

"How long had that been going on?" Ms. Johnson asked.

"I'd been on the crew for about six months. After the first month or two, Harkness let me sleep whenever I needed to."

"Did the other inmates know about it?"

LeBlanc chuckled. "Yeah, they knew. They kept saying they were going to try my con. They thought it was a way to get out of work."

"Who is the leader of the inmate crew? Not the corrections staff, but the inmate leader."

"Hammer," LeBlanc said, not even pausing to consider the question. "Charles Hastings, his real name. But we call him Hammer. He'd as soon hit you on the head as look at you. Everybody is afraid of him in here. Guards and inmates."

Mercy looked at LeBlanc. "Are you afraid of him?"

"Not really. I probably should be. But there isn't much he can do to me but kill me."

She thought about the calm way he said that, then took up her legal pad, and made a note. She turned back to LeBlanc. "Now tell me what you can about this bus incident."

LeBlanc looked at his hands. He had started to twist them, then he steadied them in his lap. "I was asleep. The lieutenant woke me up. Cops were everywhere. The crew was gone. Harkness's body was in the funeral home van. The FBI agent and some local cop talked to me. Accused me, really. I told them I was asleep. They didn't believe me. Then the crew got picked up and they started squeezing me, afraid I saw something, I guess. Between Nash and the crew, I haven't had much rest."

Mercy made another note on her legal pad. "Alright, let's get to the tough question. Who killed Harkness?"

"I don't know. I didn't see it. But it had to be Hammer and his guys. No one else was around. Unless Strafe and Pockets did it. They are the two guards on the bus. But why would they knock themselves out afterwards? And why would they kill Harkness? Hammer and his guys escaped. That seems like a motive to me."

"Yeah, that's what the FBI is saying. But, they're putting you in the escape plan. They say, 'Okay, let's assume LeBlanc really does have this sleep thing. He was in on the plot, but he couldn't carry through because he fell asleep. He's still guilty. He's an aider and abettor. If he was in on the planning, it doesn't matter whether he actually carried out his part in the scheme. He's guilty of murder one and felony murder, as an accomplice.'"

LeBlanc looked confused. "How can I be guilty of a crime," he asked, "just by being in the place where the crime was committed, with the people who committed the crime? I'm guilty by association, is that what you're saying?"

"Not exactly," Mercy said. "You have to know what is happening, want it to happen, and take some role in making it happen. It's not enough that you were there while somebody else did the crime. You see the difference?"

LeBlanc sighed. "I'll think about it, Ms. Johnson. Do they really think Hammer would share his plot with me? He never has trusted me. I think he knows I am not afraid of him. That worries him. Why wouldn't I be? Everybody else is. He can't handle that. He'd never let me know if he planned to commit a crime."

"Can we prove that?" Mercy asked.

"Everybody in here knows it. Now, would they testify to it? Not if Hammer told them not to."

"I'll think about how to show a jury that you would not be in this Hammer's inner circle. It may be that the State will not pursue a murder charge against you. Nash may be bluffing, thinking he can get you to give evidence against the men on the bus. So for now, let's concentrate on proving your sleep disorder. I think we can show that you really do have a serious sleep disorder and that you are not faking when you say you don't know what happened on the bus. If we can show that, maybe Nash will stop harassing you to get you to give information you don't have. I have a Records Release here. I need you to sign it, so I can get your files and any evaluations that have been done about the sleep problem. Depending on what the prison records show, I may get my own doctor to examine you. She could come here, do an interview, give you some tests, the usual psychological work-up. I assume I won't have any problem getting your cooperation for that?"

"Are you kidding?" LeBlanc seemed genuinely surprised at the question. "I'll do whatever you say. You're trying to help me. Why wouldn't I cooperate?"

Mercy laughed. "I've been in this business a long time, Theodore. Some people don't seem to be able to act in their own self-interest. But I don't think you're one of those. I think you've been used by Hammer and his crew, and Nash would like to use you to further his own career goals. Close the case, lock everybody up, get one rung up on the FBI ladder. If we can show that your sleep disorder is real, and that you were not involved in any crimes on the bus, maybe we can stop him."

LeBlanc looked relieved. Mercy hated to bring up the prospect of a murder prosecution but she wanted him to be prepared for whatever might happen. She started with the practical—could Theodore afford to contribute to his own defense?

"Now, let me ask you some questions about money. I will agree to represent you with the understanding that you will pay me when you are able. But if you are charged with murder, and we have to prepare for trial, we will probably need a psychologist to testify. Any expert witness will expect to be paid. If you are charged, I will file a motion with the court, asking that the court appoint and pay a psychologist, because you are without funds. The legal term is indigent. I'll need to file an affidavit from you, detailing your financial circumstances."

"Sure, I don't mind. I'll tell you whatever you want to know. I used to have a house and a savings account. But when my wife and I divorced, after I came in here, I signed it all over to her. What good was it doing me? Eight years sounded like eternity to me. Plus, it was so hard on her, me coming in here. She didn't know what to do. She worked, too, but she was used to me taking care of most of the financial stuff. She needed the security. So it seemed like the right thing to do."

LeBlanc stopped, catching his breath. Mercy got the sense he was rushing through the explanation, that he didn't like to talk about how his marriage had ended.

Mercy took a form from her briefcase and handed it to LeBlanc to sign. "This form is an affidavit of indigency. Please sign it after I fill in the blanks. Then I'll attach it to my motion for a court-appointed psychological expert. In a murder case, we should be able to get the court to appoint the expert. The court may want to hold a hearing on the motion, so that we can show that we need the expert."

Mercy filled in the blanks and LeBlanc signed the form.

"Theodore, is there anything else you want to tell me?"

"I can't think of anything, Ms. Johnson. I hated it about Harklness. He was not a nice man but I didn't wish him any harm. I honestly don't know who shot him. I wish I could help, because shooting him wasn't right. But I can't make myself know what I don't know."

Mercy heard a tinge of what sounded like despair now. "Of course you can't, Theodore. That would be lying and that would make a bad situation much worse."

As Mercy stood to go, she extended her hand. LeBlanc's big hands swallowed hers.

"Ms. Johnson, I don't know what to say. Rosie is a true friend. I knew he wanted to help me, but I didn't really believe any lawyer would be willing to help without being paid up front. I just don't know how to thank you."

"You don't have to. Thank Rosie. He cares a lot about you."

"I will thank him. I'll try to do something for him, too. He's in here for nothing, just like I am."

"Sam told me all about Rosie's situation. Don't you worry about Rosie for right now. We'll try to get your situation straightened out. Sam won't let me forget about Rosie, you can trust in that."

Mercy signaled the guard at the desk in the visiting hall that she was ready to leave.

"Theodore, I'll be in touch with you soon. Meantime, do not

discuss your situation with anyone but me or Sam. If anyone else tries to talk to you, tell them to call me. Here's my card, with all my numbers."

LeBlanc nodded. Mercy watched him leave the room and go to the guard for his pass back into the institution. For someone who had been dealt such a bum deal, he didn't seem angry. She wondered how that was.

Chapter Ten

Mercy spotted a roadside café on the sparsely-traveled road from the prison to the motel. She would get some food to go, and share with Walter if he was interested. She stopped at the café, and called Walter on her cell phone. She was pleased to get reception down here in the foothills.

As she opened the door to the little restaurant, she saw a large black man sitting at the counter. He smiled at her and she smiled back. Since he was wearing an apron, she assumed he worked here.

"Good evening," she said to the man. "Do you work here?"

"When I feel like it," he replied. "Today ain't one of them days. That's how come I'm sittin' here at the bar, watchin' the screen door go back and forth. Today I ain't feeling like it." He laughed, and the sound rumbled down in his large frame and settled deep. It was a pleasing sound. Then he winked at Mercy, and smiled at her again. "Even though I'm not working, I don't mind helping a pretty lady. What can I do for you?"

Mercy smiled back. "I'm here to get some dinner for my husband and me. He's not feeling well so I'm carrying dinner back to him."

"Well, ain't he the lucky one." That twinkle again, and with it an easy smile that held a hint of devilment.

Mercy made her way to a booth in the back, and scanned the menu. A waitress brought her coffee, and she placed her order. She told the waitress she would take it to go, and headed for the bathroom before she got back on the road. Just as she came out of a stall, and was headed to the basin to wash up, a large black woman came into the bathroom. The room was small, and there was not much room for her to pass Mercy to get to the stalls. Mercy stepped back to let her pass. But instead the woman stopped in front of her, so close she was inches away from her.

She towered over Mercy and outweighed her by at least fifty pounds. Mercy tried to back up but there was no place to go. The woman was frowning. She crossed her arms, and Mercy noticed that she had muscles like someone who worked with weights. Hers more likely came from hard work, not exercise. Mercy tried to get past her, saying, "Excuse me, ma'am." The woman did not budge.

Mercy was annoyed now. "Can I help you with something?" she asked, her tone exasperated.

The woman looked down at Mercy. "I seen you flirtin' with my man." She was speaking in very low tones. "You'd best be out of here, 'fore I have to hurt you."

Mercy was more than annoyed now. But she knew she was no match for this woman. She had to finesse this, if she could.

"Ma'am, I don't know who your man is. I don't think I flirted with any man, but if it looked that way to you, I'm sure sorry. I don't want your man, whoever he is. I'm sure he's a good man, don't take offense. But the man I've got can be a handful, sometimes. I sure don't want another one to have to get used to." Mercy spoke matter-of-factly, looking up at the woman's tired face. She was relieved when the woman's eyes started to show a smile.

Just then the woman broke out into a belly laugh. She uncrossed her arms, moved back from Mercy, and wiped at her eyes. When she smiled, Mercy noticed that one of her front teeth was missing. She wiped her hands on her apron. Mercy figured the woman must work here, given the apron. When she could get her laughter under control, the woman said, "Tell the truth, honey, tell the truth. Half the time they ain't nothin' but worriation. You go on now, and I'll tell Macie to bring you some supper. What you want, honey? I'll fix it myself, make sure it's done like you like it."

Mercy didn't let on, but she surely wasn't eating anything prepared by a woman who thought she had designs on her husband. "Thanks but I'm on my way to my man now. I figured to take him some supper. He's been sick and I'm making sure he eats enough."

"Sorry for scaring you," the woman said. "I just get crazy sometime. I think it's my hormones. They up and down like a see-saw these days. Hot one minute, freezing the next. Sad one minute, giddy the next. Doc says it's normal when you going through the change. Ain't that just like a man? Your body done took you hostage, and some man calls that normal. Normal for the insane asylum, maybe. That must be what he meant." She laughed again, and touched Mercy's arm. "I really am sorry, though. Don't know what comes over me sometimes."

Mercy smiled. "No problem. No harm done. But maybe you

ought to find a woman doctor. She might have a different definition of normal."

"I think I will, honey," she said. Then she frowned at Mercy. "You trying to help me, I can see. Let me try to help you. You see, I got powers lot of folks don't have. I see things. Most times I see things before they happen. My peoples called it a sixth sense. Whatever it is, I see some things about you."

Mercy was so shocked she could barely breathe. Was this woman trying to tell Mercy she was some kind of fortune teller, or some kind of clairvoyant? She stared at the woman until she realized she ought to look away, before the woman left because she took offense. Mercy felt her skin prickling, and her scalp tingle. She was afraid, but something in her willed the woman to continue.

"I see a woman, light-skinned, looks like she might be Chinese. I see a young black man, in some kind of uniform. They ain't keepin' comp'ny, but they's sweet on each other. Some kind of problem is driving a wedge between them. I see the woman, somewhere nearby. She's scared. But she's tough. I think she's going to be alright."

The woman turned to Mercy then. "Sorry. I can't see no more. I get these flashes, they speak to me, then they go away. Always has been like that. Most times, I don't really get enough information to warn people. But just so you know..."

She straightened her apron, looked in the little bathroom mirror to align the hair net on her head, and turned from Mercy. And then she was gone.

Mercy paid for the food and drove back to the motel. When she told Walter the story, he couldn't stop laughing. "I'd like to have seen that. That woman didn't know who she was up against."

Mercy didn't share his humor. "Walter, who do you know that is in uniform? It's got to be Toby. And a woman who looks Chinese. That's Helen. Walter, that woman was warning me about Helen and Toby. I don't like the feeling I have in the pit of my stomach."

"Mercy, that woman was pulling your chain. She thought you flirted with her man. Or maybe she just thought he wanted to flirt with you. Either way, that other-worldly stuff was just get-back. Don't pay her any mind."

"Easy for you to say," Mercy huffed. "You don't have mischief following you around waiting for you to let down your guard."

"And neither do you. How many times have you told me about

this mischief, and nothing happened?"

Mercy looked at Walter, then she spoke, her voice barely above a whisper. "Last year Toby got shot. He almost died." A tear slid down her cheek.

Walter reached for her and held her. He patted her back. "Mercy, don't go getting all worked up, now. Toby is a police officer. He knows how to take care of himself."

Mercy knew there were some things Toby couldn't guard against. But she decided she'd get nowhere arguing with Walter. She changed the subject.

"Let me tell you about Sleepy LeBlanc. You know how mad I get when some high-toned lawyer takes a client's money and sits on his butt. Well, that's what happened here, I think. I doubt LeBlanc or his people can pay us much. But I'm mad now. I'm gonna do this case, and if I have to, Ill do it for free. He's been cheated out of years of his life. I'm gonna do my best to get those years back for him."

Mercy was still thinking about LeBlanc's case when the lighted dial on the alarm clock showed 2:00 a.m. Walter was snoring softly. She had a sense that LeBlanc's case was going to upend her for awhile. Maybe that was the mischief she was fearing. Or maybe it was the encounter with the woman at the café. Either way, she hoped her premonitions wouldn't come to anything.

Chapter Eleven

Sleepy was lying on his bunk, trying to read, but thoughts of the legal visit kept interrupting his concentration. Was he dreaming? Had Ms. Johnson really said she could help him? He replayed the visit in his mind.

Everything about Ms. Johnson made Sleepy want to trust her. The first thing he noticed was how she dressed. Her outfit was one Brenda might have worn. Grey slacks, a light blue shirt of some silky fabric and a short navy blue jacket with tiny pearl buttons. Even in her high heel shoes, she was much shorter than Sleepy. Still tall for a woman, maybe five feet eight or so. She was slender, which made her seem smaller next to him. She was a pretty woman, medium brown complexion, short hair in twists. Her hair was streaked with silver, signaling that she was not as young as her unlined face would suggest.

Everything about her said that she was comfortable with who she was, and confident. She looked good, but now showy. His family had hired a fancy uptown lawyer for him when he was charged with burglary of the department store. The guy wore five hundred dollar suits. He always had his nails buffed. His hair never moved from its perfect place atop his head. He didn't do jack for Sleepy. He showed up in court, told him to take a plea, got mad when he said he was innocent, and let the State run roughshod over him for what passed for a trial. But Sleepy had to hand it to him. He looked good while he let Sleepy flounder and die. Sleepy got a different feeling from Ms. Johnson.

Sleepy was heartened, too, by her age. He took from the grey in her hair that she didn't start in this business yesterday.

She put him at ease, even when he was discussing unpleasant things like the details of his financial situation. He was careful not to sound like he was pitying himself. He hated that attitude in anybody, especially himself. What was, was. That was all he could say. He used to be comfortable enough, when he had a job, and at the time it had seemed he had a bright future ahead with Brenda. But this sleep thing ruined it all. He'd lost one job, then another. Brenda was getting more and more frustrated. Then he got locked up and came here. He couldn't explain what was happening. The doctors his family had consulted hadn't helped. Why play the bagpipes over it? Plenty of people in here were worse off. Ms. Johnson seemed to just want information, not to make any judgments about his situation.

He remembered how she had taken the financial affidavit form from her briefcase and given it to Sleepy to sign. Seeing her small briefcase caused Sleepy to remember the high-gloss reptile skin briefcase his other lawyer had carried. All Sleepy ever saw him take out of it was the New York Times financial section.

He got the feeling, from his meeting with Ms. Johnson, that she would really work for him. He believed in her, partly because Rosie said she was okay. He trusted his own instincts, too. Any woman who put him in mind of Brenda, he had to trust. For the first time in days, he felt lighter. He picked up his book and found the page he had bookmarked. Today he could concentrate on the story, and not be distracted by his own problems. For a little while, he would let the story take him away from this place, and he would be free.

Chapter Twelve

Nash was still furious at LeBlanc's refusal to tell him what happened on the prison bus and who was behind the murder and escapes. He drove the few miles from the prison into downtown in minutes. He stopped off at his favorite coffee shop, ordered a latte to go, and was in the District Attorney's office right on schedule. The Assistant District Attorney tapped to handle the Harkness killing was waiting for him, pacing his office, twisting a rubber band into a figure-eight and frowning. Jonathan Blume was one of the senior trial attorneys in the DA's office. Unlike the District Attorney, who was elected, Blume was a hireling and one who had stayed well beyond the two to three year stint that was a stepping stone to the big firm partnership track. He had a reputation for toughness, and for impatience.

Before Nash could even shed his raincoat, Blume was asking questions. "What is the Task Force doing to wrap this case up? I read that all the cons are back in the joint. That's just the beginning. Those men shot a prison guard. We are no closer to proving which one, are we?" His irritation was obvious, and it irked Nash.

"Look, Blume, we are working this case round the clock. We got all the escapees within forty-eight hours of the shooting. You know one of them will probably want to deal. Even if we can't deal with the escapees, we got a witness. We're making good progress."

Blume's response was not enthusiastic. "Nash, don't try to con me. From what I hear, this Hastings has a tight-knit group. Don't put your hopes on one of them turning snitch. For a guy with a pretty mild record, Hastings seems to rule with an iron hand. He must be one of those who does his dirt, then gets somebody else to take the fall. That's how he's kept his sheet clean of violence, I'm guessing. But he's working on his boys now. They know if they tell who did the shooting, they'll have to do a long sentence in protective custody. Even there, he's got friends in the system, and in other states. There's no way we can guarantee their safety, unless they're willing to go into prison witness protection. But you know what that means? Limited family contact, limited visits with girlfriends or wives. Who's gonna sign on for that?"

Nash leaned back in his chair and put one ankle on the other knee. He examined his boot for smudges. He appeared to be thinking. What he was really doing was trying to contain his resentment at being second-guessed by this bureaucrat.

"I think LeBlanc will break. Yesterday his cell was firebombed. Now that Hastings is back, LeBlanc will be the center of his attention. He's smart, and he knows LeBlanc is dangerous to him. LeBlanc claimed to be asleep, but how long will he stick to that story, if he's facing a capital murder charge? I had a chat with Hastings. He knows LeBlanc is not talking right now, but he also knows he can't trust him to be stand-up. You know snitching is a way of life in the joint. Hastings will figure LeBlanc for one of those cons who will know what the State needs him to know, so he can get out from under a rack of time. I think he'll put some serious pressure on LeBlanc. Then we'll start getting some information. Just to make very sure Hastings has the tools he needs to scare LeBlanc, I'm dropping some tidbits to the media, so they can apply some pressure on LeBlanc. I'm going out to see LeBlanc's family in the next day or two. That should tighten the squeeze. Once his aunt and uncle, who are getting up in years, let LeBlanc know that we're talking to them, he'll open up. He won't want them to be bothered with us."

Blume did not look pleased. "So you've been talking to the media? I wondered who this 'highly-placed source within the investigation' was. I guess that's how you got dubbed the lead investigator on the case, too." Blume's voice had a definite edge now. "Listen, agent Nash, I don't know how those federal prosecutors operate, but I don't cotton to messing with the lives of innocent people. Especially old innocent people. Do you have any information that leads you to think LeBlanc's relatives know anything about this case?" Before Nash could answer, Blume continued. "Because I don't. I think you just want to use them to get to LeBlanc. I don't operate like that. If you have a genuine need to speak with them, go ahead. But do it gently. Do not pressure those old people. If I hear that you did, I will speak to your supervisor and try my level best to get you off this case. This is still a state investigation. You are here only because you are on the Violent Crimes Task Force. But for that assignment, this case would be handled by local law enforcement. And no more chats with the media, okay?"

Nash returned Blume's stare. "Mr. Blume, I have the full authority of the Federal Bureau of Investigation behind me in this case. I am on the Task Force, which gives me the right to investigate this crime as if it were a federal offense. I intend to conduct this investigation as I would any other criminal investigation. That means throwing as wide a net as possible, when searching for information. If that net snares a couple of old people, so be it. I don't intend to torture them. I intend to question them. If they don't have any information, fine. But at least I will have covered that base. And as for the media, I'll direct all future inquiries to you. If that meets with your approval."

Nash's face was set, and he felt his face flushing. Blume must have decided not to push him, because all he said was, "Let's meet the end of the week, and see where we are."

Nash took out his calendar, they agreed on Friday noon, and Nash left. Only when he was outside the county judicial building did he let off steam. He kicked the tire of an unmarked police car that sat at the curb. Then he focused on his objective, as he'd been taught. Anger diffuses energy, unless it's focused on the opposition. Who is the opposition here? Not that jerk Blume. He's inconsequential. LeBlanc is my opposition, because he's keeping me from breaking this case. I have to focus on him. I have to break him. I'll make him scream to talk to me.

This exercise made him feel better. Another couple of years, he told himself. Two more years in this swampland, running the regional office, and then back to civilization. How the hell he survived six years in the South, he did not know. People didn't even speak English, as far as he could tell. Back in Brooklyn, he could understand anybody. Italians, Caribbean islanders, even those refugees the government settled near his family home when the crap hit the fan in Bosnia. But these crackers were another story. They talked around marbles, it sounded like. He got the assignment as punishment, that he knew. One little screw-up, one suspect who grabbed his gun and shot another agent, and he was on the Magnolia Express to this wasteland. Agent didn't even die.

This case could be just the break he needed. Maybe he'd been a little rash, claiming the full backing of the Bureau. Truth was, he wasn't filing his reports like he was supposed to do, and the current regional director was not really in the loop. But once he got the regional director position, what would that matter? A dead prison guard ranked near the top of the Bureau's list of domestic priorities. Make a bust, get the publicity, get the attention of the guys in Washington, get the regional director's job. The plan was simple. But to solve the case, he needed LeBlanc's help. Maybe the little old auntie could help.

Chapter Thirteen

Nash pulled the grey unmarked sedan up to the front door of the small brick bungalow. According to the prison records, this address was where LeBlanc's aunt and uncle lived. Prison records were notoriously inaccurate, he'd found, so if this was the wrong house, he'd have to go to the techies at the FBI to get him a good address. He hated to do that, because he hated the fact that the old timers like himself were beholden to this new breed of agent geek.

Nash knocked twice sharply on the wooden edge of the screen door. He tried the door, and it was locked. Through the glass side panel to the front door, he saw movement in a hallway. The front door opened, and an elderly white-haired woman stood before him. Her pale skin was wrinkled. Her blue eyes squinted at Nash as she undid the apron that had been tied around her small frame. She reached up and removed the glasses from atop her head, adjusting them so she could see him. "Yes, sir?" she said. She kept the screen door closed.

Nash took out his leather badge holder and showed her the badge. "FBI, ma'am. Can I come in?"

"FBI?" her voice trembled slightly. "What in the world is the FBI doing looking for me?"

"You are Ruth LeBlanc, aren't you, ma'am? Mrs. Samuel LeBlanc?"

"Why, yes, of course I am. I never said I wasn't. But what does that have to do with the FBI?" Her tone was not unpleasant. She was obviously unused to official attention of any kind, and genuinely puzzled by his visit.

Nash didn't want to state his business out here on the stoop. The nearest house was about fifty yards away, but he was concerned for privacy, even so.

"Ma'am, it's about Theodore."

A look of worry crossed her gently-lined face. She opened the screen door. "Come on in, then."

Nash entered the short hallway off the front door, and was led into the living room to the right of the hallway. The room was stuffed with antique furniture, and knickknacks covered every surface. A worn floral rug covered the floor. The room showed its age, but was very clean. He took the least spindly of the several small upholstered side chairs. Mrs. LeBlanc seated herself on a love seat, next to a large grey cat. The cat did not wake up, or acknowledge Nash. She rubbed the cat softly, made cooing noises, and moved it slightly to sit back on the love seat.

"Yes, sir? What has happened to my nephew?"

Nash thought she was holding her breath, waiting for his answer. "Oh, he's fine, ma'am. He's not hurt or anything."

She held her hands tightly in her lap, and he noticed that they trembled in spite of her grip. Her voice broke when she spoke. "Thank God for that," she said. "He was my sister's child. She died a few months after he was born. My husband and I took him to raise as our own. We could not have children, you see. We could not have loved that boy any more if we'd made him ourselves. I hate that he's off up there in that place. Samuel can't travel anymore, and I don't like to drive because of my eyesight. So we don't get to see him hardly."

Nash looked down at the rug, tracing the footpaths made by years of walking around the furniture placed exactly as it was now. "Ma'am, the FBI is investigating your nephew. There's been an incident at the prison. I need to ask you some questions about it."

"Oh, you mean that escape from the bus? I knew Theodore was working on a road crew. When I didn't get a phone call from him, like I do once a week, I figured it out. He couldn't call because of something to do with that bus thing. I sure hate what happened to that guard. Theodore must be real upset, being nearby when that happened."

She looked genuinely distressed. Nash wondered how much LeBlanc had told her.

"Ma'am, what did your nephew tell you about the incident?"

"Why, Theodore hasn't told me anything about it a'tall. I haven't talked to him. I just told you he didn't call last week like he usually does. I'm the one guessed it had to do with that bus thing, since I knew he was on the prison road crew. I never figured that one out, either. My nephew would be useless working on a road crew. He never held a job for more than a few months at a time. He can't stay awake to work. My husband and I spent what money we had getting him to doctors about it. But nobody could ever tell us what was wrong with him. We just knew he fell asleep at odd times, and nothing we could do would rouse him. I knew it would get him in trouble one day. I knew he would be at the wrong place at the wrong time, because of it."

She stopped talking, and looked down at her hands, still gripping each other in her small lap. Nash noticed that tears were now falling softly on her pink cheeks.

Damn, he thought. A whole family of actors. Don't this beat all? LeBlanc's got this sweet little old lady in on his gig. Either that, or he has her fooled, too.

"Ma'am," he tried again, "can you tell me when you last spoke to your nephew?"

She looked up, wiped her eyes on the sleeve of her housedress, and seemed to calculate. "I think it was last month. You see, he usually calls every week. But week before last I had to take my husband to the hospital for a test, and he had to stay overnight, so I stayed there with him. That would have been Theodore's usual day to call, and I missed that call. Then last week, when he would have called, I heard about that incident on the news, so I figured that's why I didn't hear from him. So, I haven't really talked to him in over two weeks. That would have been at the end of last month."

"And when you spoke to him, what did he say?"

"You mean, all of it?" She looked like she had been asked to recite the catechism, Nash thought.

"No, ma'am, just the gist of it. Did he ever mention the crew boss, for example? Or any of the people on the road crew?"

"Not by name. He told me that the man who was in charge was very mean to the prisoners. But for some reason, he wasn't mean to Theodore. He let Theodore stay on the bus and sleep. Theodore figured it was because he didn't want him to cut himself or one of the other inmates with the tools they used to cut the grass along the highway. Paperwork for the boss, you know. And he said the other men on the crew were jealous that he didn't have to work and they did." She paused, as if thinking. "That's all I remember."

Nash was irritated now. This old broad had talked to LeBlanc, he knew it. They had hatched up this explanation. He was not buying it. Time to turn up the heat.

"Mrs. LeBlanc, I need to know what your nephew told you about this escape. I know you've talked to him. I got his phone records from the prison. They keep track of all calls inmates make. I just need to know what he told you about the escape, that's all. Tell me that, then I'll be on my way."

She looked puzzled. "I'm afraid you're wrong, agent Nash. There is no way the prison records could show such a thing. I haven't spoken to my nephew since last month. He may have tried to call and not gotten through, but I definitely know that I have not spoken to him."

"Mrs. LeBlanc," his tone hardened. "Do you know the penalty for aiding and abetting?"

Again, the puzzled look. "I don't even know what it is, sir." Behind the puzzlement, Nash caught a hint of steel. This wasn't working. She might be a little old lady, but she was nobody's fool. He might have to get really nasty.

"Look, ma'am. I don't want to play games here. If you know something about your nephew's role in this escape, and you don't tell me, you are committing a crime. You could be in trouble yourself. Is protecting your nephew worth going to jail, leaving your husband with nobody to take care of him?"

Nash realized from the look on her face he'd gone too far. But it was too late. He made the threats, and now he'd have to try to back them up.

"Agent Nash, I haven't done anything wrong. And I'm sure you know that. You came in here thinking you could bamboozle a little old lady into telling you what you want to hear. Well, it won't work with this little old lady. I'm old, but praise God, my memory is still fine. I know when I talked to my nephew, and I know what we talked about. You can threaten me 'til the Lord returns for me, but that won't change. Now, I think you'd better get out of my house.

My husband will wake up any minute, and when he does, he won't want to know that you've upset me. He is very sickly, and I don't want him upset by you and your foolishness. So go on now. Get out. And don't come back here unless you've got a warrant. Sir," she added firmly.

"I may do just that, ma'am," Nash snapped. He slammed the door on his way out. Of course, he knew the chances of his getting a warrant were slim to none. Unless the prison taping system happened to work for a change. The prison was supposed to tape inmate calls randomly. They saved the tapes for ninety days. He had asked the prison records clerk to get the tapes for the time around the escape, to see if anybody had been talking about it on the phones at the prison. Maybe he'd get lucky and uncover a conversation with auntie here. He was bluffing when he said that the records showed calls to her house. He did not have the prison telephone records yet, to compare with her telephone number. He hoped the bluff would work. Now he was disappointed. Oh, well. Next time he'd try for her husband. He'd have to find a time when the old man was home alone. Maybe when the old lady was in church. Maybe he'd have better luck pressing him.

And of course, there was LeBlanc's wife. Ex-wife, really. She would probably know something that he could use. He checked the notes he made from LeBlanc's prison file. "Midway," he said aloud. Brenda LeBlanc lives in Midway. Where the hell is Midway? He got out his map, and was pleased to see that he could be there in under an hour. Let's just see what Mrs. Sleepy has to say for her dumb cluck husband, he thought. The prospect of shaking her up made him forget for the moment his lack of success with auntie.

Chapter Fourteen

Nash sat hunched down in the seat of his Crown Victoria. The grey sedan blended so well with the surrounding trees that when he got out to answer nature's call, he nearly didn't see the car on his return. He doubted Brenda would notice it when she drove into her driveway. The driveway was long, and he was at the end, just near her garage, but pulled into the trees. He was glad it had not rained in a while, and the ground was firm. He sure as hell did not want to get stuck in this backwater town, and have to wait hours for a tow truck.

Just as Nash was about to settle himself for a short nap, he heard the crunch of tires on gravel, and the soft strumming of an engine moving slowly. He looked up just as a white Toyota, vintage 2000 or so, came into the driveway and stopped outside the garage. A man got out the driver's side door. Nash recognized the passenger as Brenda LeBlanc from the picture he got from the Department of Motor Vehicles. Brenda waited for the man to come around and open her door. The man reached out his hand and helped her from the car.

Nash was dumbstruck. He let out a very soft whistle. Well, I'll be damned. Look at that. How in the world did that cracker LeBlanc end up with this looker? Brenda LeBlanc could be in the movies. Blond hair, thick and shiny. Eyes looked blue, from where Nash was sitting. Perfect size six, he guessed. Perfect, whatever the size. She was dressed all in red—red dress, with a short jacket, red sling-back pumps, red straw purse. She was probably coming in from work, Nash thought. The man got two bags of groceries out of the back of the car, and they went inside. Must be planning a cozy little get-together.

Nash gave them a minute to get settled. There was no way they could leave without his seeing them. So why rush? Maybe she'd take off some of the clothes she was wearing and put on something comfortable. It didn't hurt to hope.

Ten minutes later, Nash gathered his badge and one of his cards, and made for the door to the neat white bungalow. It was small, but surrounded with great landscaping, including a bed of purple and yellow flowers which were in full bloom. "Better Homes and Gardens," Nash muttered with a snort.

He reflexively checked his shoulder holster to make sure the Glock nine millimeter was in perfect place. Why he'd need it, he couldn't guess, but he never abandoned his training as far as his weapon was concerned. Every encounter was a potentially dangerous one, in his mind.

He knocked on the polished oak door with the brass knocker. He didn't see a doorbell. He was about to knock a second time, when the door opened. There stood the lovely Mrs. LeBlanc, clad in blue jeans and a sweatshirt. Damn, Nash thought. What happened to Daisy Dukes? To Brenda, he said, "Good evening, Mrs. LeBlanc. I'm FBI agent John Nash. I need to ask you a few questions, if that's alright."

She hesitated and looked back into the house, to what Nash guessed was the living room. "Uh, sure, agent, no problem. But what is this about? I know the FBI doesn't investigate parking tickets, and that's the only trouble I've ever been in." She said this with an earnestness that irked Nash. What was this? Why did she think a senior FBI agent would be investigating parking tickets? He must be in for another run-around, like the one he'd just gotten from auntie. The whole freaking family must be actors, he thought.

"No ma'am," he said calmly. "I'm here about your husband."

At that, the man poked his head around the door jamb, and looked at Nash. Nash looked at him levelly, and raised his FBI identification so the man could see it. "Agent John Nash," he repeated. "Who are you?"

Brenda spoke before the man could answer. "He's a friend. Why do you need to know his name? He has nothing to do with my husband. Ex-husband, that is." She looked pointedly at the man when she said that. He draped an arm around her slight shoulders, and she moved closer to him.

Nash wondered what LeBlanc would do if he witnessed this

scene. He said to the man, "I just like to know who's around when I'm conducting my business. If you don't want to give me your name, perhaps you'd be good enough to leave us. I just have a few questions for Mrs. LeBlanc, then I'll be on my way." His tone was firm, and as he spoke, he closed the distance between the man and him. The man backed away slightly.

"Look, agent, I don't want any trouble. I'm Jedd Buffett. I'm a friend of Brenda's. I work down the road there, at the Circle K Fast Mart. I'm the manager. About to be the owner, actually."

"Whose car is that in the driveway?" Nash asked evenly.

Brenda looked at Jedd, then said, "It was Theodore's car. When he went away, he signed it over to me. Like he did everything else. Everything we had is now in my name."

Her tone was matter of fact. She was conveying information she thought he might need, not gloating over victories some lawyer wrung out of her ex-husband in a divorce court.

"Generous guy," Nash couldn't help remarking. Brenda looked at him hard, then straightened to her full five feet four and change, and said primly, "Indeed. Now what is it you want from me?"

"May I come in?"

"Oh, of course. I'm sorry. Jedd, can you get us some iced tea? We'll sit on the side porch. It's cooler out there."

Nash noticed that the house was not air conditioned, but there were ceiling fans, and the windows were opened enough to let in a nice breeze. The side porch was actually a screened in porch, comfortably furnished with wicker furniture that looked like it was vintage, not reproduction. Bright cushions made the space look inviting. She can keep house, too, Nash thought. Man, that LeBlanc was one dumb S.O.B. leaving a woman like her. He took a seat in the chair, leaving the sofa for Brenda and Jedd. They sat side by side, nearly touching. Jedd watched Brenda carefully.

"Ma'am, I don't want to keep you," Nash said. "I just have to ask you some questions about your husband's escape and the killing of the prison guard. What do you know about that?"

She corrected him quietly. "My ex-husband, if you please, agent."

Nash ceded the point. "Sure, ma'am. Sorry. What did he tell

you about the crime?"

Brenda sat straighter and looked directly at Nash. "Nothing. I haven't spoken to him in weeks. I usually go visit him on the major holidays. He's so lonely there, and his aunt and uncle are older, and in poor health. They can't go like they'd like to. So I try to get up a few times a year. We are divorced, but I still consider him my friend."

At that, Jedd rested his arm lightly on the back of the sofa, nearly touching Brenda's neck. Nash wondered what Jedd thought of these little pilgrimages.

Nash thought he'd try a different tactic, since he assumed Jedd's presence would make Brenda somewhat nervous about admitting contact with her ex. "I have the prison records. It looks like LeBlanc called here a day or two after the escape. What did he have to say?"

Brenda was not fazed. "Prison records? You mean of the telephones there? If he called here . . ." she began.

Nash interrupted. "Oh, he called here alright. What I want to know is what the two of you talked about."

She stood her ground. "Agent, I am very clear about this. I did not speak with Theodore after the incident. I read about the incident in the paper, and I knew right away what happened. The same thing that always happened to him. He fell asleep. I know he was on the road crew, and I know the head of it, I guess that was Harkness, let him sleep most of the time, because he didn't want Sleepy, Theodore that is, to cause an accident."

Nash held his temper. "Sleepy? That's what you call him?"

Brenda smiled slightly. "Sometimes. I use his given name some, too. I call him Theodore sometimes, but he's been called Sleepy since he was a child. I knew him by that name in school, so I guess it stuck. Come to think of it, we didn't call each other by name that often."

Then she blushed, and cast a quick glance at Jedd. If he reacted, Nash couldn't tell it. He could imagine what Jedd was thinking. All those "honey"s and "sweetie"s were probably getting to him.

Nash steered her back to LeBlanc. "So, that's what he told you? That Harkness let him sleep on the bus so he wouldn't cause an accident?"

Nash should have known she'd be too quick for that old saw. "Agent, " she said sternly, "I just told you. Sleepy didn't tell me anything about that day. I just know. He fell asleep everywhere. He lost jobs because of the sleep disorder. He's in jail because of it. The disease, and that rotten lawyer his family hired. He didn't believe Sleepy had anything wrong with him. We all tried to tell him, and tried to get him to get the medical records, but he wouldn't listen. Just kept telling Sleepy to plead guilty, he would get probation. Sleepy said, no way. He wasn't guilty. He wasn't going to say he was. Then the man just quit trying to help Sleepy. I could have done a better job at the trial than he did, and I didn't even finish college, let alone go to law school."

She was worked up now, and her face had taken on a slight moist sheen. Jedd looked at her with what might have been alarm. He patted her hand. She glanced at him, and smiled slightly.

Then she turned back to Nash. "And now he's in this mess, and once again, nobody's listening." She looked directly at Nash.

"Ma'am, it's not up to me to decide what to do. I just have to get the facts. And a fact is that telephone records show a call to this residence number from the prison within hours of the escape and killing."

"Can I see them?" Brenda asked.

Nash didn't even blink. "Well, ma'am, the government obtained them via subpoena, so they're what we call work product. So no, we won't reveal them at this stage. Just tell me what you and your ex-husband talked about, and I'll be on my way."

"Agent Nash," she emphasized his whole name, like his elementary teacher might have done. Nash wondered if she taught school. Probably not, since she said she didn't finish college. She was looking at him hard now. "I don't know what records you have. If there was a call to this number, it would have been Theodore, or maybe someone from the infirmary calling for him, to let me know he was alright. I did not speak with him. I have no information about what happened on the bus." She paused. "And, if the report is accurate that Theodore was asleep, then he won't know, either. These sleep episodes can last an hour, even longer.

And when he comes out of them, he doesn't remember anything about what happened right before. I think you're just harassing him, and harassing his family, hoping you can make him confess to something he didn't do, and you can close the case. You don't know Theodore, if you think that."

She sat back calmly, waiting for Nash to speak.

He tried not to show his irritation. "Ma'am, the FBI does not harass people. We have to get information, and sometimes people don't want to give it to us. But we don't harass."

"Well what do you call this, then? You know we are divorced. Why would you think he would confess to me, even if he did have something to do with this crime? Which he did not," she added stubbornly. "I think you are trying to force me to say something that is not true. If you don't have a warrant to arrest me, I think you'd better leave." Her resolve was obvious.

Jedd stood then. "Agent, Ms. LeBlanc has asked you to leave. Now I'm asking you, too. And don't come back here without a warrant."

Nash was furious that these bumpkins thought they could tell him what to do. He wanted to show them who was boss here. But he knew Blume would get his shorts in a knot if Mrs. LeBlanc and her friend complained. He could tell he wasn't going to get anywhere here anyway. Best to cut his losses. At least his visit might get the missus to speak with LeBlanc. If LeBlanc thought the FBI would come down on her, he might loosen up a little. Maybe all was not lost.

But it was not in his nature to concede. Nash had to have the last word. "Fine. If you want to play hardball, hardball it will be. I'll be back. And next time, it won't be for a chat." When he got to his car, Nash called his office. "Get me everything you can on a Brenda LeBlanc—credit records, driving records, assets listing, the works. And I need it right away. I need to put a little pressure on Mrs. LeBlanc. She's a possible witness in a murder I'm working."

Chapter Fifteen

Sleepy met the housing board first thing in the morning. He had been in solitary confinement for five days. Under prison rules, he was entitled to a review of his housing designation after that time. The board listened to him repeat his story, that he was asleep at the time of the escape and knew nothing about it. They questioned him about the fire that was set in the cell near his. He told them the truth, that he was unaware of the problem until he smelled the smoke and called for the guard, that he was led to the atrium to wait for the fire crew, and that the fire crew put out the fire and used an exhaust fan to clear the smoke away.

The housing board consisted of three senior officers. All three said the same thing to Sleepy—the fire was obviously meant for you. Why else would it be set in that corridor? There wasn't anybody else on that corridor. It was used for emergency protective custody. Sleepy had been put there because Hammer and his crew would be less likely to find him and be able to get to him.

Sleepy didn't point out that the best laid plans had gone seriously awry. He wanted to be moved to open population. A smart remark now wouldn't help his cause. "I'll sign a waiver," he said to the board members. He knew that a primary concern was that the prison would be held liable if something happened to him. The waiver relieved them of responsibility because he was voluntarily electing to leave protective custody, after the fire incident and after their advising him that he could be in further danger.

The officers looked at each other. The chair of the board nodded, looked into a folder, pulled out a long form, and handed the form to Sleepy. "LeBlanc, read this and if you choose to do so, sign it. But remember, it's your funeral. We are advising you to remain in protective custody. We have reason to believe that you are still in danger."

"I know, Sir. I'll take my chances."

The chair continued, "As for the other matter, your possible involvement in the escape and the shooting and assaults, we have considered the evidence against you and we find, at this time, that we will not hold you in disciplinary detention for those events. You are not in the clear on the matters, LeBlanc. The FBI is here every day, investigating the escape and killing. If they can connect you to the escape, you're going back into detention until we can arrange a transfer to the Hill. You'll do the rest of your time there…however long."

Sleepy got his meaning. If he was found involved, the administration would transfer him to the super-maximum security facility up the hill from this prison. He would surely have new criminal charges, and if he was convicted as an accomplice in Harkness's murder, he'd either get life without parole or a death sentence. Either way, he'd leave the Hill in a box.

He just nodded. The chair handed him a pen, and he signed his name on the waiver. He didn't read it. He knew what he was giving up. The right to a civil suit if he was harmed or injured. So what? What would be the likelihood that any jury would award a convict any money if another convict attacked him? Or give his family any money? He'd gladly give up that slim chance for the relative freedom of open population.

The chairman conferred briefly with the other two hearing board officers, then announced the decision: Open Population, Block A, Cell 10. Sleepy tried not to show his feelings. He stood, nodded at the board, and left the room to wait for his escort. Home! He thought. He was going back to his old block. He'd check with the block officer about his property, and he'd probably have his books and paperwork by the end of the day. His good shoes and good underclothes, especially the insulated kind, he could kiss goodbye. He learned when he went to segregation before not to expect property worth anything to be given back to him. But nobody wanted his books and writings so they weren't worth stealing. He'd get his stuff back, get his house organized like he liked it, settle in and wait for Be-Bop to figure out he was back.

The escort took him directly to cell 10. In open population, he could shower daily. As soon as his property arrived, he got his soap and towel and headed for the showers. When he was done, he went back to his cell, hung up his towel to dry, put away his soap, and laid down on his bunk. He had made it up fresh before he left for the showers. Showering alone was a luxury he would not be able to afford from now on, he knew. He'd have to rely on Rosie to watch his back. He would be glad to see Rosie. Rosie would find him as soon as he was able. In the meantime, Sleepy wanted to take a short nap.

He was awakened by a slight pinch on his left hand. He realized immediately what it was. Be-Bop was nibbling at his finger. Be-Bop liked to nip but he never actually bit him. He was so happy to see his rat. He was very afraid that someone would catch him while he was gone, or that one of the prison cats would find him and make lunch of him. When he was in his cell, Be-Bop stayed close to home, waiting for the dinner crumbs that he knew were going to arrive, like clockwork. Sleepy felt at ease now. He had all the comforts he could provide for himself in his environment—a clean bed, a clean body, clean clothes, his books and writings, and his pet.

The best thing about being in population was that he got a weekly telephone call to his family. His aunt would be worried, since she read the papers and watched the news religiously, eager to keep up with what was happening in the world. He wanted to get word to her that he was okay.

When he got to the head of the phone line, it was almost too late to call. He didn't want to wake her, but he wanted to ease her mind if he could. When she answered, he felt a huge sense of relief. Hearing her voice made him want to cry. "Aunt Ruth?"

Before he got out another word, she had started to sniffle. "Theodore? Theodore, is that you? Oh, I've been worried sick. Honey, tell me what is going on. How are you? Are you hurt?"

Sleepy was about to cry himself. "Aunt Ruth, don't you worry about me. I'm fine. That's why I called. I wanted you to know I'm alright. I knew you'd be worried. But I can't really tell you anything. I was asleep on the bus. I didn't see what happened."

Her tone of voice changed suddenly. "Well, you should tell that

FBI agent that. He surely thinks you know something."

Sleepy felt his heart rate increase, and realized he was sweating. "What do you mean, FBI agent?" His mouth was dry, and had a sour taste. What could she be talking about? It must be something she read in the papers.

Before he could think on it any more, she continued. "Yes, that agent Nash fellow. He came here, you know. He came here yesterday, acting all-important. I took him down a peg or two, you can bet."

Sleepy couldn't help but smile. His aunt had been a junior high school teacher. Dealing with bullies was second nature to her. He could almost feel some sympathy for Nash, if he were not so blindingly angry. So that was Nash's tactic. Harass his family, to get to him.

"Aunt Ruth, I'm sorry he bothered you. It won't happen again. How's Uncle Samuel?"

"Honey, he hasn't changed. He's maybe a little weaker. He's still really alert, though. He will want to speak with you. Let me go tell him to pick up the other phone."

In a second, his Uncle Sam's voice came on the line. He sounded weak. Sleepy could hardly stand to hear how much he was going down hill. But he knew his uncle could sense his upset, so he tried to sound cheerful. "Uncle Samuel, how are you?"

"Boy, I'm weak of body, but not of spirit. That's the best I can say. Your aunt takes real good care of me. I just wish I could get up to see you. Maybe one of these days."

They both knew that would not happen. But if it made his uncle feel better, he would go along. "Uncle Samuel, I would really enjoy that. This place is not so bad. I've made peace with being here. I have a friend here, who is a good man. He got into some trouble when he tossed the governor's aide out of a topless bar for manhandling the dancers. Next thing you know, there is cocaine in his locker. He never touched the stuff in his life, but there it was, in his locker."

"Lord, son, your experience has colored my view of our criminal justice system. I used to think that if you were innocent, you couldn't end up in a place like that. I surely know different now."

"Well, Uncle Samuel, you taught me that things happen for a reason. I'm just trying to make the best of this situation, and get back home."

Unspoken between them was that Sleepy wanted to get back home before Uncle Samuel died. From Aunt Ruth's reports, that might not be possible.

Sleepy told his uncle goodbye and promised to call again next week. He told his aunt that if she got any more visits, to call the prison and ask for the chaplain, and ask the chaplain to get a message to him. That means of communication was usually available only for family illness or death, but he was pretty sure the chaplain would put this in the category of family emergency. What he would do to protect his aunt and uncle, he did not know right now. But he would think of something. And to hell with agent Nash and his plan.

Chapter Sixteen

The more Sleepy thought about his aunt and uncle being bothered by Nash, the madder he got. Those sweet people never troubled another soul. They did not deserve to be treated as pawns in Nash's games. Sleepy was taking a walk on the rec yard, aware that he would be happy to be back in population and able to get a small dose of sunshine each day, but for Nash and his antics. He spotted Rosie moving slowly toward him. Rosie's bulk slowed him at times, but if he needed to get someplace quickly, his years in the ring kicked in and he could maneuver with lightning speed. Today, ambling seemed more comfortable for him.

When Rosie got in earshot of Sleepy, he called out his name. "Sleep. Good to see you back."

Sleepy approached his old friend and gave him a brief hug. "Rosie, you know you're in trouble when you miss the likes of you!"

Rosie grinned. "Yeah, I know. What's up?"

"That jerk Nash contacted my people. You know my uncle is sick. And my aunt worries herself half to death about him, and about me being here. Now Nash is troubling them. I don't know how to help them, and it's driving me crazy."

Rosie slowed his walk. "Sleep, did you talk to Ms. Johnson about what Nash is doing?"

Sleepy stopped walking altogether. "Rosie, I can't believe I didn't even think of that. Do you think she would help me?"

"Course she would, Sleep. She's your lawyer. That's what good lawyers do, they help people. You and me didn't know 'bout that since we had bums for lawyers, but I hear tell that's how good ones operate."

Rosie smiled at his sarcasm, and slapped Sleepy on the back. "Go get on that phone, boy, and tell her what Nash is up to. I'm betting she'll put a stop to it right quick."

Sleepy did just that. He went to the banks of telephones just off the rec yard. There was one phone with no line. He used his prepaid phone card to call the Washington office number Mercy had given him. Rosie followed a few paces behind Sleepy, and tried to look unobtrusive. The fact that he was guarding Sleepy was clear to anybody with an intent to harm him. That was what mattered.

When Sleepy reached Mercy Johnson's office, a young woman answered the phone. "Can I speak to Ms. Johnson? This is Theodore LeBlanc."

"Just one minute, please."

Sleepy waited less than half a minute, and Mercy Johnson came on the line.

"Hello, Mr. LeBlanc. How are you?"

"I'm not too good, Ms. Johnson. I got out of the hole today. I called home to check on my aunt and uncle and to let them know I am fine. My aunt told me agent Nash came by to see them, and that he acted like he was gonna come back 'til they told him what he wanted to hear. Well, that won't happen. Aunt Ruth and Uncle Samuel won't bend to his pressure. They don't know a thing about the prison break, I didn't tell them anything because I don't know anything. The agent is gonna cause them hurt, if he keeps pressuring them. I'm real worried, Ms. Johnson."

"Don't be, Theodore. Let me handle it. Call me back tomorrow. I'll have good news by then, I expect."

"Yes, Ms. Johnson. I will do just that." Sleepy was glad legal calls didn't count against his one call per week limit.

LeBlanc put down the phone and gestured to Rosie. Rosie came to the phone bank and the men walked onto the yard, to a corner where no other inmates were around. Sleepy looked around to make sure they could not be overheard, then he said, "Rosie, thanks, man. She said she would handle it. She told me to call her again tomorrow. I feel a whole lot better. If I know my aunt and uncle are not going to be upset, I can handle everything here."

Rosie nodded. "I got your back, Sleep. Now Ms. Mercy's gonna protect your peoples."

Chapter Seventeen

Mercy put the phone down and headed for Sam's office. He looked up as she entered. "Uh-oh," he said. "Is that war paint I see? Who is the unlucky target?"

"That FBI agent, Nash. He visited Theodore LeBlanc's elderly aunt and uncle, tried to scare them into telling him that LeBlanc knew something about the prison escape and that he told them about it. They held firm. But those old people are not well. They do not need to be worried by Nash and his foolishness. I'm going to put a stop to it myself, or I'm going to find a judge who will put a stop to it."

"Anything I can do to help?"

"That's why I walked down here. I needed to let off steam, but I also needed to get your help taping my conversation with Nash. I want you to listen to my end of the conversation, so you can testify to exactly what I said, if it becomes necessary. But I want to get it on tape, too. I'm going to give him fair warning. If he fails to heed the warning, I intend to make life very uncomfortable for him. I don't trust him. He will lie about what I said, if he can. We will make sure he can't do that."

"Seems like a plan," Sam said, reaching into a drawer behind his desk and extracting a tape player. He set up the player, put in a fresh tape, attached the unit to the telephone, and nodded to Mercy.

Mercy dialed the number on the card Nash gave LeBlanc. He answered after two rings. "Nash," he barked into the phone.

Mercy wasted no time. "Agent Nash, this is Mercy Johnson. I am a defense attorney practicing in Washington, D.C. I am associated with the firm of Holland and Pearce, a Virginia law firm, in the representation of Theodore LeBlanc. I understand you have spoken to my client. I am calling for two reasons. First, to ask that you not attempt to speak with him again. He is represented by counsel, and I have advised him not to discuss his case with anyone but me. Any further attempt on your part to communicate with him will be futile. I'd like to ask if we are clear on that point before we proceed."

Mercy could hear Nash breathing hard. "Well, well, The-oh got him some big city lawyer, huh? Guilty people usually do, don't they, counselor?"

Mercy resisted the urge to engage. "Agent, I assume at some point in your training, someone mentioned to you a document known as the United States Constitution. I don't think it's my job to educate you, if your education was otherwise lacking. I am simply asking you a question. Do you understand what I have just told you, that I am counsel to Theodore LeBlanc and that he has been instructed not to speak with you?"

"Yeah, counselor, I heard you. Of course, you and I know you can't keep me from talking to your client. If I decide to talk to him, I will. It's up to him whether he talks back."

"True enough. If you choose to waste the tax payer's dollars by repeated, futile attempts to speak with him, go ahead. I'll just include that bit of information in the rather lengthy letter I intend to put together to your director. And while we are speaking, I want to ask that you refrain from any further contact with Samuel and Ruth LeBlanc as well."

"Oh, so now you represent the whole flippin' family, huh?"

"Agent Nash, you know I do not represent the family. I am asking you nicely to refrain from harassing people who have not one shred of useful information to impart, as they have tried to explain to you. If you choose to continue in another fruitless endeavor, that is your option. I will add that to the list of complaints I intend to put forward in my letter to your boss. I should tell you that I know your boss. He and I are former adversaries. We went toe to toe several times when he was an Assistant United States Attorney here in the District. Knowing him as I do, I believe that on this issue he and I will see eye to eye. He is very well grounded in the Constitution. Moreover, he will strongly object to one of his underlings terrorizing old people. Sick old people at that. Anything else we need to talk about today?"

"Nope," Nash said curtly. "Since you are so worried about

taxpayer dollars, I'll end this call and get back to something important."

"Suit yourself, agent."

Mercy hung up. She looked at Sam, who was smiling broadly. "Lord, I almost feel sorry for that man. He don't know it yet, but trouble done called his name."

"He's probably calling me a few names right about now," Mercy said. "Every name but a child of God."

Sam laughed. "You right about that."

Chapter Eighteen

Hastings paced in his cell. He was used to solitary confinement, so it wasn't the cramped quarters that bothered him. He paced to think. He needed a plan to get to the plowboy. He pulled the little piece of sharpened metal from between his two longest toes and carefully stowed it away underneath his mattress. He got the standard body cavity search when he was moved to the hole. The guard was new and not used to inspecting all the various parts of the human anatomy where prison-made weapons could be hidden. He missed the shank.

Hastings sat down on the bunk, and put his shower shoes on. Prison floors were notorious for creepers and he slept in his shoes, in case he had to get up and get somewhere quickly. He made his bed, straightening the blanket military-style over the steel slab and thin mattress that served as a bed in the segregation unit. He learned years ago, when he first started jailing, that a well-made bed often deterred officers from looking inside the cover, or underneath the bed. "Clowns probably think cleanliness is next to godliness," he muttered. Hastings usually slept soundly. In a world where fear was the paramount emotion, he was fearless. He had the safest life a prisoner could have. He had a crew of men working for him, to keep him safe. He was the boss, because he was the smartest and the meanest. He didn't flinch at hurting his opposition. He loved his nickname. He was dubbed "Hammer" after his first prison fight. He was given a job in the shop, working on the prison vans. He qualified because in one of his short stints on the street, he worked as a mechanic. When the shop boss, a trusty, tried to tell him that he put the wrong nut on the wrong bolt, he slammed the guy in the head with a hammer used for loosening tires from wheel rims. Gave the guy a concussion and got himself fired from the shop. Of course, he also got the maximum in detention, six months. What did he care? He was alone there, like he had been for as long as he could remember. Only difference from the street was he didn't have to scuffle for meals and a bed. He didn't complain about the hole. It was a five-star hotel, compared to some of the places his mother had called home.

Hastings laid back on his bunk, and closed his eyes. He needed a plan. If he could get to open population, he could take care of that dumb plowboy himself. With an escape charge, and maybe a murder charge coming down the pike, he knew he would be in the hole for at least six months. He would probably be transferred to super-maximum security, even if the State didn't indict him for murder. Wouldn't that be a joke! Harkness was the meanest man he'd ever met, next to himself. The State should write if off as a mercy killing. Mercy for all those poor convicts the pervert would torture in some dark corner of the showers, or the laundry room, or wherever else he could find them without any backup. Hastings knew the system wouldn't necessarily agree with his definition of mercy killing, but he sure wasn't sorry Harkness was gone.

So how to keep that Sleepy creep from deciding he needs a time cut, and working a deal with the State? His boys from the bus crew were all in the hole themselves. Thank god, the crew members who weren't on the bus could still move about. Like Exxon, his ace fire setter. Exxon was doing time for burning down his own mother's house, for the insurance money. She had been in on the plan, except the part about his setting the fire while she was upstairs asleep in her bed. Exxon didn't care who he burned, as long as he got to set the fire and watch it. Crazy as a bed bug, that one. Hastings got the word to him, "#1 Burn the biscuits." Just a little fire, for starters. He put the kite in the slit in his pants waistband. He then took off the pants, and with the heel of his shoe, put a mark on the left front pocket. Exxon worked in the laundry. He knew Hastings was in the hole. Exxon was on the look-out for messages, when he saw the footprint, he looked inside the waistband for the kite. The signal was one Hastings's gang always used when one of them was in the hole and trying to get a message out. Each message had a number, which told his crew who was to receive it. #1 was Exxon, #2 was Nut, and so on. The system was the best he could devise, without the chirp phones he used to communicate with his underlings on the street.

Hastings was thinking about Exxon, and his love for fire, when he heard footsteps pounding down his corridor. What the hell? he thought. Must be a Code Blue. Maybe Exxon got to Sleepy, after all. He suddenly felt a glimmer of hope. If Sleepy got burned, he'd be on his way to the infirmary, maybe even on his way to a hospital on the outside. Soon Hastings would know about that. Whatever was up, the news would get to him before it got to the warden. The prison grapevine was the most efficient in the world at getting out information.

Sure enough, it was only a minute before a balled up message rolled underneath his door. He opened it carefully. The message said, "Wrong house." Now what the devil did that mean? Wrong house! Did Exxon torch the wrong guy? Exxon knew all about the escape plot. He was smart, and he would figure out that Sleepy was trouble for them all. Hastings had trusted him to take care of the guy. Apparently, that trust was misplaced. Time to go to Plan B. Then they could all breathe easier. Maybe the guy really was asleep on the bus. But why take the risk? What was that guy to him? Hastings hadn't lived this long by giving people a break. The plowboy didn't get one either.

Plan B was Nut. Hastings pulled a piece of paper towel from his shoe. He got the pencil stub, and wrote a kite to Nut. "#2 Old Lace." He figured the guards were all too young or too ignorant to know the reference. The poison Nut had wasn't arsenic, anyway, but it was good enough. He'd sure seen some rats wish they hadn't eaten it. Probably wouldn't kill Sleepy, but he'd be sick enough not to forget what Hammer was telling him.

He balled up the paper spit-ball size and scooted it like a marble under the door of the cell across the corridor from him. An inmate would clean the cell eventually. When he found the message, he'd pass it on 'til it got to Nut.

Chapter Nineteen

Hastings was worried. He should have heard from Nut by now. Nut always carried out his assignments. He never let Hastings down. He smiled when he remembered the snitch who told on him for getting marijuana into the visiting room through one of the many women who visited him. He got caught with the marijuana because two of his women showed up at the same time. One was supposed to come that morning, for the family church service that the chaplain arranged for inmates who had been sixty days without an incident report. Instead, she waited for the usual family visiting hours in the early afternoon. Hastings told another woman she could come to see him then. All hell broke loose when they collided. The one who was smuggling the marijuana in her bra threw the plastic baggie at Hammer and stormed out, yelling "bitch whore" at the other woman and threatening to wait for her in the parking lot. He was quick enough to get the baggie and put it in his underwear while the guards were still watching the two women, hoping for a fight. But one of the inmates with a short sentence saw the baggie. He wanted to do the rest of his time in a camp, not in the correctional institute, a fancy name for pen. So he informed on Hastings. Nut found him in the shower one day and shanked him. The guy bled so fast he nearly died before the medics got the bleeding stopped and got him to a hospital. Hastings heard they had to give him so many transfusions they replaced every drop of blood in his body before they were done. Nut was good like that. You could trust him to do a job right. The snitch didn't die, but that was okay, because he was taken to another prison, not a camp, and kept in administrative segregation, protective custody, for the rest of his tour. The word got out quick. Don't tell on Hammer. And of course, if you were part of Hastings's crew, you got the same protection. They could pretty much do what they wanted, as long as the guards didn't actually see it, because no one was going to let on that they knew.

Nut almost killed another inmate by poisoning his food. He got hold of some poison meant for the rats that ran rampant in the old prison. A guy owed Hastings some money for heroin he had convinced one of his harem to bring in. The guy kept promising to pay. He told Hastings he would get his wife to send money to Hastings's account. That was how debts usually got paid in prison. But the money never came. Hastings waited a month. He couldn't wait any longer. If he did, people would take him for a chump. Then nobody would pay his debts. Hastings got no regular money from anybody on the outside, except these payments by inmates. Of the many women on his visitor list, one or two a month would scrape up twenty dollars, or even fifty dollars. But he couldn't count on it. They were always complaining that they had bills, their car quit running, the kids needed shoes. Something to get in the way of sending money to him. So he had to take care of himself. That meant he had to collect his debts. So he told Nut to get the guy to pay up. Nut meant to teach the guy a lesson, not to kill him. That he nearly succeeded in killing him was more accident than anything else. But it worked out for Hastings. Everybody knew why the guy got poisoned. Nobody else wanted to get so close to death's doorstep, so they started paying up right away. Get the drugs one day, have somebody put a money order for Hastings's account in the mail the next. Sweet lesson, Hastings thought, smiling.

There were one or two other guys Nut had worked on for Hastings, but he couldn't remember the details. He didn't need to. All he remembered was that when he needed some heavy lifting, Nut was his man. So what happened with that dumb Sleepy? Why ain't Nut got the message to the guy?

He needed to talk to Nut. It would have to wait 'til he got his shower. Then, he'd tell whoever was in the shower before or after him to pass the word to Nut that he needed more information. Was it tomorrow he got out to shower? He tried to reconstruct the events since he was picked up at his old lady's house. That was Monday night, when he slapped the bitch so hard her bridgework came out of her mouth. Then she called the cops on him. He still couldn't believe it. Women these days, man, you really had to watch them.

If it was Monday night when the cops locked him up, then today would be Saturday. He got showers Wednesday and Sunday. So tomorrow he could get a message to Nut. Nut's last name was Jefferson, so he would shower tomorrow, too. Maybe they could actually speak to each other. Hastings was so relieved at that possibility, he laid down on the hard steel slab and went right to sleep.

When he woke, he took out the newspaper one of the guards on his payroll had dropped off. He laughed when he saw the headlines and the questions about the road crew. "Whew," he said aloud, "they're roasting that S.O.B Watts. Using his butt for firewood." He smiled a satisfied smile. Then he got to the section which profiled the escapees. "Damn," he said, when he got to the story about him. "They make me look like some kind of mobster! I ought to sue for character defamation!" He laughed aloud. He was pleased with the coverage, especially the frequent use of his nickname. The worse he looked on paper, the less work he had to do to get what he wanted in here. He ought to send the reporter some roses. She had hyped his image better than he could have done.

Hastings was still smiling when he got to LeBlanc's profile. When he finished the story, he was shaking his head. Now if that don't beat all, he said to himself. Dumb sucker's in here because he fell asleep in a department store and when he woke up, couldn't get out. He was still there in the morning, in a dressing room with clothes his size. Got prosecuted for burglary one, on a fluke. So happened the department store had an occupied penthouse apartment. Should have been prosecuted for felony stupid. Hastings laughed at his joke.

He read the other profiles. His crew looked bad. Some of them had convictions even he did not know about. No wonder the public was upset. Hastings hoped they didn't investigate too thoroughly. He had paid a king's ransom to get his boys on the road crew. He hoped the guards he tipped would keep quiet. He doubted they'd risk talking, since it would mean their jobs, but if they did, he had people on the outside to take care of them.

Hastings re-read the article about LeBlanc. This highly-placed source was probably that greedy FBI agent, he thought. He was trying to squeeze LeBlanc to cooperate with him. Hastings had to get word to his crew. The way they protected themselves was to squeeze harder. It was time to get LeBlanc. He didn't want to hear any more excuses. He underlined part of the profile on LeBlanc, and tore the whole profile from his paper. He rolled the profile into a tight ball, and waited for a way to pass it to Nut. Nut needed to get busy. He had work to do.

Chapter Twenty

Sleepy woke up hungry. He went to the dining hall early, but because the lines were so long, he just got a bowl of oatmeal and stashed it, bringing it back to his cell so he could nap first, then eat breakfast. He still felt foggy from sleep, but he reached for the bowl he left on the ledge just above the bed. It wasn't there. He sat up, and when he saw the bowl, his heart sank. It was lying on the floor, upturned. He cursed himself. He had forgotten that Be-Bop liked oatmeal. Be-Bop must have found the bowl while he slept, and got into it. Where was the little guy? Sleepy knew he liked to stay in the cell after he ate, and clean himself before taking a nice long nap. Where was he hiding? He got up and looked under the bed.

Then he sat back down, almost falling onto the hard bed. Be-Bop was underneath the bed, on his back, all four feet in the air. He was not moving. Sleepy knew he would not move. He also knew that whatever was in the oatmeal had been meant for him. His shoulders heaved, and his breathing came fast and shallow. "Bastards!" he said. "Those damn bastards!"

He sat on his bed without moving for a long time. He tried not to think of the hours he had spent teaching Be-Bop tricks. He tried to think of only one thing. How to get back at that Hammer creep? It would not be easy. He was well-protected. But Sleepy meant to put a stop to him. The only questions were when, and how.

*　　　*　　　*

Rosie exploded when Sleepy told him about Be-Bop. "Sleep, man, you know I hate that. I was afraid of the little guy at first, but he grew on me. I didn't mind taking care of him while you were in the hole. Whoever did this is a sick sucker."

Sleepy was clenching and unclenching his fists. "Rosie, I don't remember ever wanting to hurt anybody 'til now. I know the oatmeal was meant for me. That makes me mad enough. But to think that Be-Bop was the one who suffered, it kills me. I want to find the guy who did this and make him pay."

Rosie punched Sleepy's shoulder lightly. "We make him pay, Sleep. We in this together. Now it's war. We just can't fight like these guys do. We ain't like them. We got to out think them, hit them where they're weakest. You and me are two smart country boys. We'll figure it out."

Chapter Twenty-One

Hastings was asleep in his bunk, trying to find ways to accommodate his bony frame on the steel plate, when he heard a noise in the hallway. Then the door to his cell swung open, and the SWAT team was at the door. Wearing gas masks and carrying night sticks, they managed to scare even him. If he'd seen them coming, he wouldn't have been shook up. But to sneak up on him like they did, that gave him a start. He recovered quickly, and put on his most sullen face.

"What'd I do?" he demanded to know.

Insolence to an officer was sure to land him in the hole for a few days. But he was already here for the duration, so what did it matter? The guards knew not to smack him around, even when they came in numbers. They knew that sooner or later, he'd get them alone, and he'd do a lot more damage than they would. Word in the prison was that Hammer had been home-schooled by Attila the Hun. He liked the rep. It saved him having to prove himself all the time.

The leader of the SWAT team spoke to him. "Hastings, we have reason to believe that there's some contraband in your cell. We're going to search it. Please step outside. You don't need to make trouble for yourself."

Hastings nodded. "Search all you want." he said, refusing to acknowledge what he knew to be true, that they would search regardless of whether he cooperated. He held his hands out to be cuffed, and then followed one of the guards to the hallway, where they stood together while the rest of the team searched every nook and cranny of the cell. In just a few minutes, the lead guard stepped to the hallway. "All clear," he said to the hallway officer, ignoring Hastings.

"So, can I have my house back now?" Hastings asked.

The guard did not answer, but the lead guard went to a clip on his belt, retrieved a key, and unlocked the handcuffs. He held the door, and motioned Hastings back into his cell. Then as quickly as they had appeared, the SWAT officers left and Hastings was alone.

He sat on his bunk, savoring what he knew must be true. Someone had been hurt. Someone that Hastings wanted hurt. Otherwise, why the police presence? He'd get the news soon enough. But now, he could rest, knowing that his orders had been carried out. What more could you ask of foot soldiers?

Chapter Twenty-Two

Mercy hung up the phone and called for Sam. She was pacing when he rushed into her office.

"Tell me, Sam, what I can do to protect Theodore inside? There's been another incident. He just called. Someone poisoned his pet rat. The poison was in the oatmeal on his breakfast tray. It was obviously meant for him. He thinks it's this Hastings character, the leader of the group of inmates who escaped the bus. We can't get into the prison to watch over him. Your cousin is doing his best to watch his back, but he can't be with Theodore 24-7. What would you suggest?"

"Mercy, you know how prisons are. No one is safe if someone wants to do him harm. Guards can be bought, other inmates turn their heads, inmates run in gangs for their own protection and don't want to refuse orders from their protectors."

Mercy knew Sam was right. "This Hastings character probably got his flunkies to hurt Theodore. I hate it about the rat, it was his pet. He's very sad about it. But thank God it wasn't him. And it could well have been. We have to do something."

"You want me to go talk to him?"

"If I can get you into the prison. I think I will have to go with you. You are a licensed investigator, but you are still a convicted felon. It may be dicey, getting you in on your own."

"I go into the jail here all the time."

"Yes, we've worked that out with the Department of Corrections. I just don't know about the authorities down there. Let me make some phone calls, and set something up."

An hour later, Mercy was standing at Sam's desk, a form in hand. "Here, I downloaded this from the internet. It's a visitor request form for the state prison system. Fill it out, and fax it to the Visitor Control Officer. Her name and the fax number are on the form. I'm already on file as his attorney so I don't need the form.

Let's try to get down there tomorrow. I don't have anything in court. I was going to use the day to catch up on office work. Oh, well."

"Yeah, me too. Can't say I'm upset about not getting to write up a bunch of reports, though."

Sam smiled slyly.

Mercy grumbled. "If you'd do them as you go, it wouldn't be such an issue."

"Yeah, I know. I know."

Chapter Twenty-Three

Sam drove Mercy's car while she used her smart phone to answer a backlog of emails. "Multi-tasking gets harder and harder at my age."

"Our age," Sam corrected her. "If you think it's hard for you, what about me? I'm learning a whole new world. Technology I only read about when I was locked up. That phone is nothing short of a miracle, in my eyes. But I'm getting there."

"Sam, you know more about computers than the average fifteen year old. Don't sell yourself short. To prove my point, pull over and let me drive. I want you to look up something on the Internet. I have an idea about how to get to this Hastings character."

"Care to share it?"

"What do you suppose scares Hastings the most?"

"No contest. Losing face. That's the way with prison honchos. They have their underlings, usually dumber than they are, and in order to keep their power, they have to look tough. Anything that makes them look weak threatens their hold over the masses."

"Yep, that's what I was thinking. Now, I just have to figure out how to tarnish Hastings's tough guy image. Get to him, make him want to leave LeBlanc alone."

"Mercy, you are one devious woman. I feel for Walter if you ever set out to get him."

"Why would I do that? He's the best man I know. "

"And lucky for him."

Mercy handed Sam the phone and got behind the wheel. He made a show of fastening his seat belt. "Alright, Danica, let's roll."

Mercy just grunted and kept her eyes on the road.

They arrived at the prison with time to spare. "Sam, before we see LeBlanc, I want to speak with the warden. I want to alert him about Hastings's threats to our client. I didn't make an appointment with him, so I hope he's available."

"Might be a good idea for us to introduce ourselves, anyway. Since our client could end up charged with the murder of one of the prison staff, we should let the warden know we will be diligently monitoring our client's safety."

"Right."

When they had been screened and searched, Mercy asked the visitor control officer if she would call the warden about a quick visit.

"Did you have an appointment with the warden?" the woman asked suspiciously.

Mercy decided humility would probably trump insistence as an effective means of persuasion, so she said politely, "I'm afraid I forgot to ask about that when I called for our appointment. But something has come up concerning our client's health. I want to make sure the prison administration is aware of a potential problem. I think it could even be a life-threatening problem. I know I won't rest until I've done what I can to alert the proper authorities. I think this is something the warden will want to know about."

Either Mercy's gentle demeanor persuaded the officer, or she had a vision of the warden learning that she had advance knowledge of a life-threatening situation she did not report. She used her radio to call the warden's office.

"You're in luck. He's in. I'll show you how to get to his office."

Raeford Watts was not the man Mercy would have pictured as the prison warden. He was tall, and moved like an athlete when he crossed his office to greet Mercy and Sam. He extended a large hand to shake their hands. His charcoal suit fit his slim frame perfectly. His light blue cotton shirt matched his eyes. His face was tan and his body looked like it benefited from the attention of a good trainer. Impressive man, Mercy thought.

"Ms. Johnson, my visitor control officer said you have an urgent matter for me. How can I help you?"

Mercy sensed she needed to get to the point quickly. Everything about Watts's demeanor said that he was a man with a crowded calendar. She told him what Hastings was doing to Theodore LeBlanc.

He listened without comment. When he did speak, he sounded

almost weary. "Hastings is a menace. I can't watch LeBlanc around the clock. He does not want to be in protective custody. I'm going to think about how to incapacitate Hastings. If you have any ideas on that subject, I'd like to hear them."

"I think whatever you do to warn him off, it has to threaten his image. He wields power because he instills fear. If you can somehow make him look weak, maybe you can negotiate a truce with him."

"My thinking exactly. Scares me, to be on the same page as a defense attorney."

Watts's smile lit his lean face. Planes that would fit together to make him look hard were softened by the smile. He seemed to enjoy his own joke. Mercy liked that in the man. She was willing to trust that he would try to help her client.

"Warden, are you willing to let me know when you have something in place? I won't share it with Mr. LeBlanc, but I will sleep better at night if I can be confident he is safe."

"If I can, I will."

Mercy knew that meant that if he could without compromising the running of his prison, he would. She wouldn't push for more right now.

"Then if you will direct Mr. Lester and me to the visiting hall, we will be on our way."

The warden buzzed his secretary and told her to send in an escort. Mercy thanked him and left. She waited until she and Sam were seated in the attorney booth, waiting for Theodore, to ask Sam's opinion of Watts.

"A cut above what I was used to as a prison warden. But let's see what he does. If he can figure out how to rein in this Hastings fellow, my hat's off to him. I've seen these prison toughs take over a prison to the point that even the administration and the guards are afraid of them. I don't see that happening with Watts."

"Good. That's my view, too. Now let's make a plan with LeBlanc, and make sure he knows how to get help if he needs it."

A visit Mercy had meant to be brief stretched to two hours, but at the end, she and Sam were comfortable with LeBlanc's ability to get the word to them if he needed more protection than Rosie and

Watts could provide. As they were leaving the prison, Mercy asked Sam, "So, what do you think about our client? Is he part of a plot to murder a prison guard and free a bunch of prisoners, or was he asleep on the bus like he says?"

Sam looked thoughtful. "I don't get the sense from him that he's hard enough to be in on such a plot. I think he's telling us the truth about being asleep. My only concern is whether he uses sleep to avoid anything unpleasant. If that's the case, he could be operating on a level of consciousness that seems like sleep to him but is really more avoidance."

"You mean he may know something, but not know that he knows it?"

"Yep."

"Well how would we know if that is the case?"

"My fear is, we won't. Let's just hope it doesn't matter in the long run."

"Sam, I've been thinking about our investigation. Nash has focused on the road crew, and he won't expand his search for suspects, I'm guessing. That's why he's so determined to squeeze LeBlanc. We need to do his work for him, on that score. We need to identify other people who might have wanted Harkness dead. You know the first rule. Start with the person closest to him and work outward in his circle of family and friends. Can we try to find out about his family and friends?"

"I'm ahead of you there. I already got the newspaper articles about his death, and learned that he has a grieving widow. Much younger, very pretty, and the complainant in at least two domestic violence charges against Harkness. She seems like a good place to start."

"Definitely. If Harkness had the standard State employee package, he had life insurance. See if you can check out her credit, her spending habits, whether she looks like someone who lives beyond her means. Check him out too, since they may have separate bank accounts, credit cards, store accounts."

"Will do. I'll get back to you on that tomorrow."

Mercy agreed. "That's soon enough. I doubt we will have any use for the information until trial, but it will be good to know whether there's a third party with motive and the opportunity to kill Harkness."

"Huh," Sam laughed. "From what I'm hearing of the guy, there may have been a waiting line to do him in."

Chapter Twenty-Four

Nancy Carmichael was new to the job. In June she earned a second master's degree, this one in psychology, and before the ink dried on her diploma, she aced the civil service examination and placed near the top of the list for a job with the state government. She had to start somewhere, she reasoned, and until she could get her complicated life arranged so she could pursue a doctorate, she would take the first civil service job she was offered. She might not have been so quick to join the workforce if she had known that the first offer would come from the prison. But once she got the offer, and looked at the pay scale, she couldn't say no. And her mentor and advisor, a woman to whom she looked when any decision had to be made, was comfortable with the prison assignment. So here she was, settling into an office the size of a cell, trying to get used to a computer that must have served Caesar, and trying not to swear loudly enough to be overheard.

She was underneath the desk, fiddling with some of the wires to the various ancient components, when she heard a knock on the door to the office. "I am not scheduled for any appointments today," she muttered. "I need to get this stupid machine up and running."

But she got out from under the desk, brushed off her new pantsuit, and took the step between the desk and the door, opening it carefully so as not to dislodge the only other chair in the room besides her desk chair. A tall man stood at the door, wearing a suit, and holding a hat in his hand. Nobody wears a hat these days, she thought, irritated at the interruption.

"May I help you?" she said, in her best imitation of a professional voice. It didn't work as well as she had hoped, since she was a sliver over five feet tall, and the man standing much too close to her was well over six feet. She stepped back as far as she could, to put distance between them, and rephrased the question.

"Were you looking for me? I'm Nancy Carmichael, the prison psychologist."

"I know who you are," the man said, smiling. "Can I come in?"

"Well, I'm sure you can. But do you mind telling me your name, and what your business is with me."

Nash smiled even more widely. "I'm agent John Nash, of the Federal Bureau of Investigation. I need to ask you some questions."

His smooth manner unnerved Nancy. She didn't have a doctorate in psychology yet, but she had some sense. What was an FBI agent doing at her door, hat in hand? Whatever he wanted, it wouldn't be pleasant.

She stepped aside to admit Nash to her tiny office. He filled the empty spaces, making her feel crowded. She stepped behind her desk and sat in the desk chair, nodding toward the straight-backed visitor chair. "I didn't want my guests to get too comfortable. The chair is part of my interviewing technique," she apologized. "How can I help you?"

Nash rested his hat on the corner of her desk, and smiled at her. "I need the benefit of your expertise," he said. The emphasis on the last word could have been mocking, but she couldn't be sure.

"In what way?" she asked, guardedly.

"To solve a murder," he said bluntly.

She was startled. Without thinking, she blurted out, "Who got killed?" In an instant she realized her mistake. Nothing could have marked her as the new kid on the block better than that she had not been working at the prison when the guard was killed. Mentally, she kicked herself. You idiot! The guard, of course. What other murder would bring the FBI to the prison? Trying to regain some ground, she forced her voice to be calm.

"I'm sorry, I was distracted. Of course you are talking about Officer Harkness's killing. I was sorry to hear about his death. I want to help if I can, but I don't have any knowledge at all about the incident."

Nash looked at her for a shade too long, before he said, "I'm aware that you were not employed here when the killing took place. It's your expertise as a psychologist that I came for. There's a guy in here, claims he was asleep on the prison work bus when the guard was killed. The entire work crew escaped after the killing, although all but one are now back here. That one got shot, trying to make a stand. This witness is playing dumb, probably because he's in a hell of a bind. We want information from him, and if he gives it, he's got to watch his back constantly because the rest of his crew is in here, all of them worrying what he's going to tell. I think he's a smart guy. He's made up some sort of nonsense about having a sleep disorder. Even got the brass here believing the story. I looked at his records, and the story is that he falls asleep standing up. I don't buy it. The shotgun that killed the guard makes enough noise to be heard in Kansas. This guy is conning, I'm sure of it. I just need your help to figure out how to get to him. He's a hard nut to crack, I'll tell you that."

Nancy knew when she was being flattered. Nash obviously thought she'd be eager to help if she was presented with a challenge. He must not have read her professional canon of ethics before coming to her. "Cause no client harm," was at the core of it. Of course, this inmate was not yet her client. But he well could be someday.

"I don't believe I've met any client here with a sleep disorder, agent Nash. I don't see how I can be of any assistance to you."

"I didn't see in his records that he was a client, ma'am," Nash said. His emphasis on "client," irked her, but she let it pass. She could figure out later whether it was a slap at her profession, or just her.

Nancy refused to defend. She said, "He is not a client, I have not reviewed his records, and I know nothing of him or of any sleep disorder. Again, agent, I fail to see how I can help."

"You can help," Nash said, his irritation visible now, "by telling me what you know about this sleep disorder. Then you can review this con's records, talk to him, and tell me what methods I might employ to get him to talk. Your mission, if you choose to accept it, is to assist me in solving this heinous crime."

Nancy knew for sure now that he was ribbing her. He assumed she would be too young to remember that line from the television show on which at least four recent movies were based, but she let it pass.

"Let me get this straight, agent. You want me to contrive a session with an inmate, interrogate him for you, and soften him up for cooperating with you?"

The muscles in Nash's jaw twitched. She could see she had gotten to him. She was not displeased to have landed one blow in this sparring match.

"You could put it that way. But here's how I would put it. I want you to talk to him, review his records, and advise me how to reach him. There's nothing illegal in that. You are the prison psychologist, after all. I cleared this with the commander. He suggested I approach you."

So that was it. She had no choice. Nancy didn't like the orders from her boss being delivered by a go-between, but she didn't say so. "Do you have his records?"

Nash agreed to drop them off within the hour.

"When I get them, I'll look through them. Then I'll call him in for a meeting. After that, I'll talk with the commander about my ethical obligations, then I will share with you what I can."

"Fair enough," Nash agreed. His look said that he would not be persuaded by anything as high-minded as ethical considerations, but he didn't say so.

Nancy was relieved when he left. Something about him made her mad. He was definitely condescending, probably sexist, and totally lacking in appreciation for her role in the prison. But it was more than that. She sensed he wanted things to go his way, and when they did not, he could be troublesome. She'd have to be very careful of him. She would have to figure out how much he knew about her, too. He wasn't in the loop, so far as she knew. Nothing in his treatment of her suggested that he was.

She busied herself with the computer cords, and by the time Nash returned with the prison folder, she had the computer up and running. Meandering was more like it, but at least it worked. She would learn to live with the cords snaking every which way under her desk.

Nash must have sensed her wariness of him, because this time, he skipped the chit-chat. "Call me when you're through," was all he said, and he left.

Nancy opened the prison folder and began to read. Before she knew what had happened to the time, it was lunchtime. She was hungry, but not hungry enough to eat prison cafeteria food. She took the folder, got her purse and jacket, and left for the staff eating area in a courtyard off the atrium of the prison. She took her tuna salad sandwich and diet soda from her locker and walked to the outdoor eating area. It was chilly, but in her jacket, she was comfortable enough. She took a table apart from the few guards who were seated in the area. She wanted to read the file without anyone else seeing it.

The episodes of LeBlanc's falling asleep at the wrong times and in the wrong places were documented. The guards who had found him did not think he was faking. Prison guards were not easily hoodwinked, and if they decided LeBlanc was really asleep, he probably was. Of course, he could use sleep to manipulate. He might be one of the people who fell instantly asleep when he set his mind to it. She had certainly heard of such people. She would question him about the episodes. If she could see a pattern, a motive to use sleep as a weapon of some kind, or as avoidance, she would explore it. She would find this guy, and set up an appointment with him.

Nancy was not allowed in the housing areas of the prison. She had been given the media tour, shown all the places that touring dignitaries were allowed to see. But she had not seen the innards of the place. So to schedule a meeting with LeBlanc, she telephoned his housing unit, and spoke with the officer in charge.

"This is Nancy Carmichael," she said pleasantly.

"Who the hell is Nancy Carmichael?" came the surly reply.

"I'm the psychologist, officer. Who the hell are you, to speak to me in that way?"

There was silence on the other end of the telephone. Then the surly tone again:

"So what do you want, Miss. Psychologist?"

She ignored the insult. "I want to set up a meeting with an inmate in your housing unit. His name is LeBlanc. His number is 5789. I want him in my office tomorrow at 9:00 a.m. Can you arrange that?"

The surliness left him. Must be because my request doesn't cause him to do any work, Nancy thought. "Yes, ma'am. I'll bring him there myself. Hate we got off on the wrong foot. See you tomorrow."

Nancy had an idea about where he could put his wrong foot, but she didn't say it. "Thank you, officer. I'll look forward to seeing you and Mr. LeBlanc tomorrow."

Nancy spent the rest of the afternoon poring over the records. Mother died of cancer when LeBlanc was just months old. Father gave baby to mother's family. Not heard from again. Boy raised by aunt and uncle who had no children of their own. Finished high school, two years at technical college learning drafting, married for three years, divorced without children. Ex-wife on visiting list, and visits on holidays. Aunt comes more regularly. Two incident reports, for being out of bounds and for fighting. Nancy found the actual write-ups. The out of bounds related to his being minutes late returning to his cell for count. The fight was apparently self-defense.

There were no write-ups for violence in his record. She went all the way back in his file to his admission processing. The conviction which landed him here was for first degree burglary. The indictment said that in the early morning, a cleaning woman found LeBlanc in the dressing room of a department store, sleeping on the floor. There were several items of clothing underneath him, all with store tags. The State's theory at the trial was that LeBlanc deliberately stayed in the store after hours, so that he could remove the merchandise without paying. The prosecutor used some arcane statute to convert what was at most a breaking and entering into first degree burglary by claiming that the department store had a penthouse apartment where the store's CEO sometimes stayed overnight. LeBlanc did not testify, on the advice of his counsel. The jury convicted, although they deliberated for two days before reaching a verdict. Because LeBlanc was sentenced before the advent of the structured sentencing scheme, and the judge was pissed that he went to trial at all, he gave LeBlanc close to the statutory maximum, even though he had no prior criminal record.

Nancy put the file down and rubbed her eyes. She realized that it was nearly three o'clock, and that she had not moved since she sat down with the file after lunch. The former prison psychologist, who was now in private practice, had done an entry evaluation for placement into general population or specialized housing. He had determined that LeBlanc could be confined in general population without harm to staff or other inmates. He had written a cryptic note on his copy of the psychological report, above the part of the report where he questioned LeBlanc about the conduct leading to incarceration. "Check for sleep disorder." If he had done any follow-up interviewing or testing, the results were not in the file. Nancy made a mental note to try to locate the doctor and see if he remembered the case.

But for now, she had other work to do before she could leave for the day. When she was finished with LeBlanc's file, she got her jacket and purse, took out her ID so she could use it at the atrium control window if the officer did not recognize her, and found her way back to the prison exit. As she did so, she wondered, Why is LeBlanc here? If he really fell asleep in the department store, why couldn't his lawyer show the jury that? She made another mental note—find the attorney, and see what he had to say about LeBlanc's case. She had read the newspaper article about him in the file. She would find his phone number, and call him.

Chapter Twenty-Five

Sleepy was up early. He was told he had to report to the prison psychologist this morning, so when he woke up at 3:00 a.m., he just stayed up. That way, he was sure to be ready. He couldn't shower until 6:00 a.m., but his shift in the dining hall for breakfast was at 5:30 a.m. so he just had a few minutes to wait. Once he had eaten, he would shower and get presentable.

Who was this psychologist? he wondered. And why did he have to meet with the person? Then Sleepy remembered something that had happened to another inmate, some months back. The chaplain was on leave, and when the man's mother died, it was the psychologist who brought the bad news. Sleepy thought of his aunt and uncle—his uncle's bad health, both of them getting on in years. Suddenly, his heart was pounding so loudly he could see the heartbeat against his cotton shirt. He could hardly breathe. He fell back on his bunk, knowing he would fall onto the floor if he didn't. His legs would no longer support him. That must be it, he thought. There was news of his family. Someone was hurt, or dead.

Sleepy did not remember falling asleep. When he was fully awake, the guard at his cell door complained, "Damn it, LeBlanc. I'm tired of standing out here banging on this freakin' door. Get your butt up. You're supposed to be at the psychologist's office, ten minutes ago. Let's go!"

Sleepy splashed cold water from the tap in his room onto his face, wiped it dry with a paper towel, ran the damp paper towel over his hair to tame it, rinsed his mouth out with water, and presented himself at the door. "Sorry," he mumbled, reaching for the pass the officer had written to permit him to go to the administrative office building.

When he had the pass, he flashed it at the control booth in his housing unit, which caused the door to the administration corridor to open. Sleepy went through the door, trying to remember where the staff offices were. He saw a sign up ahead for the chapel, and recalled that the office of the psychologist was in that direction.

When he found the door with the plate indicating it was the psychologist's office, he knocked on it lightly. The door was opened by a petite woman Sleepy had never seen. "I'm here to see the psychologist," Sleepy said. He glanced around the tiny office, and realized she couldn't be the receptionist, since there was no reception area. She must be the psychologist. He guessed she was new.

"Come on in, Mr. LeBlanc," she said politely.

Sleepy knew then that she was new. Nobody on the staff addressed inmates as Mr. Rarely did anybody speak to inmates politely. At best, you got a chilly reception from the professional staff. At worst, downright hostility.

"Take a seat there," she said, pointing to the only other chair in the room besides the one behind the desk. "Yup, she's new," Sleepy thought. But she seemed nice. He was glad of that. He prayed he was wrong about the reason for the visit, but the sooner they got down to business, the sooner he would know for sure.

Sleepy sat down, and looked at her, waiting for her to speak.

"Mr. LeBlanc, I'm Nancy Carmichael. I'm the psychologist here at the prison. I'm glad to meet you. I've read quite a bit about you in your records here. I wanted to meet you and talk with you about your situation."

Sleepy felt weak with relief, and ecstatic at the same time. He managed to get his voice to work. "Is that all?" came out with a slight squeak.

Carmichael looked at him blankly. "What do you mean, is that all?"

"I mean, you want to ask me questions? You don't have any news for me?"

"Why, no. I don't think I do. Were you expecting news of some kind?"

"Not expecting, ma'am. Dreading is more like it. But that's okay. Go on with what you wanted to talk about. I'll tell you whatever I can."

"Mr. LeBlanc, I'll get right to the point. The staff is concerned about your sleep problem. We need to address the problem, to see if there is any way we can help you. I'd like to hear what you think the problem is, how it affects you, and so on. Is that okay?" When she looked at Sleepy, waiting for his answer, he noticed that her eyes were somewhere between gold and brown. He wondered if that was because she was wearing colored contact lenses. He had read that women were doing that now.

"I don't really know what happens to me," he said. "I am fine one minute, and then the next I am fighting to stay awake. My eyelids feel like they are glued shut. When I try to keep my eyes open, the glue pulls them back together. My head feels very heavy, as if my shoulders are not strong enough to hold it. Then my body becomes limp, and that's all I remember until I wake up. Sometimes it's a few minutes later, sometimes an hour or more later. If I dream, the dreams that I can remember are sweet, like about my mother, or about my aunt and uncle. And I feel really peaceful when I'm asleep. When I wake up, I feel sad that I've waked up. Does that make any sense?"

Carmichael did not answer. She was busy writing on her notepad. But when she looked up, she was smiling. "So you prefer what is going on when you're sleeping, to what is happening when you are awake?"

Sleepy grinned at her. "Well, ma'am wouldn't you? I mean, when I'm awake, I'm in prison. Sometimes when I'm asleep, I'm with people who love me. Not much of a choice, huh?"

She didn't answer. "Let's talk about your childhood. Your mother died when you were a baby, so how is it that you remember her?"

"My aunt kept her picture on my bedside table, and every night we said a prayer for her. When I'm awake, I can see the picture when I try to, but when I'm asleep, the picture is real. She's alive in my dreams, and talking to me."

Ms. Carmichael poised in her note taking. She looked thoughtful. "What exactly does she do in your dreams?"

"She sings, she dances, she laughs a lot."

"All happy things. Do you do any of those things yourself, when you dream?"

Sleepy thought about that for a minute. "No, ma'am. I don't dream about myself."

"What about when you are awake, do you do any of those things?"

Sleepy felt his face getting hot. He knew he was blushing. He ducked his head, hoping Ms. Carmichael wouldn't see that he was embarrassed. "I write songs," he mumbled. "And I sing them to myself. That's all."

"I'd like to see some of the songs sometime, if you would allow me to." She was smiling at Sleepy, and the smile did not seem forced or phony. But the fact that she seemed nice did not mean he would show her his songs. Nobody got to look at his songs. That was all he had of his own in here, and he meant to keep them to himself. He wore uniforms that were worn by other people, slept in beds where other people slept, ate food that other people had not eaten the day before. His songs would stay just that, his songs.

To her, he said, "Maybe one day."

She smiled and changed the subject. "I hear you were on the prison work crew when Officer Harkness was shot. Do you want to tell me about that?"

Sleepy wondered why he suddenly felt disappointed. And then he knew. For just a minute, it seemed that someone in here was treating him as a human being. But now her purpose was clear. She wanted to get him to talk about the shooting and escape. That creep Nash had probably put her up to this. Okay, he thought. This should be quick.

"Ms. Carmichael, did you say your name was?" He worked to keep his tone neutral.

"That's right. Nancy Carmichael."

"Well, Ms. Carmichael. I'm afraid I can't help you there. I've told everybody here, and that FBI agent and a boatload of cops, what I know about that. What I know is nothing. I was asleep. I was on the bus when the cops got there. The lieutenant had to wake me up. I didn't see or hear anything. I didn't like Harkness, nobody did, but he was okay to me. He let me sleep on the bus, and that made him alright by me. As for Strafe and Pockets, I never had any trouble with either of them. So I'm afraid I can't help you."

The psychologist must have sensed the change in Sleepy, because she pushed a piece of paper across the desk to him and asked him to read it. "This is a consent form. It allows me to speak with you and to get records about you that would help me understand your situation. Look at that last line. Everything you tell me is in confidence. Only if you confess that you are about to commit a crime can I tell anybody else what you have told me. That certainly includes agent Nash."

Sleepy felt relieved. He had not wanted to believe that she was a dupe for Nash. But in this place, the best rule was to trust only yourself. With the exception of Rosie, Sleepy had followed the rule.

He signed the form and handed it back to the psychologist. He sat quietly, hands in his lap, waiting for her next question.

"So your first memory of that event is when the lieutenant woke you up?"

"That, and the dream I had that day."

"Do you remember the dream?"

"No, ma'am. Not now, I don't. I remembered it for awhile after I woke up, but nobody asked me about it then. That FBI agent didn't believe I was really asleep."

Carmichael nodded, her pen poised above her notepad. She paused for a moment, then made a quick note. "Was agent Nash the first to question you that day?"

"He tried to ask me some questions. When he didn't get the answers he wanted, he left."

She laughed. He liked the way her face changed when she laughed. He wondered what he had said that was funny.

"I see you have had the same experience with agent Nash that I've had," she said. "He does seem used to getting what he wants. Do you think if you took some time, you might remember the dream?"

Sleepy thought about it. Sometimes he could recall his dreams, even days or weeks after the fact. But this was different. He didn't want to remember anything about the day Harkness was shot.

"I don't know. I might. I could try." He hated to disappoint her by flat-out refusing to remember the dream. Maybe he would try to remember it, and if it was not bad, he would tell her about it.

"I think we should meet again in a few days, Mr. LeBlanc. You try to remember. I'll try to get some more background information on you. When we talk next, I'll try to have some answers for you, about this sleep problem. Do you want to know what is going on with the sleepiness, or would you just rather sleep?" She was smiling that smile again. Sleepy wondered that she would understand that maybe he wanted to be asleep. Maybe she was smart, as well as pretty.

The thought that she might understand made him chuckle.

"Did I say something funny?" she asked.

"Oh, no ma'am. It just tickled me that you could see that there would be a choice to be made there. See, most people who talk to me about my sleeping think it is a problem for me. Actually, it's a problem for them. For me, I'd surely rather sleep than have to face this hell hole all day long. It's not that I'm lazy. I've always tried to work. I don't mind the sweeping and mopping. I don't even mind the road work. But I can't stand the constant noise, and the constant fussing and fighting, and always having to watch what you say to somebody or how you look at somebody. Everybody's on edge, so the slightest little thing will set off a riot, if you're not careful. It gets on my nerves."

Now it was Carmichael who chuckled. "Well, I don't doubt that it would. It would get on my nerves, too. Why don't I just do what I can to figure out why you are sleeping, then you make the choice whether to fix it, if it can be fixed. Is that a deal?"

Sleepy nodded. That made sense to him. He was always ready to listen to somebody's ideas. Sometimes they were even ideas he liked. So he'd see.

When he stood to leave, he noticed a small silver frame on Carmichael's desk. It had a photo of a small boy in it. The little boy was wearing a robe of some kind. He debated whether to ask her, but she had been nice so far, so maybe she wouldn't take offense. "Is that your son, ma'am?"

She looked at the photo for a long minute, then at Sleepy. "No, Mr. LeBlanc," she said softly. "That's my father when he was little. He died two years ago, from a heart attack. I keep that picture to remind me that he was once a child, a happy child."

Sleepy didn't really know what to say. He was cursing himself for prying, and for causing her to think of something sad. "I'm sorry," he muttered, looking at the floor.

"Don't worry, Mr. LeBlanc. You didn't know. Now, let's decide on a day next week when we can get together again, and talk more about this sleep issue." She checked a small desk calendar.

Sleepy didn't have a calendar to check. "I'm available any day," he said.

She smiled at him again. "Yes, I guess you are, aren't you?"

Chapter Twenty-Six

After LeBlanc left, Nancy got her textbook on sleep disorders and read the chapter on narcolepsy. LeBlanc's symptoms seemed to fit. He fell asleep at inappropriate times. He described an overwhelming urge to sleep, an urge he could not fight. His eyelids felt like they were glued shut. He felt muscle paralysis, and could not order his body to move. Narcolepsy was a fairly common sleep disorder, although his symptoms were more severe than many sufferers. She wondered why he had never been diagnosed. Diagnosis was admittedly difficult, but there were tests available which were considered accurate. If he had been properly diagnosed, he could have been treated with medications. There was no known cure for narcolepsy, but his life would surely have been easier if someone had figured out what was going on and gotten him some help. She remembered he told her his aunt and uncle had taken him to several doctors about the problem. With LeBlanc's permission she could get access to his medical records. But for now, she would call the psychologist whose position she filled, and ask him what he had done.

Her conversation with Dr. Blake could not have been less helpful. He was on his way to the golf course, he had only a vague recollection of LeBlanc, and he knew so little about narcolepsy that she was sure he never followed up on his suspicions, as the note in the file reminded him to do.

She hoped for better luck when she called the office of his attorney in the burglary case. A woman answered, rolling off the eight or so names that made up the partner roster. I would surely hate to have to manage that mouthful every time the phone rang, Nancy thought. "Could I speak with Mr. Harbaugh please?"

The receptionist was abrupt, probably because she was about to have to repeat the line-up to another caller. "He's on another call. Would you like his voice mail?"

"If I may, I'll hold for a moment. Perhaps he won't be long."

"Suit yourself, honey," the receptionist said, and clicked off. Nancy wondered if she'd ever remember that she had a call on hold for Harbaugh.

She felt lucky when Harbaugh came on the line in less than a minute. "Harbaugh here, what can I do for you?"

"Mr. Harbaugh, this is Nancy Carmichael. I'm a psychologist at the Walton Correctional Institute. I'm calling about one of your former clients. I need some information about a medical condition, and I'm hoping you may have gathered some records about him during your representation. I have a release signed by the inmate."

"What's his name?" Harbaugh was obviously in a hurry.

"Theodore LeBlanc."

"LeBlanc? I don't know the name. Are you sure I represented him?"

Nancy was about to believe she had made a mistake, but she checked the file again quickly, and there it was, no mistaking it. Lawrence Harbaugh, of Harbaugh, etc. Odd he couldn't remember LeBlanc. Not your usual client, she would think.

"Mr. Harbaugh, he is a very tall gentleman, who has what appears to be a sleep disorder. He falls asleep at all the wrong times. He was convicted of burglary of a department store. The State's evidence was that he was found sleeping in a men's dressing room when the store opened, and he was surrounded with clothes belonging to the store, still with price tags attached. Does that ring a bell?"

"Oh, yeah. LeBlanc. Now I remember. His aunt and uncle paid my fee. Paid promptly, I recall that much. What was it you wanted to know?"

Nancy tried to control her irritation. "Do you recall anything about the sleep disorder? That's the reason for my call. I'd like to gather his medical records, and since I figured you had already done that for his trial, I thought I'd start with you."

"Why would I need his medical records? Open and shut case, as far as I was concerned. He insisted on going to trial. I told him to take the plea. Would have been out in eighteen months. His stubbornness got him several extra years. What was his sentence, anyhow?"

Nancy spoke patiently, like she had learned to do with raving patients. "His sentence was eight and a half years. He has served a little over a year now. But it sounds like you won't be able to help me. I will try to get the records some other way."

"Yeah, I guess you'd better." Harbaugh seemed bored now. "But call me if you think of anything else I can do. Be happy to help. Always happy to help the folks out at the prison."

She rang off politely, but she was fuming. "Help the folks out at the prison!" the jerk said. She had no doubt he was doing that. Helping to fill the place! What kind of decent defense attorney would not remember his client a year after he represented the man, and what kind of decent defense attorney would not get medical records for a client who was found asleep in a department store, had no prior record, and said he was innocent? She was still furious when she dug out the newspaper article where she first found Harbaugh's name. She re-read the article. It said next to nothing about LeBlanc's case, but touted Harbaugh as the most highly-paid defense attorney in town, the one the bigwigs turned to if their children got a little off track, the one at all the charity functions and political campaign events. She made a mental note. If ever in trouble, shoot Harbaugh if he shows up!

Chapter Twenty-Seven

Nancy's next call was to LeBlanc's new lawyer, Ms. Johnson. As she dialed the number LeBlanc had written own for her, she wondered how many Johnsons there were practicing law in a large city like Washington, D.C.

A male voice answered. "Mercy Johnson and Associates."

Nancy tensed. She willed herself to speak calmly. "Is Ms. Johnson available?"

"May I tell her who's calling?"

"Nancy Carmichael. I'm a psychologist at the Correctional Institute where one of her clients is confined. Theodore LeBlanc. I understand she is his attorney."

"I'll see if she is in."

Nancy was surprised at how quickly the call was answered. "Mercy Johnson. How may I help you?"

"Ms. Johnson, I'm Nancy Carmichael. I am the psychologist at Walton State Prison. I am calling about Theodore LeBlanc. The prison staff asked me to speak with him, because of his sleep issues. Knowing that he is under investigation for the murder of a prison guard, I wanted to alert you about that. I explained confidentiality to him, and that my work with him would be for treatment, not investigation. He signed a consent form. But given the seriousness of the potential charges against him, I did not want to proceed without at least giving you an opportunity to talk to him and advise him."

"I appreciate that, Ms. Carmichael. Can you tell me why you are meeting with Mr. LeBlanc?"

"Certainly. You know about the episode on the bus, of course. Mr. LeBlanc told the authorities that he was asleep and did not know what happened. The FBI agent assigned to the case believes he is faking sleep. The prison officials do not agree. I was asked to meet with him and see whether in my opinion he has a genuine sleep disorder, and if so, whether it can be treated. The sleep disorder does interfere with his progress here in significant ways."

"So you will not be questioning him about events of the guard's killing and the escape?"

"No. My concern is how the sleep episodes start, what causes them, their duration, and how we might prevent harm to him. I did ask him if he recalled anything of that day. He told me the same thing he has told all the law enforcement officers and agents. He was asleep. He woke up when the lieutenant came on the bus and shook him awake. He did mention one other thing that I do not think he told the authorities. He said he had a dream, which he was trying to remember when he woke up. He was unable to recall the dream."

"When do you intend to meet with him again?"

"Next week, if that suits you."

Nancy could hear the click of computer keys. "That will be fine. If you can schedule your meeting for the end of the week, I can meet with Mr. LeBlanc before then and we can decide what our response will be."

"Fine. If you want, I can transfer you to the officer who makes appointments for legal visits. That way, you won't have to call back."

"Thank you. I appreciate that. And Ms. Carmichael, thank you for calling me. A lot of prison employees would not have done that."

Nancy laughed. "I'm not a prison employee first. First, I'm a psychologist. I have a masters degree. I hope to earn my doctorate in the next few years. Treating patients is my goal. If investigation were the goal, I'd have joined the FBI myself. Of course, if I'd met agent Nash first, I'd probably have run the other way."

Mercy laughed and Nancy liked the sound of it. Rich, like her speaking voice. One reason she's so good with juries, Nancy thought. Her looks and her voice, and she had them eating out of her hand.

"I can tell we are on the same page about the agent. I warned him not to speak with LeBlanc. He ignored the warning. I suspect he'll show up there again before long."

"If he does, I'll call you. I don't like it when agents like him try to run over people."

"Fair enough. I appreciate the help."

"Ms. Johnson, it's not help. I'm not on anybody's side here. I am just trying to assess an inmate with a possible psychological problem. That is how I see my job."

"Good. Then we will get along just fine."

"I surely hope so. I'm glad Mr. LeBlanc finally has a lawyer who wants to help him. I spoke to Mr. Harbaugh a little while ago. If he was still involved, he'd be playing golf with Nash."

Mercy laughed again. "Yeah, I've checked him out. Let's just say if I was in trouble, he would not be my first choice."

"To put it mildly. Goodbye, Ms. Johnson."

Nancy let out her breath, and sat down. Her hand trembled slightly. Her next move would be to call her mentor. If she approved of Nancy's plan to have further conversations with Mercy Johnson, Nancy would not feel so anxious about the prospect.

In fact, as long as there was no need for a face-to-face meeting, all should be well.

Chapter Twenty-Eight

When Mercy hung up, Sam appeared at her door. "Well, what did the psychologist have to say?"

"Sam, you will appreciate this. She said she did not view herself as an agent of the investigation, but as a treatment person. She wants to help Theodore deal with his sleep issue. She does not like Nash. As skeptical as I am about prison psychologists, I'm inclined to trust her. I'll have to speak with him first. And check her out, of course. But it could be useful to us, to have the prison psychologist diagnose a sleep disorder, and to verify that he is not malingering."

"Malingering. I saw a lot of that from the prison shrinks. Never mind that some of the guys I did time with were as crazy as bedbugs, the shrinks always started with a diagnosis of malingering. Faking was a lot easier for them to treat than genuine mental illness. Do you know how many people in prisons today are certifiably mentally ill?"

"Scores, is all I know. And most are not in prison mental hospitals. Most are in open population, where they are a real risk to themselves and other prisoners. The handful of prison mental hospitals could not possibly contain all or even most of the people who need treatment. Veterans are an especially large group. People who are so damaged by their war experience they get caught up in the legal system and can't get out. But, we are preaching to the choir."

"Yep. But I see why Ms. Carmichael's approach might let you trust her. She is a rarity, in my experience."

"Mine too. I made an appointment to go down and see Theodore the end of the week. Why don't you come along? We'll see what his take on her is."

"Love to. Meantime, I'm gonna cruise the information highway, see if she's got a presence there. Some background might make us both feel better."

Mercy smiled at Sam. "Just what I was thinking. In fact, let's do a quick search now, and then we can do a more in-depth investigation after we meet with LeBlanc."

Mercy sat in the chair beside Sam's desk while his fingers danced across the keyboard, and waited for him to look up from the monitor. When she saw him frowning, she asked, "What? Bad news? What's that face about?"

"Not bad news. No news. I can't find anything on her. Nothing about college graduation, nothing about a masters degree. No articles published by her or even co-written by her. I'm checking the state licensing agency now, but nothing is coming up. She's a ghost, looks like. What do you make of that?"

"I don't know enough about internet background searches to draw any conclusions. But it worries me." Mercy got up from the chair and paced Sam's small office.

Sam sighed. "Okay, I guess I'll have to act like a real investigator and invest some shoe leather in finding out about Ms. Carmichael. I'll get on it when we get back from the prison. She can't be a non-entity. The prison would surely have checked her background before hiring her. I'm going to start with the state licensing agency and work my way back from there. We'll know her as well as her own mama does, just give me a few days."

Chapter Twenty-Nine

Hastings paced the small isolation cell. When word reached him last week that his crew set fire to the wrong cell, he was so angry he tried to tear the steel bunk from its bolts. But he quickly calmed down, because he remembered that in prison, there's always a second chance to take somebody out. So he sent the kite, "Old Lace?," knowing his crew would read it right—poison the plowboy. And what did he hear back? Just thinking of it sent his blood pressure off the charts. What he heard back is that the idiots poisoned LeBlanc's rat! LeBlanc is walking around, healthy as a horse, and the rat is in rodent heaven! So this time, instead of attacking the bunk, he went for the slit of a window high above it on the wall. He took off his shoe, and threw it with such force it bounced off two walls of the cell before landing with a thud on the bunk. "Dumb, dumber and dumbest," he shouted. Lucky for him, his cell was at the end of the isolation corridor, and no guards were passing by to observe his temper tantrum. Otherwise, he would get a write-up for attempting to destroy prison property, and that would get him another two weeks, at least, in the hole. Not that it mattered. Just that the disciplinary process was a pain in the butt. Get the write-up, answer the write-up, request a hearing, set a hearing date. He didn't have time for that crap.

The burst of energy seemed to calm him, and he laid down on the bunk, to think. How to get to LeBlanc? Could his crew carry off anything more complicated than they had tried so far? He doubted it. Nobody was an Einstein. They usually did what Hastings told them to do. He was the genius behind the operation. He was the brains, they were the brawn. So why were they having so much trouble getting his message to LeBlanc?

He thought about a plan that would be as close to foolproof as he could come up with. If his guys couldn't do this right, they couldn't do anything right. He had to figure out how to get the message onto the sliver of paper he had scrounged from the disciplinary report the guards had served on him last week. His pencil was still in his shoe, but he was wearing the nub down too quickly. He needed to conserve what few materials he had, he thought. So he wrote just two words, "Squeeze Play," and folded the tiny sliver of paper to the size of a speck.

He waited a while before trying to decide how to get the kite to the crew. He heard through the grapevine that LeBlanc was back in population, which meant he got access to the yard for recreation. Hastings's crew that did not work on the road was still in population. Only the ones who participated in the escape were actually locked down. Of course, they were his best men. The hard core guys who would take risks for their freedom. Some of the guys who were in population were only in the crew for the protection it provided. There were one or two stand-up guys who would do what Hastings wanted, partly because they respected him as the bad-ass he was, and partly because they liked violence and hurting other people. Hastings selected two from this group.

When the guard brought his supper tray, he knew how he would get the message to the crew. He laid the tiny speck of paper on the tray, and said simply, "Day-Day." The guard looked at him, then nodded. He would get the paper to Day-Day, and next week, somebody from Hastings's network outside would see that an envelope made its way to the guard's car, top of the right front tire. For simple favors like this one, cash would do. For something more major, Hastings could get more creative.

He finished his tray, and laid back down on the bunk. He hoped that Mack truck Rosie wasn't on the yard when the play went down. LeBlanc was big, but not too coordinated. He wasn't much competition for a skilled fighter like Day-Day. Rosie was another matter. Not as tall as LeBlanc, who was 6'8" probably, but built to break rocks. Rosie had to weigh over three hundred. Word on the block was that Rosie had been a bouncer in a nudie bar. The governor's aide came in, and started feeling up the dancers. Rosie didn't know the S.O.B. was the aide to the governor. Probably wouldn't have mattered to Rosie anyway. He tossed the guy, bodyguards and all. Next month, cops found some suspicious white powder in Rosie's locker at work. Wouldn't you know it, when the lab guys tested it, it was cocaine. Rosie never used anything stronger than weed in his life. Didn't even drink. Everybody knew it was a set-up, but Rosie's family hired some high-class suit and haircut for a lawyer, and the guy was afraid to take on the governor's aide. Should have taken the public defender. All the trouble he'd been in, he never hired a lawyer. Always got the guy from the PD's office. He was doing time, but not more than he deserved.

Hastings thought he ought to work out a contingency plan. If Rosie was on the yard, chances are he would need it.

He thought about Day-Day. The man was big, but not as big as Rosie. He was devious though. Like a snake, creeping up, striking quick. He would warn Day-Day to take Rosie out first, then concentrate on LeBlanc. To get that long message to Day-Day would cost him. He would probably have to do it by telephone. In the hole, he lost all his phone privileges. He would have to claim a family emergency, get the guard to let him call, talk to one of Day-Day's friends on the outside, and wait for Day-Day to call the friend, who would relay the message. It was the only way he was sure Day-Day would get word. He could bribe a guard here and there, for favors, but no guard was stupid enough to let him out of the hole to make a regular telephone call. He would say he got a letter, and that his mother was real sick. She probably was real sick. If she couldn't get the crack she needed, she'd be crazy sick.

Hastings banged on his cell door. The guard who was on this shift was the same as the one who took the message to Day-Day. That was a stroke of luck. When the guard opened the door, Hastings said, "I need a phone call. I got word my mom is sick. Can you get me five minutes?"

The guard looked up and down the corridor, to make sure they were alone. "Yeah, Hastings, but it's way against regulations to let somebody in the hole make a phone call. How did you get word about your mom?"

"I got a letter from my sister last week."

"Do you still have it, so we can show it to the case manager if need be?"

Hastings looked through the little property he was allowed in the hole. "Yeah," he said, waving the envelope in the breeze. "It's right here." The envelope did contain a message from his sister that his mom was sick. He got the word last week, and didn't care enough to try to call then. But he could explain that by saying he was in the hole, and afraid to ask for a telephone call. Maybe the case manager would go for it.

"Okay," the guard said, "I'll arrange it. Five hundred dollars for this favor, though, since I have to put myself out for it. This is different from getting a message to somebody. This could blow up on me."

"Have I ever stiffed you for your money?"

The guard shook his head. "You're a fast pay, Hammer." The guard was smiling now. When he was gone, Hastings laid back down on his bunk. The plan was taking shape. He would call home, talk to his brother and ask for the money to be put in the usual place. Then he would ask his brother to call Day-Day's main man, and get the message to Day-Day. By next week, Sleepy's rec time ought to get real interesting. "Dumb plowboy," Hastings was muttering, as he dropped off to sleep.

Chapter Thirty

The recreation yard was overflowing with inmates. Sleepy was at a picnic table, head on his arms, eyes closed. Whether he was asleep was not obvious, but since everybody knew he was often asleep, it was a safe bet. Day-Day watched him for a few minutes, and saw no signs of movement.

A stroke of luck made Day-Day smile. Sleepy had picked a table right next to the rec yard closet. It wouldn't look unusual for Day-Day to move in that direction, since footballs and other equipment, such as it was, were kept in the closet. He checked his pocket for the shiv he made from the can lid one of his crew smuggled from the dining room. The shiv was only two inches long, but it was very sharp, and if he hit Sleepy just right, it could do some major damage. Hammer asked him to do the job because he was the best at aiming the shiv for a major organ. Even if he didn't kill his prey, the damage would send a powerful message. And that's all Hammer wanted him to do to Sleepy anyway. At least for today.

He sidled up to Sleepy, keeping his hand on the object in his pocket. As he did, he glanced around, to make sure there was no one else within range who could intervene. The guards were all talking to clumps of inmates. They were probably reviewing last night's game. Every now and again the prison broadcast something from the cable channel, as a reward for a quiet two or three weeks. Day-Day smiled, thinking what effect his stabbing Sleepy would have on that carrot. The rec yard would be off-limits for at least a month, 'til the officials got the stabbing sorted out, and the inmates who were not in Hammer's crew would be pissed as hell. For Hammer's crew, it was a cost of doing business. If any of the crew complained, it would be out of Hammer's hearing and to someone who would not carry the word back to him.

Day-Day was almost to Sleepy. In a few seconds, he could get to his back, pop him with the shiv near his kidney, and be safely in one of the clumps of inmates standing about. Hammer would owe him for his work, and it was always good to have Hammer in debt to him. He was much safer that way.

He was within feet of Sleepy when the closet door opened, and Rosie stepped out. Rosie's huge foot drove directly into Day-Day's left shin bone. He screamed in pain and stumbled, grabbing the edge of the picnic table for support. When a guard looked his way, he waved him off, signaling that there was no problem. He couldn't afford to get caught with the shiv, and there was no convenient place to hide it right now.

Rosie's big head was wrapped in a do rag. His face was nearly as black as coal. Sweat sat on this upper lip like a mustache. His face and head were shaved. Rosie growled at him. "Get the hell away from here, Day. You ain't got no business over here. You want to get hurt up real bad, come back 'round here when we're here."

Day-Day knew Rosie meant business. He was quiet, he didn't ask for trouble. The last guy who tried to get past Rosie hadn't come back from the hospital in town. Might not come back, word was. Rosie did his stint in the hole, but even the disciplinary board could see it was self defense. Rosie was no worse for wear.

Day-Day backed away from the table, and went over to one of the groups of inmates clustered nearby, where he could watch the picnic table. The guys were all in Hammer's crew, so it was alright for him to join them mid-way of their recap of last night's game. No one acknowledged him, so he stood quietly, waiting for an opportunity to recognize the inmate who was speaking, one of Hammer's lieutenants. As he listened to the play-by-play from last night, he kept an eye on the picnic table. Sleepy did not move. Rosie sat on the other side of the table, reading a newspaper.

When the group broke into laughter, Day-Day joined in. He was not listening and missed the joke, but if the crew thought it was funny, he did, too. The lieutenant had rank with Hammer, and if he told a joke, it was best to laugh along with the others. Once the laughter ended, the lieutenant looked at Day-Day.

"What's up, Day?" he asked.

The acknowledgment gave Day-Day an opening, and he took advantage of it. He pointed toward the picnic table with a brief nod of the head.

"I need to get rid of the plowboy's sidekick for a minute."

The crew members looked toward the table, then back at Day-Day. One of them spoke. "Man, I ain't messing with Rosie. That man got to weigh three hundred pounds. And ain't none of that fat. He's as quick on his feet as a pro, man. Ever watch him hit the big bag? Scared me, man, and I don't scare easy. I ain't going against him 'less I got something, man. Something heavy."

"Man, you don't need to do nothing by yourself. We need to go after him together. If we can put him out of circulation for a minute, I can get to Sleepy. You know what Hammer wants. Now who's gonna help me make it happen?"

They all looked at Day-Day. "Man, if Hammer wants you to do the plowboy, you got to figure out how. Hammer didn't tell me to do nothing. If he did, I'd find a way to do it. You know what I mean?"

Day-Day knew only too well what he meant. And he had tipped his hand to the crew. If he didn't act now, word would get back to Hammer in a flash. There would be hell to pay, no doubt about it. Day-Day turned and started back toward the table. There was no sign of Rosie.

Sleepy was in the same spot he had left him. If he had moved at all, Day-Day couldn't tell it. He heard soft sounds coming from the table, and knew Sleepy was snoring lightly. Day-Day advanced toward the table, looking over his shoulder to make sure the guards were still occupied. He was poised, ready to strike, when he hit the ground with a hard thump. For a minute, he couldn't get his breath. He raised his head and looked toward his crew, but they were still listening to jokes and laughing. If anyone was noticing him, they weren't coming his way.

Rosie got hold of his arm and pulled him to his feet. He sat Day-Day onto the picnic bench, and then sat down on the other side. If the guards saw them, they'd think Day-Day tripped and Rosie had helped him up. With both of them seated, the guards wouldn't bother with them.

"Crap," Day-Day muttered aloud.

"That's right," Rosie said. "Crap it is. You're full of it. Now let me give you some meaningful advice, young'un. You get from here right now. We don't need no cops handling this. You just go on 'bout your business. That way, won't nobody know 'bout that shiv you got in your pocket. And you're alive. That's the best part. But you hear me, now. You mess with my friend again, you won't be alive for long. I'll take you out myself. You might be tough enough for that Hammer idiot, but you're no match for me. Think about it. Hammer will be mad you didn't accomplish your mission. But he won't kill you. I will. The choice seems pretty obvious to me. 'Course, I got the sense God gave me. You ain't. So however you play it, I'm ready."

Day-Day looked at Rosie's face. There was no expression there. It was the calmest face he'd ever seen. Day-Day scrambled to his feet, anxious not to be seen by Hammer's crew. He shuffled backwards, keeping an eye on Rosie 'til he was well away from the picnic table. As he walked, he tried to figure what to tell Hammer.

Suddenly he knew what he had to do. He took the shiv from his pocket, closed his eyes, and jabbed it into the flesh of his thigh. The pain nearly caused him to pass out. Blood spurted from the wound. In seconds his prison uniform pants were drenched with blood. As quick as he had stabbed himself, he buried the shiv deep in the soft earth at the end zone. He limped toward one of the guards who was putting fresh lines on the playing field, hollering to him as he went. "Sergeant, help me. I'm cut." The guard turned, saw the blood on Day-Day's uniform, and raced to him. "What's up, Day? What happened? How'd you cut yourself?"

Day-Day was calmer now. "I didn't cut myself," he said indignantly. "I was asleep. Some dude come up and stabbed me in the thigh. By the time I was awake, he was gone. I didn't see who it was."

The guard looked at him hard, but didn't question him. "Let's get you to the infirmary. Can you walk?"

"Yeah, but a stretcher would be mighty handy right now."

The guard called for help. "Get a medic over here! Now!" The bleeding had slowed to a trickle, but the wound had bled so much that the medic paled when he saw Day-Day's leg. He went immediately to the medical cabinet along the wall, opened it with his key, took out the folding stretcher the prison kept in the cabinet for emergencies on the yard, and ran back to the sergeant with it. They loaded Day-Day on it and made for the infirmary. Day-Day sighed with relief. Now he would go to protective custody. That was the rule whenever an inmate was assaulted. If he participated in the assault, he went to the hole. If he did not, he went to PC, where he could be watched until the administration sorted out the assault, who was beefing with whom, who meant to harm whom. In PC, Hammer couldn't get to him, at least right away. He would stay there while he made up a story. If Hammer bought it, fine. If not, Day-Day would have to figure out a way to get transferred to another joint. Hammer would have contacts wherever he went, but if he could get far enough away, he would have a chance to serve out the rest of his eight years without getting killed.

Chapter Thirty-One

Rosie sat next to Sleepy, who was finally awake. Rosie hung his head, and spoke so softly Sleepy had to work to hear him. It always amazed Sleepy that somebody so big could speak in such a quiet voice.

"Sleep, man, what's up? Why these guys trying to hurt you? You ain't talking, are you?"

"Talk about what, Rosie? You know I was asleep on the bus when the hit went down. I told you that. I didn't see a thing. I'm getting pretty pissed off about this. That FBI jerk, Nash, keeps bothering me. Went to my aunt's house, and threatened her. Then these morons in here think I know something. They're putting the squeeze on me. I'm 'bout ready to lose it, Rosie. They killed Be-Bop, that was bad enough. Now they want to kill me, too."

Rosie snorted. "Man, they been trying to kill you. It wasn't Be-Bop they was after. The poison was in the oatmeal, your oatmeal. It was an accident that Be-Bop ate some of it before you could. They meant to kill you, or at least make you real sick. Lucky for you these guys are as incompetent as criminals as they were at whatever they did on the streets. Else you'd be going out of here in a box."

"Thanks for that image, Rosie. It's comforting."

Rosie shot a glance at Sleepy, but he didn't seem to be offended by the sarcasm. "Now you listen to me. You ain't no match for these scum suckers. You big, that's true, but you ain't a fighter. Me, I fought for fun in the Golden Gloves competitions, then I fought some clown every night, when I worked at the nudie bar. 'Scuse me, 'gentleman's club.' People I was throwing out weren't no gentlemen. Especially your governor's boy. He was everything but a gentleman. But I learned some tricks working there. I can take care of myself, and I can take better care of you than you can take of yourself. So what I need to do is watch you more. I can't be there 24-7, but I got to work it so I'm around more. And don't go into this yard without me, you hear? You know the rec yard is the best place to get hurt. These clowns are getting word from Hammer, and they'll have to tell him his plans ain't working. They'll step up the assault. You know Hammer don't play. They got to make his plan work. So the pressure's on, Sleep."

Rosie looked at Sleepy. Sleepy's face, which had been so set with the stress of the attack, was relaxed now. His eyes were open, but he had slumped down into himself, like a rag doll. Rosie spoke louder. "Hear me, now, Sleep. This is serious business."

Sleepy did not turn or acknowledge Rosie. Instead, he started to incline to the right. Before Rosie could grab him, he had fallen onto the picnic bench. Rosie grabbed his arm, and pulled him upright.

"Damn, Sleep, you know how dangerous it is to sleep on the yard?"

The frustration in Rosie's voice would have bothered Sleepy, if he had heard it. Instead, he heard a soft drone, and felt very glad to have such a good friend as Rosie. He was about to try to say thank you when he lapsed into unconsciousness.

Chapter Thirty-Two

Nash drove up to the prison gates and announced himself on the speaker box. "Agent Nash, FBI. Got a warrant to make an arrest." As he said it, he fingered the paper on his lap. Just looking at it made him happy. The State versus Theodore LeBlanc. The charge, Murder I. The vic, Harkness, late of the State prison. "Yes!" he said for the fifteenth time. He punched the air, feeling like he was front row at the NCAA finals. "Nobody knows what I had to go through to get this warrant. Freakin' DA was a wuss. Didn't want to get a warrant. Wanted to put the case before a grand jury, when he had enough evidence. Why get a warrant, he said, when the perp is locked up anyway? Wait, get the indictment, get the case on track for trial. Get the drop on the defense."

That might have been an okay strategy, if he had a case to make. But Nash knew damn well that the case they had right now against LeBlanc was the best it would get, without a confession. That's why he needed the warrant. Once LeBlanc was served with the warrant, he would know that Nash could deliver on his threats. He might even think that Nash could arrest his aunt, for withholding information and accessory after the fact. LeBlanc was probably too smart to think that, but you never knew. Some of these guys knew next to nothing about the legal system that chewed them up and spit them out. You'd think the way they came back time after time, they'd learn a little something about the process.

Nash flashed his ID at a blue light on the speaker stand, and the gates swung open. He drove through and parked in the officials parking lot. This time he tried to avoid the warden's spot. Thinking back on how mad the warden got when he parked in the spot last time, he chuckled. But today, no time for fun and games. He was all about his business today.

He went directly to the warden's office. Watts's secretary looked at him crossly, and without speaking, buzzed her boss. "Sir, there's an agent Nash to see you."

"Send him in, Betty. And get me a Tylenol from the first aid kit, will you?"

"Right, sir." She nodded at Nash without speaking, and turned her attention to a desk drawer, fishing out a First Aid box and snapping open the lid.

Nash was already seated in Watts's office when Betty came in with two caplets, and a glass of water, which she placed on Watts's desk. She looked sharply at Nash, but said nothing. She closed the door behind herself.

Watts swallowed the pills in a gulp, and then turned to Nash. "What's up, agent?"

Nash was irked at the tone, but even the chilly reception did not spoil his delight at having the warrant. "Got a warrant for the arrest of one of your inmates, sir," he said, exaggerating emphasis on the "sir" ever so slightly.

Watts still caught it. He seemed to be taking care to breathe slowly. He didn't speak right away. Then he said, "Warrant for which inmate? LeBlanc?"

"Right, how did you guess?"

"Because I'm not as dumb as you think I am, Nash. What's the charge? "

"Murder one," Nash said, trying not to sound smug. Watts frowned, but he didn't say anything.

"So, here's the plan," Nash continued. "I'll serve the warrant on him. He'll have a court date next week. Counsel will be appointed, if he doesn't already have a lawyer. I talked to some big-shot woman lawyer up in D.C., but LeBlanc wasn't charged with murder then. I'm entitled to try to speak to him about this charge, even if she represents him on something else. It's up to him whether he wants to talk to me. I want to talk to him before she even knows about this warrant. I'm sure once she finds out about the murder charge, she'll warn him off speaking with me. I want to strike while he's the most vulnerable, right after he knows he's charged with murder, and before he has the benefit of legal advice as to that charge. I think he's more likely to come off this sleep nonsense if I get to him right after he knows the murder charge is official. "

Watts read the warrant carefully. Then he handed it back to Nash.

"Our rules don't permit him to be served by outside law enforcement. This is a tricky situation. We've never had any problems out of LeBlanc, but you never know. If you tell a man who's already serving time that he's about to face a murder charge, that can set off a reaction. We have a rule that we serve warrants using prison staff. Somebody the inmate already knows, and is used to dealing with. We have staff standing by, in case there's an outburst. I seriously doubt that will happen with LeBlanc, but the policy will be followed in this case, like in every other."

Nash tried to contain his outrage. "Warden, this is my arrest. This is my investigation. I got this warrant after presenting the evidence to the DA, and then to the magistrate. Federal law allows me to serve the warrant, even though right now the prosecution is state rather than federal."

Watts was unmoved. "Here's what I'll do, Nash. I'll let you meet with LeBlanc in my office. I'll have two officers here to serve the warrant. Then you get the benefit of seeing LeBlanc's reaction, of telling him whatever you want to tell him to soften him up. Then you can use the interview room if he wants to talk to you."

Nash knew he'd been trumped by Watts's nearly absolute control of how the prison ran day to day. He wanted to protest, but he knew Watts wouldn't budge. Instead, he tried to smooth feathers, thinking that he might need Watts at some point down the road in this investigation and prosecution, and maybe others.

With effort, he said, "I appreciate it, warden. I'll be glad to be here with your men as they serve the warrant. And I will use the interview room to talk to LeBlanc. Thanks for making the facilities available."

Nash didn't like the taste of humble pie, but if it got the job done, he'd eat it this once.

Watts called his secretary. "Betty, get me the unit commander of Block A, please. Tell him to get one of his officers and bring LeBlanc as quick as he can."

To Nash, he said, "He'll be here in a minute. Why don't you get some coffee or something, and I'll return a few phone calls.

Harkness's wife is calling me every day about his insurance money. I need to see what I can do to help her."

Nash resented the dismissal, but he sure wouldn't show it. "Okay, warden, I'll be right outside in the waiting area."

He didn't want to just sit here, and feel Betty scowling at him. What had he done to her? he wondered. Watts must have complained to her about the parking space. These damn locals had way too much control, in his opinion.

Nash sat in the chair farthest from Betty's desk, and closest to the waiting room door. He read his case file and refused to look in her direction. He knew if he did she would be sour-faced. Within minutes, the unit commander and another guard appeared with LeBlanc. Nash was irritated that LeBlanc was not in cuffs, shackles or leg chains. Being able to move about the institution when you were about to be charged with murder didn't seem like a good idea to Nash.

Watts's door opened as the unit commander spoke to Betty, and the warden ushered him, his officer and LeBlanc into his office. Nash followed. Watts told them all to take a load off.

What is this crap? Nash thought. Tea and crumpets? He refused to sit, and instead, stood next to his chair, so he could face LeBlanc directly. When everyone else was seated, he looked at Watts, and when he received a nod, he took the warrant papers from his notebook, handed them to the unit commander, and looked hard at LeBlanc.

"The-oh," he began, noting once again that his disrespect got no rise out of LeBlanc. He repeated the offensive nickname. "The-oh, we're here because I have some news for you. I just handed to the commander a warrant for your arrest. It is signed by the magistrate of the Superior Court of Wyatt county. It charges you with the first-degree felony murder of Officer Harkness. The charge is based upon your participation in a felonious prison escape in which Harkness was killed. The warrant directs that you be held without bond on the charge, and arraignment is set for next Thursday. The arraignment will take place by closed circuit television, here at the prison. Any questions?"

Sleepy sat still in his chair, his head in his hands, elbows on his knees. He was the picture of despair. Good, Nash thought. We're breaking him. Won't be long now 'til he'll be ready to tell us all about the escape. He waited for LeBlanc to answer his question. Maybe he hadn't heard it.

"The-oh, did you hear what I said?'

"Yes, sir, I heard you," Sleepy responded without raising his head.

"Then do you have any questions?"

"I guess not, sir," he replied, barely loudly enough to be heard through his hands covering his face.

Nash looked at Watts. "I'd like to use the visiting room to advise LeBlanc of his rights. May we go there now?"

Watts was looking displeased. His frown was directed at Nash when he said, "Sure, agent, you can use our facilities to speak with LeBlanc. If he wishes to speak with you, that is. It's up to him."

"Well," Nash said, working to control his anger, "I have to advise him of his rights. He's now formally under arrest for murder. Once I've done that, he's free to leave and return to his unit, if he wants."

Watts nodded at LeBlanc. "You heard him. It's your choice. Just tell the man what you want to do."

With that, the unit commander stood, and lightly tapped Sleepy on his shoulder. "Let's go, Sleep. I'll walk you down to the visiting area. You can speak with this agent if you want. I'll wait for you, and take you back to your unit when you're done."

LeBlanc finally raised his head from his hands. "Thanks, sergeant," he said to the commander. He stood up, and waited for the commander to head first for the door. He followed the commander, leaving Nash to close the warden's door.

When they reached the interview area and were inside the small cubicle, Nash motioned for Sleepy to sit. "I'll stand, if that's alright," Sleepy said.

"Suit yourself, The-oh," Nash snapped. He pulled another set of the warrant papers from his pocket and handed them to Sleepy. "This is your copy of the warrant and affidavit. I'm going to read you your rights. When I'm done, you can ask me any questions you have."

Nash recited the warnings without a prompt from the vinyl-coated cards popular with police officers. He spoke as if reciting a poem, using his voice to give dramatic flavor to the rendition. When he was done, he turned to Sleepy. "Do you wish to speak with me without an attorney here?"

Sleepy sighed loudly. "I just want to know why you all are doing this to me. You know I didn't see anything. I've told you that a hundred times. If there was any kind of plan to escape and hurt the guards, nobody told me about it. I'm kind of out of the loop, I guess you'd say. I don't mix with anybody in here, to speak of. I keep to myself, do my work, try to avoid trouble."

Nash barked at him. "Can it, LeBlanc! I'm tired of this sleep nonsense. Nobody could sleep through what went on out on that highway when the work crew killed Harkness. Now, I'm giving you one last chance to tell me the truth. You know you can help yourself by talking to me. Right now, you're the only one charged with this murder. But soon, there'll be some more warrants coming down. Hastings will be charged, along with his crew. We'll need your testimony to sort out who actually shot Harkness, who drugged the two guards, who planned the whole thing. I'm telling you, The-oh, I can walk you out of here, even with this bullcrap B & E sentence, if you work with me. If you don't, I'm gonna slam you. Simple as that."

Nash left the interview room. "Take him to his cell," he told the unit commander. Nash would wait for the reality of LeBlanc's situation to sink in. He was no dummy, he would undoubtedly figure out why he was charged before Hastings and his boys. He understood a squeeze, and he knew he was in a vice. What would he do about it? That was the sixty-four thousand dollar question.

Chapter Thirty-Three

The guard shook Sleepy hard, rolling his long body back and forth on the narrow cot. "Still no response," he said into the mouthpiece attached to the walkie-talkie he carried on his hip.

"I'll send the medic," his colleague in the unit's control bubble squawked back.

When Sleepy was being loaded onto the gurney, he woke up. He tried to sit, but was strapped into the soft foam sides of the plastic stretcher, and could not move.

"Fellas, I'm okay now. You can put me back down." His voice came out in a croak. He knew that meant he had been asleep, and not using it, for some time.

The men kept bundling him into the gurney. "Oh, no, LeBlanc. That friggin' FBI agent wants you in the infirmary. He says they're going to send you out for some tests. He wants to prove you don't have a sleep problem. That creep could talk to any of us, we could tell him you ain't fakin'. But he don't want to hear from no kickers like us. He wants some New York head doctor, at $500 an hour, to tell him you are fakin' us out. Like we're a bunch of dumb rednecks. Oh well, it ain't my money."

His colleague snorted. "It sure is you're money, man. You pay taxes, don't you? Who you think is paying for the head doctor? You and me, boy. Sleepy, man, I was you, I'd run that doctor around a little. Mess with his head. Get your money's worth."

Sleepy laughed and settled back into the gurney for the short ride to the infirmary. "I'm afraid to do that, sir. If I do that, they're liable to come up with some diagnosis that will land me in the nut house. No offense, but I'd rather be here than there."

"You got that right," one of them said.

Sleepy was surprised to see Ms. Carmichael when he arrived at the infirmary.

"Bring him right on in here, gentlemen," she said, pointing to a cubicle with a curtain serving as a door. Inside, the officers unstrapped Sleepy from the gurney, and helped him onto the small bed in the cubicle. Since he was fully clothed, he sat on the side of the bed, waiting to see what would happen next. He had been to the infirmary many times, always because the guards couldn't wake him, and usually he stayed long enough to get fully awake, to describe the sleep incident to one of the techs that worked here, then he was out and back to his life on the compound. It looked like today might be a different routine, since Ms. Carmichael was here, but if they wanted him to do anything more than sit on the bed and wait for the interview, they would tell him.

Within minutes, Ms. Carmichael pulled the curtain back and came into the small cubicle.

"Mr. LeBlanc, how are you today?" she asked. Her tone made it clear that she was not making polite inquiries, but that she wanted a report on his situation.

"Good morning, ma'am," Sleepy said. "You don't have to call me Mr. LeBlanc. You can call me Sleepy if you want. I always answer to that. Have ever since I was a boy."

"Alright, Sleepy. I need to ask you some questions. I need you to think carefully about the questions, and give me your best answers. Okay?"

"Sure, I can do that," Sleepy said. He clasped his hands in his lap, and looked at them, waiting for her questions.

"Sleepy, what is the last thing you remember before you woke up this morning with the guards in your cell?"

Sleepy thought about the question. " Me and another inmate talking on the yard, during rec."

"Do you know what day that was?" Her head was bent over her pad, and he noticed that her hair was coal black, all the way to the roots. "Must be natural," he thought.

He tried to answer the question. "What day is today?"

She showed him the calendar in her leather-bound notebook. "Friday," she said.

"I work on Thursday, so I don't get rec. It must have been Wednesday."

"Did you work yesterday?"

He paused for several seconds. "I don't think so. I think I slept. When the officers came for me this morning, I was still in my rec clothes. I must have come in from rec, gone to sleep and not woke up 'til this morning."

"I'll check with your work officer, to be sure," she said, making herself a note. "Tell me, Sleepy, how do the guards deal with your sleeping?"

He sighed. "Most of them are alright about it. At first, they thought I was faking. But after a few episodes, they saw it was real, and they knew I couldn't control it. So they leave me alone now. I get hassled sometimes when a new guard comes on, but pretty soon the other officers warn him off, so they treat me alright. If I don't wake up for chow, they just give my tray away. If I don't go to work, they hold my job for me. They all know I work hard when I'm there. I can't stand to just sit around, like some of the guys do. To me, a job is a way to make the time pass faster. I guess because I do my job, the boss will cut me some slack when I sleep for a day or so, every now and then."

She nodded. "Is it really only every now and then?"

He pursed his lips, and pulled on one ear lobe. After awhile, he said, "Yeah, I think so. I mean, I don't keep count. But I think it happens every few days. I only work three days out of the week. So I guess I've been lucky so far, sleeping on days I don't have to work."

Again, she was making notes. "Well, that would sound like something you can control. Do you feel like you have any control over this sleeping?"

"No, ma'am, it doesn't feel that way to me. The thing is, I don't mean to go to sleep. I'm just doing what I'm doing, either working, or showering, or on the rec yard, and suddenly, I'm too sleepy to keep on. I sit down, and next thing I know, I'm being waked up by somebody, telling me I've been asleep for awhile."

"Isn't that dangerous? I mean, don't the other inmates take advantage of you when you're sleeping?"

Sleepy blushed. "You mean take advantage of me to do something to me?" he asked, not looking at her.

She must have realized what he was thinking, because she spoke quickly. "Oh, not necessarily that, Sleepy. I mean take advantage of you like the guys on the bus did. Get into some trouble, and leave you to take the punishment for it."

"Nah, that hasn't happened before," he said. "See, I have Rosie to help me. He's big. And he means what he says. He is not mean, don't get me wrong. He's a real good person. He never tries to hurt anybody. But he won't let anybody hurt him, either. And when I'm sleeping, he looks after me. He has some friends here, and he gets them to watch me for him. I'm almost always where I have somebody to look out for me."

"But not on the bus?" she said, thoughtfully.

"No, not on the bus. Rosie isn't on the work crew. He isn't allowed. Some nonsense about him conspiring to hurt the governor's aide. See, the aide set him up. That's why he's in here. Everybody knows it. So they think he's gonna try to get back at the governor's aide for it. But Rosie isn't like that. He's a straight-up guy. It's just that the governor's aide has people in here, and they claimed they overheard Rosie planning to get out and kill him. Never happened. But you got jailhouse snitches who will say anything for a price. One of them was paid to say that about Rosie. Now it means Rosie is never allowed outside, on any work crews, or to sing with the choir, or to go out on the art exhibits, or anything like that."

Ms. Carmichael nodded. "I see. Rosie must mean a lot to you."

Sleepy nodded. "He's a real friend."

She shifted in her chair. "Sleepy, what is the last thing you remember that upset you?"

He answered without hesitation. "Agent Nash. He brought a warrant and showed it to me. I've been charged with murder, because they say I participated in the escape where Harkness got killed."

"I see," she said again, this time chewing the tip of her ballpoint pen with small white teeth. "When did that happen?"

"Nash was here, then I went out on rec, and that's all I remember.

"How are you feeling right now?"

"Okay. I am awake, alert, I don't feel like sleeping anymore. If

I could, I'd like to go talk to my boss, make sure he's not mad about yesterday. Could you give me a pass to do that?"

"I don't see why not," she said, taking the pad from her notebook and writing him permission to see his boss. "I have to call ahead, let him know you're coming. I'll do that as soon as we're finished."

"Thank you, ma'am," Sleepy said.

She handed Sleepy a pad, and a pencil. "I want you to try to keep a journal, if you can. Try to record feeling sleepy. Try to write down what you were thinking when you got sleepy. What happened before you got sleepy. What your first thought was when you woke up. That will help me try to figure out what is going on here. Will you do that?"

He took the pad and pencil. "I will try. Most times the sleep comes on sudden, and I don't have any time to figure it out. But I will do my best."

"Good. Now, I'll call your supervisor, and tell him I gave you a pass to see him. Then you go back to your work, okay?"

"Sure." Sleepy stood up, and moved toward the door. Ms. Carmichael was still poring over her notes.

"Am I ready to go?" he asked her.

The question seemed to startle her. "Oh, sure. Sorry. I was just wondering about something. You go ahead. I'll phone now."

Sleepy went out of the cubicle, and down the hall to the infirmary exit. When he got to the control unit, he showed his pass. They waved him through.

Sleepy knew he should be worried. He'd been charged with first degree murder. The maximum penalty was death. He could fry in the electric chair, or get a needle full of some lethal concoction. But the thought didn't really bother him. Because he knew it would not happen. He was innocent, of that he was sure. What he needed to do was to prove it. He would talk to Rosie about that. Rosie always had a sharp legal mind. He'd have some ideas. As he walked, another idea hit him. He now had two friends in here. Ms. Carmichael was just doing her job, he knew that. It wasn't anything personal. But she was trying to help him, he could see. The thought made him smile. Rosie and Ms. Carmichael. What a pair.

Kind of like Maid Marion and Friar Tuck.   He laughed out loud. The guard at the control bubble to the work shop looked at him funny, but buzzed him through once he saw the pass.

Chapter Thirty-Four

Hastings was sitting on his bunk, feeling dazed. His runner guard just left. As usual, the information he brought was crucial. Hastings would gladly pay to know this. Sleepy had been arrested. And for murder. He was facing the death penalty. That meant two things, as far as Hastings could see. Sleepy was now in a real bind. Talk, or risk frying. And, the crew couldn't be far behind, as far as charges went. He knew they'd all be getting them soon.

He had to think. Everything his crew had tried to do to Sleepy in here had failed. The idiots firebombed the wrong cell. The rat ate the poisoned oatmeal. Day-Day couldn't get to Sleepy on the yard because big Rosie was watching his back. What else could they do to shut him up? Hastings lay back on the bunk, put his arms behind his head, tried to breathe slowly like he'd been taught back in the day when he went to the anger management classes the State made him attend. How to get to Sleepy?

Then the light bulb went off. Hastings slapped his forehead, the answer was so obvious. Must be slowing down in here, he thought. On the street, I'd have thought of this first thing. We got to get to his people. He's got family on the street. We got to get to them.

He pulled out his pencil, and found another tiny scrap of paper from his stash. He wrote, "Get Shorty," on the paper, rolled it into a tiny ball, put it in the empty cup on his breakfast tray, and prayed his man would be working in the kitchen still, and would check his tray for a kite. He had trained the crew hard about prison communications. He'd told them when one of the crew was in the hole, to check everything that came out—clothes to the laundry, food trays, legal papers, requests for a doctor. No need to bother with letters to the outside, since the prison staff read all those before they went out and would find anything he tried to hide. Legal correspondence was sacred. The staff couldn't check it. They could feel the envelopes to make sure there was no contraband in them, but nothing else.

Legal mail wouldn't work for Hastings. His case was over and he never wrote to his attorney. What would work was the food tray. His boys liked to work in the kitchen. There were several of them there. They could use their control of the food line to dole out extras to their friends and scrimp on the food their enemies got. Or, they'd spit in the enemies' food. Or worse. It wasn't unusual for somebody they were beefing with to spit up blood after eating something out of the food line. Ground glass wasn't that hard to find. Or poison. Or rat turds. His kitchen boys were clever, and saved him a world of grief when he was in population. He could collect debts owed to him without breaking any arms or legs. Much easier than on the street. When he was in the hole, though, that was a different story. So he had trained his boys to check over his tray for messages. They knew which trays came from which cells, because of the numbers on the tray carts. His tray was labeled, anyway, because he had a special blood pressure diet. Finding it was easy, and if they followed his instructions, finding the kite would be easy, too.

"Get Shorty," meant to get Sleepy's shorty—his girlfriend, wife, whatever. Get to her, and shake her up. Don't hurt her at first. Just scare the crap out of her. Scare her so bad she'll come running in here, begging Sleepy to make it stop. Sleepy will know right away who the message is from. If he cares for his old lady, he'll fix it so she don't have to suffer no more.

Hastings sighed contentedly. He was back in charge. He knew how to fix his problem. He had the tools to fix it. What more could a kid from the projects want, than some control over the forces in his life? He was so peaceful now, he thought he could sleep. For an hour or two at least. For him, that was a long nap.

Chapter Thirty-Five

Brenda LeBlanc walked across the tiled floor of the visitors lobby in red high heeled sandals with no back straps. They click-clacked and swooshed, as the heels hit the floor and then smacked softly back against her feet. When she got nearer the table where Sleepy was waiting, he could see that the red matched the red of her toenail polish. She was wearing a white cotton sheath with red polka dots, and a red leather belt. The effect was immediate. Sleepy remembered with a stab of pain how she always coordinated her outfits, down to the last detail, when they dressed for church, or to go out anywhere, and how proud he felt to be with her.

He waved to get her attention as she searched the visiting hall for him. When she spotted him, she smiled tentatively and walked toward him. When she got to the table, she sat quickly, not giving Sleepy time to hug her or take her hand.

"Thanks for coming," he said. He sensed her reluctance, and so did not reach across the small low table that separated visitors from inmates, to touch her.

She put her small red and white striped purse on the table, opened it and took out a tissue, which she laid in her lap. "I don't know where to begin," she said softly.

"Well, honey, just start at the beginning. There's nobody here but us. Nobody is listening. I don't care if you jumble things up."

Brenda seemed relieved. She took a deep breath, focused her eyes on Sleepy's face, and said, "He followed me home from work. I saw the car when I left the parking lot, because it was that big grey sedan like daddy used to drive when he worked for the city. I just thought it was a coincidence that the car pulled out and stayed close behind me. But after I drove awhile, I got nervous. Every time I turned, the grey car turned. When I stopped, the car stopped. I couldn't see who was driving it, but after a mile or two, it was clear the car was following me. I reached into my purse for my cell phone, to call daddy, but I'd left the darn thing at work. Then I really panicked. I decided the best thing to do was to stop somewhere, get out and go for help. I didn't want to lead whoever it was to the house. Then they'd know where I lived and could come after me, if it really was somebody following me. I couldn't figure out what in the world was going on.

"I stopped at that Fast Mart down from the house, you remember the one?"

Sleepy nodded, not wanting to interrupt the flow of her story.

Brenda reached for the tissue in her lap, held it in her hand, and went on. "I got out and walked into the store. I felt kind of foolish, you know? I mean, what if it was just somebody going home the same way I went home? I didn't want to seem paranoid. So I went to the counter, and spoke to Jedd."

She looked up at Sleepy, and paused.

He didn't react. He knew Jedd had been trying to link up with Brenda. He didn't want to let on how upset that made him. He just nodded, and she seemed relieved.

"What did you tell Jedd?" he asked, keeping his voice even.

"Well, I told him I felt a little silly. But I explained what had happened. He looked out in the parking lot, and saw the grey sedan. He said, 'That's a guvment car, ever I seen one.' You know how country Jedd always talks. I thought he was teasing me at first, but then I knew he was serious. I couldn't figure out what in the world a government car would be doing following me. So I asked Jedd what I should do."

Again, the shy look at Sleepy, checking his reaction. Again, he forced his face to remain static.

Sleepy said softly, "I know you were scared, Brenda. I'm so sorry."

She went on, not acknowledging the expression of concern. "I was terrified, but I knew I wasn't going on home alone. So I asked Jedd to come with me. He was about to get off work anyhow. I waited a few minutes, 'til he clocked out, then we both got in my car, and I headed to the house."

Sleepy didn't move, or say anything. Just nodded, encouraging her to continue.

Brenda used the tissue to wipe a small dew of perspiration from her upper lip. She fanned herself lightly with her hand. "Sorry, I just get so upset thinking about it."

Sleepy said, "You want me to get us some sodas?"

"Yes, Sleepy, that would be good. I'll take a diet drink, if they have one."

Sleepy went to the soda machines, and as he got there, he saw Hastings sitting at a corner table with a woman and small child. Hastings glanced up as Sleepy's tokens rattled in the machine, and when he saw Sleepy, he nodded, slowly and gravely. Sleepy busied himself with the sodas, and walked back to Brenda, forcing himself to take measured steps.

Sleepy pulled his chair around so that it blocked Hastings's view of Brenda. She looked at him funny, but didn't say anything. He popped the top on the diet soda, then handed it to her. He popped the top on his own drink, and set it on the table.

"Did the man follow you and Jedd?" It was hard to keep the panic out of his voice now.

"He must have gone on ahead of me, because he was at the house within minutes of the time I got home. When I got out of the car, Jedd did too. We went in the house. It wasn't but a minute 'til the man was at the door. He pulled his identification out of his pocket, and handed it to me. 'Ms. LeBlanc, I'm FBI agent John Nash,' he said. I nearly choked. What in the world the FBI would want with me, I couldn't figure. So I asked him what he wanted. Just came out and asked him, because I figured I had a right to know, since it was my house, and he was kind of intruding."

Brenda sipped the soda. "Then he asked if he could come in. I didn't want to be rude, so I said, 'Sure.' When he got in the house and we all got seated, I introduced Jedd and then agent Nash told me he was there about you. I told him we are divorced. I told him I talk to you on the phone when you have money to call, but that's our only contact, except when I can come up here for a visit at Christmas or something. He said he wanted to know about that bus escape where the guard got shot. I told him I read it in the papers, but that's all I know. He said, 'Didn't LeBlanc tell you about it?' And I said, 'No, we never talked about it.' I could tell he didn't believe me. But I didn't care. I knew I was telling the truth, so I didn't really care what he thought."

She smiled at Sleepy, then. He remembered the way she always followed the rules, and was always respectful to authority. He knew it had taken courage for her to stand up to Nash. He smiled back. "You did just the right thing, Brenda. He had no business bothering you at all."

"Well, that didn't seem to get through to him, what I said. Because he kept pressing me to say that you had told me something about the escape. Then he said you were going to be arrested for murder. Now, that really got me mad. I told him right then and there, I said, 'I don't know what kind of game you are playing, sir. But I do know Theodore LeBlanc. We were married for eight years. That man has never done a wrong thing to anybody. He's in jail because he got railroaded by some big uptown attorney his folks hired. He has a sleep disorder. That's why he got caught in that store.'

"By that time, I was so mad, I was shaking all over. I just asked him if he had a warrant for me. When he said he didn't, I told him to leave. Then he said he'd be back, and next time, not just to chat.

"Well, that upset me, just like he meant it to. Jedd got up then, and asked Nash to leave. Nash glared at me some more, then he left. I was so upset, I couldn't eat."

Sleepy knew what that meant. Brenda, with her perfect size six figure, ate like a horse. She ate morning to night. Something about her metabolism let her eat huge amounts of food, and never gain an ounce. Sleepy had little or no appetite, and was always too thin. He knew if Brenda couldn't eat, she was really upset.

"I can't tell you enough times that I'm sorry, Brenda," he said. "I don't know what they want from me. I told them I was asleep on the bus when the shooting happened. They know I sleep when I don't mean to. They know I can't control it. But the guys who were caught after the escape think I know something, and the FBI thinks I know something, and they're squeezing me. I just never thought Nash would stoop so low as to bring you into it."

Brenda smiled at him. "I know that, Sleepy. I know you didn't do anything. I meant what I said to that agent. But I sure hope he doesn't come after me again. I talked to daddy about it, and daddy said he'd come with me next time. You know daddy. If Nash steps out of line with me, daddy's liable to put a fist in his mouth. Of course, that wouldn't help anything, but it might make me feel better for a minute."

Sleepy laughed at the thought. "Your daddy is more than a handful for Nash, Brenda. But I don't want Bud to get in trouble over this thing. Try to keep him calmed down. Maybe it would be better just to get a lawyer and meet with Nash. That way, Bud can't get into it. Have you got enough left to pay for a lawyer?"

When they divorced, Sleepy signed over all his share of their savings account and investments to Brenda. She was a very wise money manager, so Sleepy figured she'd have some set aside.

"I can do that. I just don't want to spend the money if I don't have to."

"Well," Sleepy said, "it's up to you. I just don't want anybody to get hurt because of me."

Brenda looked at the floor for a minute. "Sleepy, since I'm here, I've got something else I need to talk to you about."

She looked so solemn, and the knot that formed suddenly in Sleepy's stomach told him he wasn't going to like what he was about to hear. "Go ahead," he said, swallowing.

"Sleepy, you know I've been seeing somebody. I never told you who. Well, it's Jedd. I guess you figured that out by now, anyway. Jedd is a good man. He wants to settle down, have a family. You know I'm not getting any younger. If I'm going to have kids, I don't need to wait too much longer to get started. Jedd asked me to marry him."

She looked at Sleepy, searching his face. He forced himself not to react. "Brenda, you know I want you to be happy. If Jedd can make you happy, what can I say? I don't have any right to say anything."

"But you do, Sleepy. You know I didn't want the divorce. But eight years is so long. I did what I thought I had to. Can you forgive me if I marry Jedd?"

Sleepy laughed. "Brenda, if forgiveness is needed it's me that needs it, not you. You go ahead and do whatever you need to do, for yourself. Whatever that is, I'll be wishing you the best."

Brenda dabbed at her eyes now. She sniffled as she got up to go. This time she gave Sleepy a hug, then without saying anything but a quick, "Bye," she was gone.

Sleepy sat back down. He needed to get back to his cell. He needed to be out of sight of other people. But he was too heavy to move. He sat down, just to rest for a minute. When he woke, the familiar surroundings of the infirmary stared back at him.

Chapter Thirty-Six

Nancy Carmichael read the materials she had gathered on sleep disorders. A plan began to take shape in her mind. Her job was not to be an advocate for any inmate against law enforcement, prosecutors or prison officials. Her job was to identify and treat psychological problems that were relevant to an inmate's adjustment in prison and his eventual release. Her history of privilege and her own ups and downs probably made her empathetic. Her leanings aside, objectively it was clear that LeBlanc had all the symptoms of narcolepsy. So she called the warden's office to set her treatment plan in motion.

When her call was answered, she spoke quickly. "Warden, this is Nancy Carmichael. I think I know what is going on in inmate LeBlanc's case. When you have time, I can explain my conclusions. Yes, sir, ten o'clock is fine. I'll be there." She looked at her watch. That gave her twenty minutes to assemble her presentation.

She arrived at the warden's office, her pull cart loaded with her textbook, a roll-up chart she had hastily put together, and LeBlanc's file. She spoke to Betty, then waited as Betty called the warden. "You can go on in, honey," Betty said, smiling indulgently at her.

Warden Watts opened the door for her when she knocked, and seeing the cart, stepped back to give her room to haul it through the door.

"What is this, Ms. Carmichael? I hope whatever is wrong with LeBlanc, it isn't complicated enough that you need all that to explain it."

"No, warden," she said, once she had settled herself and her materials. "I think it's really pretty straightforward. I think Mr. LeBlanc has a serious sleep disorder. I want to tell you about it, so we can decide what to do."

"Wonder why Dr. Blake didn't figure that out," Watts mused. Diplomacy argued against any comment from her on that issue,

Nancy thought, so she held her tongue.

Warden Watts motioned her to begin. She sat down in the chair across from his, and unloaded her pull cart. "Here it is in a nutshell, warden. I'm sure LeBlanc has narcolepsy."

The warden looked at her blankly. "Doesn't that have something to do with dead bodies?"

She felt herself blushing. "Oh, heavens no, sir. Narcolepsy is a sleep disorder. It causes people to fall asleep at inappropriate times. It's a brain disorder, affecting the part of the brain that regulates normal sleep patterns. People who have it try and try to stay awake, but they simply can't. The brain won't let them. Some people have such severe cases that the sleep episodes last for over an hour, or even longer. And some people have severe symptoms, like temporary paralysis when they fall asleep or wake up, or seizure-like muscle activity. LeBlanc has all of those, in my opinion. The first thing that happens is he is unable to speak or move. Then he goes rigid. That's the loss of muscle tone, followed by paralysis, I think. And of course, we know that he goes to sleep at all the wrong times. From what the prison staff has seen, and documented in his records, the episodes come on, he goes to sleep, and it is next-to-impossible to wake him. I think he has a severe case of narcolepsy, warden, which has gone untreated."

The warden looked at her without speaking. He clasped his hands on his desk, steepled his fingers, and seemed to study her comment. She didn't speak, knowing from even a brief experience with him that the warden did not welcome interruption. Finally, he spoke.

"Ms. Carmichael, that's some good work you did. It makes sense to me. That FBI agent has his head up his . . . his . . ." The warden cleared his throat. "He is just wrong, I think. He thinks we're a bunch of dumb crackers, that we don't know when we're being hoodwinked. He wants this case closed. He wants the glory. So he has decided that LeBlanc is faking these sleep problems. Well, why would he do that? Before the incident on the bus, he wasn't in trouble. I think he might have been in one fight here. But if memory serves, that was pretty clearly self-defense. The agent wants us to believe that LeBlanc faked these sleep episodes for the year or so he's been here, to prepare for the time when he'd be on the bus and need to claim he didn't see or hear anything? That's bull." He glanced at her quickly, but she smiled to reassure him that she wasn't offended by his choice of words.

"Sir, I think that's exactly right," she said, encouraging him to continue.

"But..." the warden looked hard at her now, pausing for effect. "But, Ms. Carmichael, I am not sure what we do with your diagnosis. LeBlanc has criminal charges pending now. He's facing the death penalty if he's convicted of participating in the escape plot that ended in Harkness getting shot. He's got an attorney. I met her the other day. I don't think we can do anything now, because if we do, we could be accused of interfering in the case."

"That's a concern, warden," Nancy acknowledged. "But can we leave LeBlanc to the likes of Nash, whose own interests demand that LeBlanc become a witness about the bus incident, if we know he has no information about what happened? My thinking is that because he is an inmate in our facility, we have the right to treat him for any physical or emotional or psychological disorders. I believe the law allows that."

He scowled at her. "Oh, so we're a lawyer, too, now, are we?"

She stopped, taking his point. "Okay, warden, you caught me with that one. But I do think we can justify at least explaining my diagnosis to LeBlanc, and letting him do with it what he will. Maybe his attorney would even welcome it, and work with us to get him treatment."

"Maybe. From what I saw of her, she seems genuinely concerned about LeBlanc. She may try to help us, if we're trying to help LeBlanc. But you know I'm going to get all manner of grief from the Fibbies, Nash in particular. They'll claim we're taking sides, trying to derail their prosecution. That S.O.B. Nash will probably go to the governor, then the higher-ups in the Department of Corrections will start messing with me. Probably you, too. Are you ready for that?"

She tried not to show concern. "Well, I don't want to get either of us in any trouble. But if we're doing what we think is right, I don't see how that could happen."

"Here's how it could happen," the warden interrupted. "Nash will paint me as some bleeding-heart. That's not a good label to get, when you're in corrections. He'll find out I got a degree in criminal justice, and that the masters degree is what got me this desk job, not my years in the prison as a guard. He'll make something of that, try to drive a wedge between me and my staff. Or try to drive a wedge between me and the powers that be in the capitol. Next year, when budget time rolls around, they'll remember that. If I ask for money for programs, they'll nix it, suspecting that it's coming from my liberal bias. Same if I ask for staff positions like yours, or a librarian, or teachers. Anything not purely for control of inmates."

"Oh." was all she could say. She didn't add that in her view, Nash was passing himself off as law enforcement, when really he was just a thug with a badge. She didn't want the warden to think she was acting out of anger at Nash.

"Sir," she ventured tentatively. "Maybe it could come from me. Maybe you don't have to know anything about it. I could speak off the record to LeBlanc's attorney. I could tell her to get LeBlanc's prison medical records, if she hasn't already. Then she'd have all the ammunition she needs to work with. If she wanted us to test him, or treat him, she could tell us."

"No." The tone was emphatic. Let's be up front about whatever we do."

Nancy nodded. "I guess the best way is to tell LeBlanc about the diagnosis. I'll suggest that he tell his attorney. Then they can take it from there. I won't have done anything but inform a patient of a diagnosis which I believe fits his symptoms. Doctors do that all the time. How can I get in trouble for doing that?"

The warden considered that angle. "I think that could work. You're right. Assisting inmates with mental health concerns is in your job description. Of course, you can't just set up a private clinic in here. The inmates have to be referred to you by staff. There has to be some official concern about a problem, before you can look into it. But with LeBlanc's history, we should be safe on that score. I say do it. Talk to him, and see what he has to say. Then we'll see where this goes."

"Thank you, sir. I'll get right on it." She put the items she had brought to bolster her case into the pull cart, and wheeled it out and down the hall.

Nancy was relieved that the warden supported her plan for LeBlanc. She knew that one reason was her desire to make a good impression in her first serious case in her new job. Her very first work experience had been with her father, whose work ethic helped him move from a struggling small business to a small empire. So it was no surprise that she aimed to do her job and do it well. But it was more than that. LeBlanc's vulnerability touched her. Dr. Blake's indifference troubled her. Harbaugh's naked greed offended her. And Nash's dogged determination to get up the agency ladder on LeBlanc's back, consequences be damned, was the final stone in her shoe.

When she was back in her office, she got LeBlanc's file from the cart, and looked up his housing unit number. She called the housing officer and asked that LeBlanc be ready to see her the next morning. In the meantime, she'd go back over all her data, and put it together in layman's terms. She didn't like to give patients information about their conditions that they couldn't digest. LeBlanc seemed smart, but his condition was serious. It had already had very serious consequences in his life—job problems, a hefty prison term, a failed marriage, and now the prospect of a capital conviction. If she had to give patients bad news, she liked to flavor it with some good. How to find any in this situation was the question.

Chapter Thirty-Seven

Sleepy wondered why it was that he was called to Ms. Carmichael's office. She surely wasn't the principal type, but still his stomach fluttered like it did when he was a kid and called to Mr. Olson's office. Always for the same thing. Falling asleep in class. The school couldn't handle it. Neither could his aunt and uncle. They made him go to bed earlier and earlier, but it still happened.

He liked Ms. Carmichael, though. He would not think about her like the school principal. She was genuinely trying to help him, he thought. At least, he'd give her a chance.

By the time Sleepy got to Ms. Carmichael's office, he had calmed down. She was sitting at her desk, wearing a pretty blue dress with a white collar. The dress made her look even smaller than she was.

"Good morning, Mr. LeBlanc. Come on in." She nodded to the only other seat in her small office.

"Good morning, ma'am," Sleepy acknowledged.

"Sorry this space is so small." Sleepy was scrunched up in the chair, and his long legs had no place to go except to stretch underneath her desk. "I hope to earn a bigger office soon, maybe bigger than a broom closet this time." She laughed, and Sleepy smiled at her.

"What I have to talk to you about won't take too long. If you can bear with me…"

Sleepy nodded. "Sure, ma'am. I'm alright."

She opened a text book, got a chart from her drawer, and turned to Sleepy. "Mr. LeBlanc, I think I've figured out why you sleep like you do."

He looked at her, but didn't say anything. He would wait and see what she had to say.

She continued, "I think you have a condition known as narcolepsy. It's a neurological disorder, and it causes people to fall asleep when they don't mean to. Some cases are severe, and the person doesn't wake for hours. The person can have seizure-like symptoms, also. I've heard and read about your sleep episodes, in your records here. I think I'm right. If I am, there are ways to document the disorder and there are treatments which have been very successful. What I think, Mr. LeBlanc, is that you've gone undiagnosed for way too long. It's a tragedy, too, because as I read your file, you're here because of a sleep incident. Your marriage failed because of your problem, plus your being in prison. You lost jobs because of it. It has seriously affected your life. But the good news is, it's treatable. You don't have to continue like you've done in the past."

Sleepy sat very still. Her tone was so warm. She seemed genuinely concerned. And look at all the work she had done to figure this out. Her desk was stacked with heavy medical books. She unrolled a chart, which he guessed she had prepared. He didn't know what to think about this. Except for Brenda and his aunt, he didn't have much experience with women. Her concern was genuine, he thought, but it still made him nervous.

"Ms. Carmichael, I surely do thank you for all the work you've done for me. I don't really understand this disease, if that's what it is. But I am glad to hear there's a reason why I sleep like I do. It sure has caused me a world of problems. I'd like to be normal, if I could."

Ms. Carmichael smiled. "Well, Mr. LeBlanc, 'normal' is a relative term, as I'm sure you know. But I think that with treatment, you could get some control in your life. You could work eight hours, for example. You wouldn't have to worry about falling asleep in a men's dressing room. You might even be able to stay awake long enough to spend time with a woman."

Sleepy glanced quickly at her, then looked at his shoes. He felt himself turning red.

"I didn't mean to embarrass you," she said, smiling. "But I do think this is important information. Is Ms. Johnson still your attorney?"

He wondered briefly if everybody in the prison knew about his murder charge. But of course the administration would, he realized.

Nothing sinister there.

"Yes, ma'am. She is due out here any day to meet with me."

"Well, I suggest you tell her what I've told you. She'll know what to do next. She can get your prison records. She can take it from here."

Sleepy nodded.

"Well, then. That's what we will do. Now, for the time being, I'm not going to suggest any medication for you. I think you and your attorney should talk about how you want to proceed here. I don't want to interfere in your defense at all. But if she agrees, I would want to try you on some drugs that have proven successful in treating this disorder. I would have to get the doctor to prescribe them, since I'm a psychologist and not a medical doctor. But we won't do anything like that until you and your lawyer are comfortable with it. I'll just wait to hear back from you."

"It feels good to know there may be an answer to all this," Sleepy said.

"Good. Now, I have one more question. Are you having problems with the inmates who were on the bus?"

Sleepy surprised himself by telling her about Hammer, and the attempts to harm him. She was upset when he told her about Be-Bop. And she said she wanted to meet Rosie, that he seemed like a good man. When he left her office, he felt lighter. It scared him a little, that he had let her in on some things that bothered him. But somehow he knew he could trust her. Maybe, if she had time, he'd talk to her about Brenda one day.

Chapter Thirty-Eight

Nancy Carmichael learned early that because she was petite and pretty, people underestimated her. When she was young, that treatment made her furious. As she got older, she fought the frustration by making a game of it, in her mind. She calculated the triggers that would cause people, especially men, not to take her seriously. Then she played them, one by one, 'til slowly it dawned on her opponent that she had just cut him off at the knees. It was her twist on the old saw, "You can catch more flies with honey." Most times it worked.

So she was comfortable as she sat behind her desk, waiting for Hastings to appear, and for the chance to put the next segment of her plan into effect. After she spoke with LeBlanc, she pulled Hastings's file. Piecing together the several psychological reports, a picture emerged—raised by a mother whose only concern in life was getting and staying high. No wonder the man is a mess, Nancy thought. That mother alone could explain the enuresis. Nancy was mid-way of the stack of psychological reports when Hastings knocked on her door. The escort brought in a slight man, in handcuffs. His lank brown hair hung almost to his shoulders. His clothes were wrinkled. He scowled when he saw her. The escort helped him take a seat in the straight-backed chair, then said to Nancy, "He's all yours. If there's any trouble, I'll be right outside."

"Thank you, officer," she said as she smiled at Hastings.

"How are you, Mr. Hastings?" she asked sweetly.

He looked hard at her, but didn't answer.

"I guess you wonder why I wanted to speak with you," she began.

He grunted, but the sound was unintelligible.

"I'll be happy to explain. You see, I'm the prison psychologist. I am new here, so I have set myself a goal of interviewing and personally meeting every inmate in the prison by the end of this year. I am going to start seeing three or four people every day. And of course, in preparation for the meetings, I need to read the inmate files, to get as much background as I can. Since I know you are one of the inmates who is a leader in the prison population, I thought I would start with you."

"Why me? I ain't no head case. I seen every head doctor they got in the system, ain't none of them figured me out yet. You sure ain't likely to." He snorted at her, then leaned back in his chair and closed his eyes.

"Well, you may be right, Mr. Hastings, that I can't figure you out. But I do believe that there are some things you can help me with. Since you seem to be in a bit of a hurry, I'll get right to the project I have in mind." Nancy was watching him carefully now. "I know you suffered from enuresis as a child. A number of other inmates here have, also. I want to start a therapy group, for all of you. I was hoping you would agree to be the lay leader of the group." She waited for her proposal to sink in.

"What the hell is enuresis?" he asked, looking at her suspiciously.

"Enuresis is just the fancy doctor word for bedwetting." She looked directly into his eyes, and willed herself not to blink.

He exploded out of the chair. "Look, bitch, you tell anybody about that, I'll cut your stupid head off!" He was livid now. The veins in his face swelled, and his eyes bulged. He shook his head side to side. She was afraid he would hyperventilate.

"Calm down, Mr. Hastings. Of course I wouldn't tell anybody. That's privileged and confidential. I just want to try to help you."

"I don't need your help. Leave me alone." He got up to leave.

She said quietly, "Just one more thing, Mr. Hastings. I understand you have a problem with inmate LeBlanc. He didn't tell me about it, of course. You know he wouldn't do that. But the guards have spoken to me about some incidents that have occurred recently. I'm sure you know what I'm talking about. I don't mean to meddle, but I wanted to suggest something to you. I wouldn't want to hear of any more incidents. Any more threats, or attempts to harm him."

"What the hell you think you can do about it?" He was straining at his wrist restraints now, and she held tightly to the remote for her "HELP" button. Thank God the guard was outside.

"Well, here's my thinking. I won't do anything about my support group if you leave Mr. LeBlanc alone. If you continue to try to harm him, or anyone connected to him, I will get the group up and running. It's part of my job, you know, to devise support groups for inmates. I'll start the Enuresis Anonymous, and I'll post a list of inmates who are being called to the group. Your name will head the list."

Hastings was sputtering now. His fists were clenching and unclenching. "Bitch, you do that, I'll kill you."

"You want to be careful about those threats, now, Mr. Hastings. That's exactly the kind of behavior I'm trying to curb here. And just in case I didn't make it clear, the membership in this therapy group will include those mongrels that follow you around, licking your hand. Keep them under control, also. Otherwise, the whole crew goes on the roster of EA. Any questions?"

She stood firmly in front of him, but tried to get out of arm's reach. In her small office, that wasn't easy. Hastings must have sensed that she wasn't joking. He was bright, she knew that from the various psychological tests. Bright enough to understand what a label of "bedwetter" would do to the rep he and his crew cultivated. He seemed deflated, all of a sudden. He unclenched his fists, and sat back down in the chair. "No, doc, no questions," he finally said.

With that, he got up and left. He didn't even slam the door on his way out.

"Whew," she said, when he was gone. "That was too easy. He seemed calm when he left, but I doubt that will hold. I'd better get those karate lessons scheduled. "

Three days later Nancy Carmichael was still fretting about the meeting with Hastings. "I think I got the message to him," she said, trying to look at the situation objectively. "He knows I know he was a bedwetter. He knows that information would seriously tarnish his image among his thug groupies. But what if this backfires? What if he tries to take revenge on LeBlanc, because he can't risk hurting me? Or what if he decides he doesn't care about the risk of hurting me?" Her mind was jumbled and the anxiety showed. She paced her cubicle, back and forth, arms folded, head down. Anyone watching her would have thought of a caged animal, seeking some small weakness in the cage structure to worry itself through.

Her other concern was more long-term. She had taken an oath, that her practice of psychology would bring no harm. Was she potentially harming Hastings? She knew she would never expose him in the prison population. That would be a clear violation of her oath. But he didn't know that. Was she violating her canon of ethics by bringing him to the negotiating table with threats?

As she paced back and forth, an idea began to form. "Negotiating table." She liked the sound of that. If she could negotiate a truce, if Hastings and LeBlanc would agree, she would have done no harm to anyone, and in fact, she would have done some good. She mulled the idea over. The more she considered it, the better it felt. That way, she didn't have to sort out her feelings as the former victim of domestic abuse. She didn't have to question whether she identified with LeBlanc so strongly because she had been the hunted herself. Years ago, it was true. But not so long ago that she had forgotten the abject terror of helplessness at the hands of a tyrant.

Chapter Thirty-Nine

Hastings was about to explode. His head ached, and his feet hurt from pacing the cell. Being in the hole usually didn't bother him. It just gave him time to think, to regroup, to make plans for dealing with his enemies and to keep his crew occupied. But this stint seemed like it was to go on forever. And to add to it, that bitch psychologist threatened him. She knew about him, she had his file right in front of her, and she still threatened him. Bitch must not want to live, he thought. Either that, or she's dumb as a box of rocks. Hastings figured she wasn't dumb, because she a psychologist. She had to be smart to get through all that schooling. But why would she try him like that? The only way she would risk it, he figured, was if she knew she could win. Which translated to, Hastings would lose.

Hastings idea of a loss was anything that cost him respect in the eyes of his crew. He did not like to lose. He could not, would not, let the word of the accidents he had when he was a teenager get out. He would be ruined. But the question was, how to keep his secrets, and still keep his rep? And another big question, how to get the word to the crew, so they left Sleepy alone?

He dug the pencil from his shoe, and carefully tore the corner off his last piece of paper. He'd scrounged it from the "Notes" page in the prison-issued rights pamphlet he'd been given when he came to the hole. He'd used all the corners and end pages and the last page was all he had left. He had to use it carefully.

He considered how to let the crew know that the war was over, at least for now. Did they know why he was after Sleepy in the first place? Some may have figured it out, the others were just following his lead. He wanted Sleepy hurt, they would hurt Sleepy. No need to ask why. That's what loyalty meant in here. If he had to do time, he sure wasn't going to give that up. But what could he tell the ones who were smart enough to figure out that Hammer was afraid Sleepy would say something that would get them convicted of the guard's murder? Some of his crew in the hole with him had real good friends on the compound. They would want to know that Sleepy posed no threat, or they might take matters into their own hands.

Hastings reviewed the tactics he had used before to get word to his crew, and settled on one that had worked last time he tried it. He kicked the door to his cell as hard as he could. When he got no response, he kicked the door again, and yelled as loud as he could. Kicking the door hurt his toe, and he got even more pissed. "These damn shower shoes they give you in the hole ain't even good for kicking nothin'," he muttered.

The steel door cut down the noise a lot, that was its purpose. But if he banged loud enough and long enough, some guard would wake up and come tell him to cut the noise. Sure enough, on his third round of pounding the door with his fists and his shoe, he heard, "Shut up, Hastings. You know not to make a racket like that. I'm coming in, and this better be an emergency."

Or what? Hastings thought. "You'll send me to the hole?" He laughed at his own joke, and started coughing as hard as he could. As the door to his cell opened, he croaked, "It is an emergency, man. I can't breathe. I can't find my inhaler. My throat is closing up." To add effect, he bent over and held his chest with both hands. "I'm dying, man," he rasped.

The guard looked hard at Hastings, who had held his breath long enough to begin to look very ill. "Crap!" the guard muttered. "Why you got to get sick on my shift, man? Twenty more minutes, I'm on my way home to a cold beer and a hot new girlfriend. Now you done ruined my day, Hastings."

Hastings continued to sputter and wheeze. The guard opened the cell door and looked down the corridor. "Where are the others? I radioed them five minutes ago." As he was venting his annoyance, Hastings heard feet pounding down the hall. Then he saw a welcome sight. The medics had brought a stretcher. Soon he was loaded onto it, and rolled gently to the infirmary. Once admitted and assigned a bed, he could get word to his crew. Then someone would wrangle a visit—they'd either get a job real quick as the maintenance man, or have a serious and sudden attack of something themselves. He knew he could count on his men. So for now, why not lie back and enjoy it? He'd heard one of the nurses was really hot. Maybe he'd get lucky and get her to tend to him. A few days vacation wouldn't hurt him. Even after he'd gotten the message out, hanging out in sick bay could be the right thing to do. He felt a very serious attack coming on.

Nut was by his bedside when he woke up an hour later. When Hastings opened his eyes, Nut was staring down at him. His face was a map of trouble. Nut was dressed in scrubs, and had a mask sitting on his forehead. He looked like a wanna-be, sure enough.

Hastings was irritated. He didn't like anyone watching him sleep. "What the hell?" he hissed. Nut jumped back like he'd been hit with the mop he was leaning on. "Hammer, man, it's me, Nut. I come to check on you, man. Guys say you in the sick bay, we got to see why, what's up, you know? You sick for real, Hammer?" It was almost touching, Nut's concern. But it annoyed Hastings.

"Course I'm sick for real, idiot. What'd you think? I checked into sick bay to get away from the hole, or something?"

"Nah, man, we know that ain't it. You love the hole, you always telling us that. It's like a vacation cruise, you say. But why you here, man? What's wrong with you?" Again the concern seemed genuine, and again Hastings was irked.

"Man, it's my asthma. You know I always had asthma, since I was a kid. Something about the air in my cell caused it to act up, I guess. But it's kicking my butt, I can tell you that. They're supposed to be getting me some breathing equipment in here. Then I'll be alright, once I get this bad air out my system, and get me some good, pure air to breathe."

Nut looked relieved. "Okay, Hammer, I'll tell the guys that. They'll feel better. You need anything, man? Anything at all? We got all the boys back in population but the ones on the bus. We can do just about what you need us to do, we got so many of us out."

Hastings knew how rare that was. His crew spent more time in the hole than out. Always being written up for some rule violation. He'd told them, "Don't go down on nothing small. You got to go to the hole, go for something real". But they won't listen. Always violating phone rules, talking too long to their bitches, arguing with their baby mamas, that crap. Or trying to cop a feel in the visitor hall. Telling the bitches on the phone, "Don't wear no panties this Sunday," then thinking the officers ain't on to that. Man, they're some dumb suckers sometimes. He shook his head in despair, as he often did thinking about the men under his supervision and how to whip them into shape. Oh, well, at least they sent Nut. He wasn't the brightest bulb in the chandelier, but he meant well. He at least tried to do what he was told to do.

"So, Nut, here's the deal, man. I need you to put the word out. We ain't after Sleepy no more. You understand?"

Nut looked shocked. "But Hammer, he was on the bus. He got busted for killing Harkness. Man, you know he gonna sing. You know he gonna bust you. How we ain't gonna hurt him, try to stop him?"

Hastings was irritated again. "Nut, you hearing me? I said, we ain't going after him no more. That's it. My orders. No questions. That's the way we do it, ain't it?"

"Well, yeah, man, you know that's right. But ain't that dangerous? Suppose he tells? He could get you and the other guys fried, Hammer. This ain't no baby charge they putting on you, man. This the big one. What if he tells?"

Hastings was really mad now. "Damn it, Nut, listen to me!" He was spitting his words, but trying to whisper, not to cause a commotion that would get him sent back to the hole. "Nut," he said, more calmly this time. "He didn't see nothin'. I talked to the doctor. He was asleep. You know he's got that sleep thing, always falling out when he ain't supposed to. Something the head doctor knows all about. She's treating him for it. He told her he didn't see nothing. He told the FBI he didn't see nothing. He's sticking to that man, either cause it's true, or cause it's the best for him. But we got to lay low. We hurt him now, everybody's gonna start talking about how we must be trying to shut him up, and for what? Cause we're guilty of something, that's what? Why else would we be messing with him?"

Nut seemed to be thinking that over. After awhile, he said, "Hammer, we got to trust what you tell us, man. You say he ain't no threat, he ain't no threat. Don't mean I'll sit with him in church or nothing, but I'll leave him alone. What you want us to do if somebody else tries to screw with him? Could be some other gang he done messed with."

Hastings hadn't really thought about that possibility. But the answer seemed obvious. If he or his crew did anything to Sleepy, his name was going to be posted on the bulletin board as a member of the bedwetter's anonymous, or some such. "Nut, if anybody tries to hurt him, I want you all to stop them. Tell whoever it is that if they hurt him, they got to answer to me. That should protect him pretty good."

Nut agreed. "Yeah, he all right if we got his back."

Hastings smiled. "Yeah, we're gonna be his guardian angels for awhile, Nut. Trust me on this. It's best for us. Make sure the others know the order is from me. No messing with Sleepy. If somebody else tries to mess with him, get 'em. Just tell the guys he's a stand up dude, Hammer says so. That should be all they need to know."

Nut nodded. He picked up his mop, started out of the room. "Sleepy one lucky guy, you know that, Ham? One helluva lucky guy." He swished his mop down the hall, giving the floor a lick and a promise. Hastings watched him go, and smiled to himself. Imagine me in the protection business. Who would have thought?

Chapter Forty

Sleepy was on his way back from a legal visit. He was replaying the interview with Ms. Johnson in his head. He was glad she had seen eye to eye with him about Ms. Carmichael. And when she characterized the State's evidence of his involvement in a plot to kill Harkness and escape as "too weak to get past a motion to dismiss," he felt relieved. It was so hard for him to get used to the notion that he was going to go on trial for murder. He didn't even squash bugs if he didn't need to. Why kill them, he always thought, if you can just ignore them? Of course, cockroaches were exempt from that humane policy. And fire ants. And bed bugs. But otherwise, it was live and let live, as far as Sleepy was concerned. He just couldn't get his mind to accept that he was being labeled a murderer.

After Ms. Johnson explained to him the motions she filed, and that the judge would hold a pretrial hearing before deciding the motions, he knew that the motion to dismiss the indictment was a vehicle for them to test the State's case. Ms. Johnson had warned him that motions to dismiss were rarely granted before trial. He knew not to get his hopes up.

Sleepy was thinking hard about his situation and didn't see the shadow across the hallway floor up ahead. As he got level with the broom closet, the door flew open, and slammed him full on. He heard his nose crack. Blood spurted over his mouth and chin, and ran down the front of his shirt. He felt dizzy, but couldn't find anything to grab onto. As his vision cleared, he saw the back of a tan uniform running down the hallway. His attacker was another inmate, he knew, since the guards wore green uniforms, so they could never be confused with the khaki worn by the inmates in open population. What the hell was that about? Sleepy wondered. Then he almost laughed at his own foolishness. Of course he knew what it was about. Hammer again. The inmate who hit him was working for Hammer. Hammer rarely did his own dirt.

Sleepy was stumbling now, slipping in the blood that had fallen onto the floor. He left a bloody handprint on the cement wall, trying to get himself fully upright so he could assess the damage. His nose was broken, he knew. But his knee hurt something awful, too. And his forehead. Must have hit the door head on, forehead, knees, nose, the most prominent parts of his body taking the force of the door. As he was studying the mess on the floor, trying to decide what to do, a guard ran up to him.

"LeBlanc, what the hell happened to you?" He had a walkie-talkie in one hand, and a towel in the other. He handed the towel to Sleepy as he activated the phone, and yelled "911" into it. He was giving directions to the medics, telling them the block and corridor, and looking at Sleepy. He started to feel parts of Sleepy's arms and calves. "Don't seem to be any broken arms or legs," he reported. "But there's lots of blood, I'm guessing from the nose, which sure looks broken. There's a hens egg on the forehead. The knees feel swollen. Bring a stretcher, so he won't have to walk."

The guard turned to Sleepy. "Damn it, LeBlanc, you better tell me what happened here."

Sleepy was still trying to fight the nausea and dizziness. "Somebody was behind the broom closet door. When I passed by, the door flew open and hit me hard. When I could see again, I looked down the corridor and saw the back of someone in a khaki uniform. That's all I know."

The officer was looking in the broom closet. "Yeah, there's footprints here. The closet was dusty. Whoever slammed you was standing here, waiting. How did he know you'd be coming this way?"

"I don't know. I was on a legal visit. Maybe they knew that. I had to pass this way, on the way back to my cell. That's all I can figure."

The guard looked annoyed. "Yeah, somebody tipped him. That is clear. Or he was in the visiting hall at the same time you were. Did you see any other inmates with legal visits?"

"No, sir. I was the only one." By the time people were serving sentences, they rarely saw their lawyers. The options after conviction and appeal were so few that most people just did their time, and didn't bother with lawyers.

Before the guard could comment, the medics and gurney arrived. Sleepy started to protest that he could walk to the infirmary, but the look on the guard's face told him he'd be traveling the usual way.

One of the medics looked him up and down. "Damn, LeBlanc, they're going to have to name a cubicle in the infirmary after you. You sure must like our hospitality. Seems like you're with us every week or so."

Sleepy smiled. "It's nothing personal, sir," he said.

The guard interrupted. "Now there's where you're wrong, LeBlanc. These attacks are very personal. I'm going to the warden, see what he wants to do. It may be time to transfer you out of here."

Sleepy didn't like the sound of that. The prison wasn't any better than any other, but the warden was a fair man. Things ran pretty much according to the book. Sleepy had heard about some of the other prisons in the state, and he knew he didn't want to visit them. Maybe he could talk the warden out of transferring him, because this was closest to his home. Of course, if the warden looked at the visiting log, he'd know that Sleepy's family wasn't here but once in a blue moon.

When Sleepy was on a cot in the infirmary, waiting for the physician's assistant to look him over, he had an idea. Maybe he could ward off a transfer if he could get Brenda to write the warden. She could say that she would be able to visit more regularly in the future. Maybe she could get some people from the church to come. That way, Sleepy would have an argument for the warden if the subject of transfer came up.

"Can I make a call from here?" he asked the inmate who was the trustee in the infirmary.

"Sure, if it's to family. We're allowed one call to family, when we have to come into sick bay. You want me to dial it for you?"

"Yeah," Sleepy said, writing the number on the pad next to his cot. The trustee brought the phone over to the bed. Sleepy was surprised to see that the infirmary had a cordless phone. Must be because the powers that be figured if you were in the infirmary, you'd be too weak to take the phone and beat somebody with it. Sleepy wouldn't want to test that hypothesis if Hammer and some of his boys showed up here.

No one answered the phone at Brenda's house. He left a message. "Brenda, this is Theodore. I need to speak with you. Something has happened. I'm alright, but I need you to write a letter for me, if you will. I'll call you back this weekend, if I can get to the phone."

Maybe that would be enough to soften her for his next call. If she knew all he wanted was a letter, maybe she wouldn't feel put out about it. He never asked her for anything. Most guys in here wanted their families to send them money all the time, and visit them every visiting day. Sleepy wasn't like that. He knew his family hadn't done anything to put him here. Why should they have to suffer, just because he was in a bad spot?

Chapter Forty-One

Sleepy was surprised when his name was called over the loudspeaker. He sat upright in his cell, wondering if he had heard it right. Why would they be calling his name? It was Saturday, and he didn't work Saturdays. He listened to make sure he wasn't dreaming. "LeBlanc, Theodore, report to the visiting hall." There it was. It wasn't a dream. He'd been out of the infirmary a week, and still had not spoken to Brenda about the letter. Part of him hoped the visitor was Brenda. The other part of him dreaded what she would say when she saw his face, his nose in a protective cast, both eyes black and blue. He could try not to limp, but his knee was so sore, his best efforts might not let him walk straight.

He neatened up as best he could, putting his shirt into his pants, brushing his teeth and slicking back his unruly hair. He walked quickly to the main administration building. As he entered the large visiting room, he scanned the tables and chairs, looking for a familiar face. He was about to overlook her, when she stood and waved to him. Sleepy tried not to show his excitement. It was Brenda. He didn't know whether she had come about the letter, but he was glad to see her.

She stood stock still when she saw him. Then she put her hand to her mouth, as if to stifle a scream. She walked to him quickly, and stood close to him, inspecting his face.

"What in God's name happened, Theodore?" She looked like she might faint.

He spoke quickly. "Sit down, Brenda. It's not as bad as it looks. Some guy hit me with a door. He opened the closet door just as I came abreast of it. Broke my nose. It's been a week. It's healing good. Nothing for you to worry about." He told the truth, as far as it went. His calm tone seemed to reassure her.

She smiled at him, and sat down. He noticed that she had on another of his favorite outfits, a pink suit trimmed in black piping.

She called it her Elvis outfit, because it was pink and black. She was too young to remember it, she made sure to say, but she had read that Elvis drove a pink and black Cadillac. The dress was in honor of the car, she always said.

Sleepy was smiling broadly. "Long live the king!" he said, as he took her hand in his. He liked to tease her about her passion for Elvis.

He joined her at the small plastic table, trying to wind his knees around so he wouldn't put distance between them, and trying to protect the injured knee.

"I guess you wonder why I'm here," she said.

Sleepy didn't know whether to agree with her. "Well, I'm sure glad to see you. I guess you'll tell me what brought you here when you get around to it."

Instead of smiling, Brenda took a deep breath, folded her hands on the table, and looked at Sleepy. "I got a call from your lawyer. She wanted to talk to me about this sleep thing. I told her about all the times I could remember. I know I didn't recall all of them, but I tried. She said it could help you, in your case. She seemed like she was really trying to help you. But I don't know. I was worried. I wanted you to tell me what I can do. I still can't quite get my mind to accept that you are charged with murder and that the State wants to kill you." She paused, and her lip began to quiver. Sleepy could tell she was trying not to cry.

"Now, Brenda, don't you get yourself upset over anything I've done. You know me, and you know I couldn't kill anybody. I didn't like Harkness, but I sure didn't want him to come to harm. I think that guy Hammer and his crew wanted rid of Harkness 'cause he rode them so bad when we were working on the road crew. They liked to take things easy, see, and Harkness was always pointing the gun at them, threatening them, yelling at them to get up, get busy, do this or that. I guess they got tired of being mistreated. Not like they're any angels. I'm sure not saying that. But nobody likes to be treated bad all the time. It finally came back to Harkness. But I didn't know anything about it before it happened, I didn't see what happened, and I'm not about to make something up just to please that FBI jerk."

"Would it help you, even if you did tell them what they want to hear?"

Sleepy nodded. "Sure, it would help. That happens in here all the time. The FBI or the cops want somebody to be a witness against somebody else. Suddenly the inmate is their poster child for rehabilitation. They make sure he gets extras of everything. He gets more visits than the rules allow. He gets contact visits, and sometimes the guards turn their heads if it's a visit with a wife or girlfriend, and allow for some privacy. But mainly what they get is a time cut. I've heard plenty of inmates talking about time cuts, and about diming somebody out, which means snitching on somebody, just to get out early. They don't care if what they say is true. They'll make stuff up if they need to. But you know I'm not going to do that. Nash can just come with his best shot, because I won't turn into a lying scumbag for him."

Sleepy was sweating now, and he realized he was getting worked up. He didn't usually talk about his case at all, and to have any ear, especially Brenda's, was a comfort. But he'd better cool it, he reminded himself. He still didn't know why she was here.

"Did you get the message I left you last week about writing a letter for me?"

"I did, but once your attorney called and talked to me, and I knew I was going to come up to see you, I put it out of my mind."

"Did my attorney ask you to come see me?"

"Not in so many words," she said. "She just said it would help you if I could recall all the times your sleepiness got in the way of what you were doing. Of course, I didn't tell her everything." She looked at Sleepy from under her bangs, and he could see she was slightly flushed.

"Well, no, I hope you wouldn't", he said, trying not to blush himself. "But how did she think it would help if you told about my falling asleep all the time?"

"Well," she said, pursing her lips. "She said that the FBI and the prosecutor don't have any evidence against you, but that they think you are faking the sleep thing, and that you know what went on with the killing. They're trying to force you to talk. If we can show them that you do really have this sleep problem, that you've had it since you were young, and that you didn't make it up just to get out of trouble in this case, she thinks maybe they'll drop charges against you."

Sleepy nodded. "Well, that's good to hear. I don't want to get my hopes up yet, but that's some good news, anyway."

Brenda smiled again. "Well, while I'm here, let me give you some more news. I don't know if you'll think it's good or bad, but I'll give it to you anyway. I told Jedd to put his plans on hold. I told him I couldn't even think straight, with you facing this charge and a death sentence. I told him the wedding would have to wait. He wasn't happy about it, but I guess he understood."

Sleepy could barely speak. He couldn't believe what he was hearing. Brenda would do that for him? Well, not for him, so much, as because of his situation. He was floored.

"I don't know what to say, Brenda. I'm glad you put the wedding off. But I'm sad, too, because I've hurt you enough. I don't want to be the cause of any more hurt for you."

He saw her eyes fill, but she blinked to hide the tears. "You let me worry about all that," she said. "Let's just get you out of this mess. I'll call your attorney and make an appointment to see her. Meantime, I'll go back and try to think of every time in the years I've known you that you've fallen asleep when you shouldn't have. We know there's something wrong with you. We have to be able to explain it to other people."

She got up, clutched her pink straw purse, to which she had pinned a small black flower, and said, "Time to go. I'll write you soon." She stood on tiptoe, and kissed Sleepy's cheek.

He was too dumbfounded to respond. "Thanks, Brenda," he said. He wished he was one of those clever guys who always had a good rap with the women. But he never had been. Thanks was all he could think to say. Brenda smiled at him, and when she got to the door of the visiting hall, she turned to give him a last wave.

Sleepy took his visiting hall pass to the officer's desk, so his visit could be logged, time in and out recorded, and he could get a pass back to his cell. As he walked the long corridors from the administration building to his housing area, he thought about Brenda. The one thing that kept coming back to him was that she was putting the wedding on hold. Don't make too much of that, he cautioned himself. But he couldn't pretend he wasn't glad about it. Right now, it was just a glimmer of hope. A glimmer more than he had before she came to see him. He could hold onto it for awhile, at least.

Chapter Forty-Two

Hastings slammed his fist into his bunk. He had just heard about Nut's boy and the broom closet door. He was furious. He had put the word out that Sleepy was untouchable. Now, that bitch psychologist would think he had broken his word. What if she put up the list of people for bedwetters anonymous? He'd be ruined.

Now he was sorry he had pitched a fit with the nurse and left the infirmary early. He paced his cell, back and forth between the cot and the door. He could reach the door from the cot in one stride. So pacing was really more like going in circles. He had to get to the bitch, before she did something he couldn't live with.

It was only a few minutes until the guard would deliver his supper tray. He'd put in a sick call request, and ask to see the shrink. That would probably get him a meeting with her. Then he'd have to convince her he wasn't responsible for the attack on Sleepy.

His plan to get an interview with Ms. Carmichael worked. A couple of hours after he gave the guard the sick call request, he was taken to her office. He was suspicious about that, too. He'd never gotten that rapid a response before. She must have something waiting for him, he thought.

When his escort from the disciplinary segregation unit dropped him at the door to her office, he began to get nervous. What if she didn't believe him? What if she'd already posted the list of group members? When the guard knocked, she opened her office door, and when she saw Hastings, looked curious. "Yes, officer?" she said.

"Hastings put in for sick call. You sent word you'd see him."

"Yes, of course," she replied. "I didn't recognize Mr. Hastings. I'm sorry."

How could she not recognize me? Hastings thought. Everybody in here knew who he was. And most of them knew enough about him to steer clear of him. This bitch was dissing him, he was sure of it.

Ms. Carmichael gestured for Hastings to be seated, and took her place behind the small desk. "Now, Mr. Hastings, what is it that is troubling you?" She managed a smile, but Hastings thought she didn't really mean it. Probably a nervous reaction. He had that effect on women. He either made them nervous or crazy, he thought, suppressing a chuckle.

"Well, ma'am, there's been an incident. An unfortunate incident. And I wanted to see you personally, to let you know I didn't break my word."

"What incident, Mr. Hastings?" She was clearly interested now, and very alert. Her direct gaze unnerved him.

"Well, ma'am, I heard through the grapevine that Sleepy . . . uh, LeBlanc that is, got hurt. I wanted you to know I didn't have anything to do with it. And I don't think anybody connected to me did, 'cause I warned them all off. They wouldn't cross me."

Her gaze did not leave his face. "No, Mr. Hastings, I doubt they would. I believe you on that point. What exactly is your worry?"

"I'm worried you'll go ahead and post that list. You know I'm worried about that. What man wouldn't be? I hoped I could get to you before you put it up for the entire prison to see."

She smiled. "I haven't done that, and I won't. So long as you live up to your bargain. But there has been a breach, whether it's directly linked to you or not. You'll agree with me that it looks like a breach of the bargain, won't you?"

Hastings felt like he'd been spun into a web. He surely didn't trust this tricky little bitch.

"Yes, ma'am, but appearances are deceiving. That's what I came up here to tell you."

"Yes," she nodded, "I know things happen over which we have no control. But still, a breach is a breach. I think it requires a modification of our contract." She continued to look directly at him, and if she was scared of him at all, she did a damn good job hiding it.

"What kind of modification?" Now he was genuinely pissed off. She thought she could bargain with him. And what made it worse, she could. She held the cards. Hastings was not used to that.

She must have guessed that he was between a rock and a hard place, because she nodded at him, and smiled. "I'm glad you asked. I think an appropriate modification would be that you agree to see me once a week, for counseling. We will meet and discuss whatever you wish to discuss. But you have to be actively involved in a therapeutic relationship with me for at least six months. Then we'll reassess our positions. What do you think of that deal?"

Before he caught himself, he said, "That's a load of crap. I don't talk to nobody. What is this? You want inside my head? Ain't no head shrink getting nothing from me."

He was almost yelling, and sweating profusely. Ms. Carmichael never left her desk, and showed no signs of upset at his outburst.

"I think it would be helpful if we could speak to each other without yelling, Mr. Hastings. If we could use normal conversational tones, the entire administration building staff would not know your business."

That shook him back to civility. "I'm sorry, ma'am," he mumbled, looking at his lap.

"Okay," she said, "Let's start over. I think therapy would be very helpful to you. I can promise it won't hurt you. I say, as a way to make amends for the breach of our earlier agreement, you accept the notion of a once-a-week session. If you find it intolerable, I will listen to your ideas about how to further modify our contract. That's fair, isn't it?"

Hastings was good at accepting the lesser of evils. He'd done it all his life. He recognized this as one of those times when A was bad, but B sucked big time. So he would go along, or at least act like he was. What could it hurt, really? He didn't have to actually tell the bitch anything.

"Okay," was all he could muster. She seemed happy with that.

"Fine. We'll start next week. I'll make a standing appointment for you for Monday at noon. That way, we won't interfere with your work, if you get back to population."

Hastings thought he caught a note of skepticism in her voice. He reassured her. "Don't you worry, ma'am. I'll be back in population. This trial thing is coming up next few months. Then

I'll be back to the way things were, before the cops got things all twisted up and put me in the middle of something I didn't do."

Ms. Carmichael seemed preoccupied suddenly. "Months," she said, more to herself than to Hastings. "We have a lot of work to do, then, Mr. Hastings. Be here on time on Monday. I'll make the arrangements. We'll talk then."

Hastings knew when he was being dismissed. That's one thing that bothered him about this psychologist, he thought. She acted just like a school principal. He'd had enough run-ins with them to know. They were all control freaks. Do things my way, or find the highway. Hastings did the latter. And he was no worse off for it, as far as he could see. What good would an education do him, anyway, when all he ever wanted to do was drive fast cars and carry on with fast women? This psychologist was in for a rude awakening if she thought she could control him. Bedwetting or not, she wouldn't get inside his head. She wasn't ready for that snake pit anyway, Hastings was sure. All the Ph.Ds in the world weren't enough for that.

Hastings's trial was months away. But Nancy anticipated that as Hastings's attorney prepared for it, he would want prison psychological records on Hastings. Any competent attorney would, in a capital case. The prospect made her nervous. She would need to prepare as complete an evaluation as possible, to eliminate the need for her to appear personally and testify. It was not her concern, whether her evaluation helped Hastings or the State. Her concern was that she not be put in a position where her picture could appear in the newspaper, or worse, on television. She had to avoid exposure, at all costs.

Chapter Forty-Three

Mercy was worried that LeBlanc looked so nervous. She had prepared him for this day, that this motions hearing would be a major part of his case. She filed three pretrial motions, one attacking the indictment, a second seeking to suppress LeBlanc's statements, even though they were not confessions but explanations of his innocence, because Nash violated the law in the way he conducted his interrogations, and a third asking for funds for a psychological expert witness. She told LeBlanc that it was his first opportunity to hear the State's case against him, from the mouths of their witnesses. They had reviewed the discovery—the evidence the State was required to turn over to the defense before trial—but discovery did not include witness names and summaries of their testimony, unless they were expert witnesses. Today would give them a chance to be prepared when the actual trial began, a month from now. She needed to know who the witnesses would be, so Sam could do background investigations on them. Hastings and the others on the bus would not be tried with LeBlanc, because under state law, they each got their own capital trial. Today's motions hearing was LeBlanc's alone, and she was eager to hear what the State had cobbled together to make a case.

Brenda said she wanted to come to the hearing, but LeBlanc had asked her not to. He didn't want her to hear whatever it was the witnesses would say. Mercy had backed him on that. Brenda might testify at the trial, and so should not be present for the motions hearing.

When the judge rapped her gavel and the bailiff called the court to order, LeBlanc whispered to Mercy that he was so nervous he thought he might throw up. He confided that he wished he had not eaten his breakfast of oatmeal and wheat toast. His theory was always that it was better to have something on your stomach, but today he was second-guessing that theory.

Mercy passed him an antacid tablet, and resumed making notes. The lawyer assisting her as local counsel sat on LeBlanc's other side. The judge turned first to the prosecutor. "Ms. Arrow. I understand Mr. Blume has been taken ill, and that you are now in charge of this case?"

"Yes, Your Honor."

"Is the State ready to proceed on the defense motion challenging the indictment?"

"We are, Your Honor. Our first witness is the corrections officer who was first to respond to the scene of the shooting. He is in the ante room."

"Get him, then, and let's get started." The judge's tone signaled that her schedule was too packed today for delay of any sort.

Coppedge testified about calling Harkness on the walkie-talkie and getting no response. The crew was working two miles from the prison. Coppedge got into his jeep and drove to the site. That is where he found the bus, empty except for LeBlanc, and the dead Harkness on the ground outside the bus.

On cross-examination, he admitted that he did not see who did the shooting, had no idea where the crew was when he arrived, except for LeBlanc who was in the back seat of the bus, that he went onto the bus only to check for weapons and that LeBlanc did not wake while he was on the bus.

Next the State called the lieutenant who had shook LeBlanc awake on the bus. He testified that he shook him hard several times, calling his name. On cross-examination, he admitted that he had called him some names not his own, also. He said LeBlanc appeared to be sound asleep, and that it was not the first time such a thing had happened. He read from LeBlanc's prison records, which Mercy had subpoenaed to the hearing. There were over a dozen incidents where LeBlanc fell asleep at the wrong times and slept for so long he had to be taken to the infirmary. In his opinion, LeBlanc was really sleeping and not faking, he volunteered, ignoring the obvious frown from Ms. Arrow.

The State's next witness was agent Nash. He strode to the witness chair like he owned stock in it. He adjusted his tie, pushed a stray lock of hair from his eyes, and folded his hands in a prayer pose, under his chin. Mercy couldn't accept that image of Nash, the reverent and pious. Nothing could be further from her experience of the man.

Ms. Arrow led Nash through his investigation, his meetings with LeBlanc, serving the warrant, his visits to LeBlanc's family. Nash tried to downplay what the family had told him about the sleep episodes, and when Mercy confronted him on cross-examination with his own reports about the witnesses' statements, he tried to wiggle. She kept him on a short leash, with pointed and fast-paced questioning that relied on Nash's own notes and reports. By the end of it, Nash wasn't walking the cock walk quite so obviously.

Ms. Arrow was not pleased with the presentation, Mercy could tell. She had hoped Nash would cap her case for her, and he had not delivered. When Nash was off the witness stand, the judge asked her, "What now, Ms. Arrow?"

"That's our presentation, judge," she said, looking somewhat flustered. She recovered quickly, and apparently decided to argue the law, since the facts were no longer in her favor. "Judge, I don't see why we are addressing this issue. As we said in our written response to the defense motion, their arguments may have some merit at the end of the government's case, if we fail to prove our case against LeBlanc. But they have shown no defect in the Grand Jury process so as to be entitled to a dismissal of the indictment before we even get a chance to put on our case. We are entitled to try to prove our case to the jury."

The judge seemed to be thinking about Arrow's argument. "Ms. Arrow, your legal analysis may be correct. But my concern is a more practical one. My trial schedule is jam-packed. I don't want to waste time on a case that the State can't prove at trial. Where is the evidence that this man was the shooter, or that he was involved in the plot? He was present on the bus. He denied his guilt. His family, the prison officials, and the prison records show he has a sleep problem of some sort. I guess we'll hear more about that at trial. If we get that far." The last statement was so pointed, even Ms. Arrow winced.

Mercy looked at LeBlanc. His face was a mask of calm. She had told him that if the judge did not find that the State's case was strong enough against him to force him to stand trial, she could dismiss the case. She had also explained that a dismissal at this juncture was a real long shot. He did not appear to be harboring false hope.

Mercy argued hard that the evidence was insufficient. She recapped the points she had scored on cross-examination. She quoted some jurists of the past about how death was a different kind of punishment, final and irrevocable, and that the rules of the game had to be faithfully applied in such cases. She hoped her tone and posture reflected her belief in her arguments. The judge listened intently.

"Let me hear the defense evidence," she said. "If you choose to put on any evidence, that is. As you know, you do not have to do so. It is your right to hold the State to its burden to establish that this case is strong enough to go to a jury."

Mercy huddled with LeBlanc and the local counsel. They had prepared for this point. As late as last night, LeBlanc was still considering whether he would testify at the hearing. Both attorneys had advised him in the strongest terms that he should not. Anything he said at the hearing could be used against him if he testified at the trial, to make it look like he was telling different stories. But LeBlanc wanted to know why that mattered, if he was telling the truth. He would tell it the same way, of course, because it was the truth. Mercy tried to explain that things just weren't that simple, that the prosecutor would seize on any little inconsistency, no matter how minor and unimportant, to make it look like he was lying. And jurors, with their cockfighting mentality, might be persuaded. If the prosecutor drew blood on cross-examination, they were likely to think LeBlanc was wounded, or dying.

Mercy leaned close to LeBlanc and whispered, "Have you made your decision?"

LeBlanc did not respond, but continued to look down at the table. Mercy asked again, louder this time. "Theodore, if you're going to testify, it will have to be now."

Again, no response. The judge looked down from the bench and glowered. "Counsel, is there evidence for the defense?" She was not in the mood for delay.

"May I have one moment, Your Honor?" Mercy put one arm around LeBlanc's shoulders and leaned closer to him. She said directly into his ear, "Time's up. Either we go forward, or we rest. What's it gonna be?" When LeBlanc didn't answer, Mercy looked at his eyes. They were not blinking. When Mercy gingerly removed her arm from LeBlancs's shoulder, he started to teeter in his chair. "Oh, lord," Mercy muttered. She whispered to local counsel, then turned to the judge.

"Your Honor, we have a problem. Our client is not responding. I think he's asleep."

The prosecutor jumped up. "Your Honor," she said, in a loud whine. "This is outrageous. This is an attempt to hoodwink this court. Counsel should be reprimanded for her role in this charade."

Mercy ignored her. "Your Honor, I need the bailiff's help here." Her tone conveyed that this was anything but a charade.

The judge stood, and leaned over the bench, peering at LeBlanc. Her mouth was open, and her expression was one of disbelief. But she ordered the bailiff to LeBlanc's table.

When the bailiff checked LeBlanc's eyes, and his pulse, he looked up at the judge.

"He's out, judge. Out cold. What do you want me to do with him?"

The judge sat back down, and put her head in her hands. When she raised her head, she had regained composure. "Counsel," she said sternly. "I want this man taken to the hospital. I want a full neurological examination. I want the report sent directly to me. If this is a scam of some kind, he is in more trouble than he ever imagined. Do you understand?"

"Your Honor, I am grateful for the court's concern. A neurological can't hurt. But I do want to assert his privilege here. The doctors may not question him about this offense. Can Your Honor include a paragraph in the Order preventing interrogation about the events giving rise to the indictment in this case?"

"Of course. They don't need to question him about the offense. They need to tell me whether he's faking. That's all I care about right now."

The bailiff took hold of LeBlanc's arms and tried to pull him from the chair. "Your Honor, I'm going to need help here. He is dead weight. I don't think I can budge him."

"Goodness gracious, Carl," the judge said, "if you can't budge him, we'll need a Mack truck in here!"

"I know, judge. I've never seen anything like it. Can I call downstairs and get some back-up?"

"Do it." the judge said. She looked at the prosecutor. Arrow had taken her seat, and was looking disgustingly around the room. Probably looking for reporters, Mercy thought. Arrow was known to cultivate all the publicity she could get. She meant to be judge herself someday, and everybody knew it.

"Ms. Arrow?" The judge barked her name.

"Yes, Your Honor?" she said, rising and looking at Mercy as if she had plague.

"Does the State have a position on whether this case should go forward, assuming this episode today is reflective of some neurological disorder?"

"Well, Your Honor," she said, her nasal quality scratching like fingernails on a blackboard. "The State is sure this is a phony demonstration and we are confident that when we have the doctor's report, we will all know that."

"Interesting, Ms. Arrow. I didn't know the State had medical training." The judge's emphasis on "the State" tickled Mercy. She'd always wondered how "the State," an inert entity for all she knew, was so active in various legal affairs: "the State" seeks a continuance, "the State" objects, "the State" takes offense at that, on and on. Prosecutors hid behind "the State," making defense attorneys, as opponents of the State, look like terrorists of some kind. They were against "the State." No good could come of that, in the average person's mind, Mercy was sure. That the judge needled Arrow about her use of the grandiose term pleased Mercy. It wouldn't mean anything in how the judge tried the case, but it gave Mercy a moment's respite.

The judge was not deterred. "Ms. Arrow, I am assuming, for purposes of argument, that the report will show a genuine neurological disorder, of which this instance is a part. Given that, what would the State's position be?"

Arrow seemed taken aback that the judge could think her position might not be the only right one. "Judge," whining again. "The State is sure that will not be an issue."

The judge exploded. "Ms. Arrow," she nearly shouted. "Listen to me. I don't care what you, with your total absence of medical expertise, think about this incident. And this State that you are purporting to represent includes me, Ms. Johnson and her colleague, Carl here, and the defendant, as well as all the people in this courtroom, and beyond. I want to know the answer to a simple question. What is the DA's office going to do if this report shows that this man has a sleep disorder, and that he cannot control when and how it comes upon him? That's my question. Now you may need to consult with your supervisor before you answer the question. If you do, feel free to use the clerk's telephone, or if you need privacy, to use the phone in my chambers. But today, before we get the doctor's report back, I want to know where this case is going. I have two following close on its heels. I can't afford to lag here."

Arrow seemed shocked that the judge would use such a firm tone with her. Mercy had to admit it was a rarity for a judge to dress down a prosecutor. But Arrow had tried her patience, that was clear. Mercy tried not to gloat, knowing well that this was not even the battle, let alone the war.

"May I be excused for one moment, Your Honor?" Arrow's voice, still whiny, had softened considerably.

"Certainly. We will wait for an answer from your office."

Arrow was gone for about two minutes, and when she returned, she was smirking. The judge scowled when she saw the expression. "Yes, Ms. Arrow, what is it you have to tell me?"

The whining intensified. "Your Honor, the State does not appreciate being put in this position. We are committed to the prosecution of this most serious of felonies. We do not feel it is appropriate for us to have to announce a prosecution strategy in open court, and prematurely."

The judge turned pink, then bright red. The court clerk gasped audibly. Mercy was amazed that Arrow could have the audacity to thumb her nose at the judge like she was doing. She better hope she got a judgeship, because if she didn't, she had better stay out of this courtroom.

The judge's effort at control was obvious. When she had herself firmly in check, she said in an even voice, "Ms. Arrow, does that mean that the State intends to go forward with the prosecution, regardless of the doctor's findings?"

"Yes, Your Honor," Arrow said defiantly.

"Thank you for the information. I want you to do one more thing, if you please. I want you to get Mr. LeBlanc's prison records, especially any psychological evaluations that might have been prepared. I read that there is a new psychologist at the prison. She may not have had a chance to meet with him yet. But if she has, I want her report, and I want her here, when we get the court-appointed doctor's report. See to it." She rose. "Court will be in recess until we are advised that we have information from the hospital as to Mr. LeBlanc's condition." She gathered her papers, put her reading glasses atop her head, and made for her chambers.

Mercy went directly to the hospital to see LeBlanc. By the time she arrived, he was resting in a bed in the short-term care unit. Dr. Yarborough had ordered him to remain in the hospital overnight, for observation. He was under guard, two deputies stationed outside the door. Easier duty they'd probably never had, since LeBlanc lived up to his nickname and slept the better part of the day. Mercy had to wake him to tell him the news.

"What happens if they dismiss the charges?" he asked.

"You go back to the prison, to finish out the B & E sentence. The feds would threaten to charge you for murder, because Nash is such a horse's hind end, but they don't have any basis for federal jurisdiction, that I can see. So I think he's just blowing smoke."

"Boy, he'll be mad." LeBlanc smiled when he said it.

"He'll get over it. He'll go on to the next case, abusing illegal immigrants because they want to make a better life for their families, or threatening welfare mothers for taking too long to report their little part-time jobs, something of major national significance like that."

LeBlanc smiled. "Thanks, Ms. Johnson. I don't want to get my hopes up yet, but I thank you for everything you've done for me, no matter what happens."

"You're welcome, Theodore. Since Dr. Yarborough wants you under observation overnight, we won't be back in court today. So I'll see you tomorrow. They'll bring you into court early, because the judge wants us at 9:00 a.m. Try to get some sleep." LeBlanc laughed aloud, the first time Mercy had heard that in all the months she had worked with him. She liked the sound.

Chapter Forty-Four

When court resumed, and the parties were assembled, the judge addressed them. "Counsel, I have here the report from Dr. Yarborough, the chief of neurology at the county hospital. I don't have to remind you that this is a teaching hospital, connected to one of the area's finest medical schools. Dr. Yarborough is a noted neurologist, lecturer and author. We are fortunate in that he has some familiarity with the disease of narcolepsy. And, Ms. Arrow, that is what we are dealing with here. Not a charade. Not a scam. Narcolepsy. If the chief of neurology at county hospital tells me that, I believe it. I know the defense is seeking the appointment of a neurologist as a defense expert, and that if this case goes to trial, they intend to call their own expert to explain Mr. LeBlanc's condition. But I truly don't see the need in putting the State—she emphasized the two words, smiling at Arrow—to the expense of trying a man who said he was asleep when the crime happened, against whom you have no evidence other than his presence on the bus, and who is so affected by a sleep disorder that he can't even stay awake to defend himself."

She waited for Arrow to respond. Arrow was obviously furious. "Your Honor, Dr. Yarborough is only one physician. The State would need to get its own experts to evaluate the defendant. We can't make a decision on the word of a single doctor."

"Did you get in touch with the prison psychologist as I asked you to do?"

Arrow seemed to be hedging. "I tried, Your Honor. She had some recent evaluations of LeBlanc. She was unable to be present in court today because she is ill with flu. I did not want her to get up out of her sick bed to come here, so I did not subpoena her."

The judge did not look pleased. "What is her name?"

"Nancy Carmichael, Your Honor."

"Where are her reports?"

189

"I didn't ask her for them, since she was unable to deliver them herself."

The judge was clearly upset now. "You don't have anyone on your staff who could go to the prison and get the reports?"

Arrow looked sheepish. "I didn't ask, Your Honor. I did have her read the reports to me." She looked like she did not want to say any more, but the judge was not satisfied.

"And?"

Arrow looked away. "She thinks Mr. LeBlanc has a sleep disorder," she mumbled.

The judge rose and faced the prosecutor's table. "Ms. Arrow, tell your boss I want to see her. Now. I'll wait five minutes. I'll be in chambers when she arrives."

Mercy was glad she had asked Sam to do a quick background search on the District Attorney, since she was apparently now going to be the State's voice in the decision regarding LeBlanc's future. She was an elected official, and unlike Arrow, had no aspirations to any other office. She was elected on a law and order platform twenty years earlier, and in every election since then, she had been able to rely on the results her office produced to get re-elected. More convictions in serious cases than any other DA's office in the State, more pleas to lead counts in indictments than any other county, showing that her office didn't throw away cases by pleas to lesser offenses. She had less turnover among prosecutors than any other office, and her office got good reviews from the police, which was often not the case in districts where prosecutors were so afraid to lose at trial they plea bargained serious felonies down to less serious offenses. Donna Ross was not looking at the elections in 2012 when she made her prosecutorial decisions.

Once she was seated in the judge's chambers, what Ross was looking at was one very exasperated Superior Court judge. Unlike her fledgling Arrow, she had the good sense to deal with the judge's frustration head on.

"Your Honor, my office has no interest in prosecuting an innocent man. You know that about me, and I hope you know that about those who work with me." She looked at Arrow, who seemed to find a great deal fascinating about her patent leather pumps, or the judge's floral rug, or something very near the floor. "Based on Dr. Yarborough's report, and the reports from Ms. Carmichael at the prison, we will re-evaluate this case and advise the court by mid-morning whether we intend to go forward against Mr. LeBlanc. I will undertake that review myself, in conjunction with Ms. Arrow, of course."

Arrow was still intently studying the floor. When she looked up, it was to nod in agreement with her boss.

"That's more like it, Donna," the judge said. "I've never seen anything like what happened in this courtroom. Carl couldn't budge the guy! He was absolute dead weight. Carl had to call for assistance, just to get him out of his chair. It was like he froze in the position he was in when the sleep overtook him. I could almost have ruled he was not faking, before Dr. Yarborough's report and the evaluations of the prison psychologist. But with those evaluations, I have no doubt about it. You can bet a jury will not. That's if the State can even put on enough proof to get past a motion for acquittal at the close of the evidence."

Ross nodded. "I surely appreciate the court's observations," she said deferentially. "And I will be back here at eleven this morning, ready with the State's decision."

"Good," the judge said, as Ross, Arrow, and Mercy rose to leave chambers.

"And make that 11:00 a.m. sharp, everyone. I don't want to waste any time if I'm going to have to get another case queued up."

Chapter Forty-Five

Brenda LeBlanc waited in the third row of spectator seats. Mercy had reconsidered her ban from the courtroom, in light of the new developments, and allowed her to come to court today. But she told Brenda not to sit up front because she didn't want to distract LeBlanc. Mercy went to her. "Ms. LeBlanc, how are you?" They shook hands.

"I'm alright. I read the papers this morning. I just had to be here. I was afraid somebody would think Sleepy made up this sleep problem. I thought maybe you would need my help. Lord knows, if anybody knows it's not made up, it's me. It ruined our marriage. It ruined his work. He's suffered, nobody can dispute that. I'd like to see that little snippet try to make him out a liar!" She was sending dagger looks to Arrow, who was picture-perfect in a fuchsia suit, with matching fuchsia nails and hair bows. "I hate fuchsia," Brenda muttered, staring at her with pure venom.

Mercy thanked her for coming, then returned to counsel table. She whispered to LeBlanc, who turned to Brenda and smiled. She smiled back, and gave him a thumbs up.

The bailiff called the court to order. After yesterday's newspaper article, there were more spectators than usual, and combined with the press who had attended the proceedings in numbers this morning, the buzz in the courtroom was considerable. When the hum of quiet conversation died down, the judge spoke.

"Ms. Arrow, I see you and Ms. Ross are in attendance. Has the State reached a decision as to its position in this case?"

Arrow gave the judge a disgusted look, but did not respond. She could not, because Ross had clearly silenced her. Ross rose and addressed the court. "Your Honor, I have had the opportunity over the recess to review the case file, and more importantly, to review Dr. Yarborough's very thorough report. I am very familiar with Dr. Yarborough, because he has done fine work for the State on a number of difficult cases. In fact, I reached him at his home and spoke with him at some length about Mr. LeBlanc's condition. He was kind enough to go over his report with me, as well as his examination notes and protocol. Knowing what a fine physician he is, and knowing his credentials as head of the Neurology Department at the Medical School, I have no doubt whatsoever as to the accuracy of his findings. The State has an obligation to its citizens and to the victim's loved ones to bring the perpetrators of this outrageous crime to justice. But as Your Honor has heard me say many times, the State has no interest in prosecuting an innocent man." She paused, giving the reporters adequate time to record her remarks, knowing there would be some in the "hang 'em all, and let God sort it out" camp who would second-guess the decision she was about to announce, and wanting to explain her decision in terms even they could not quibble with too loudly. She also cast a long glance at her underling, who was busy inspecting her fuchsia nails and did not look up.

"Then is it your conclusion that Mr. LeBlanc was indeed asleep when this homicide occurred?" To Mercy, it looked as if the judge wanted no room for wiggling if the State tried to come back later and re-open the case against Mr. LeBlanc.

"Your Honor, that we will never know. But there is no evidence that he was involved in the escape and killing, he was found asleep on the bus when the police and FBI agents arrived, he has maintained from the beginning that he slept through the incident, and Dr. Yarborough's report gives his contention sufficient weight that I do not believe the State could convince a jury otherwise. Nor do I think we would be right to try to do so. I believe that on the evidence we have before us, and based particularly on Dr. Yarborough's examination and his comments to me about the exam, as well as the prison psychologist's report, the State has no choice but to dismiss the murder and conspiracy charges against Mr. LeBlanc. That is our decision, and we stand by it, Your Honor."

The judge was still not through with Ross. "Ms. Ross, I appreciate your assistance in this matter. Yesterday, we seemed to be stalled." She looked at Arrow, who this time was looking at the judge, and the defiance in her face might have gotten her a few hours in lockup if she'd been a defense attorney. Lucky for her she had signed on with the D.A.'s office, Mercy thought.

The judge cleared her throat. "But I must make sure for the record that we are on the same page. Does the State's position include a dismissal with prejudice?"

Ross did not even hesitate. "It does, Your Honor. If I thought there was other evidence out there that we might bring to bear on the question of Mr. LeBlanc's role in these matters at some future date, I would dismiss without prejudice. But I do not think that is the case. We know all we are ever going to know about this situation, I believe. With that, the State will take a dismissal with prejudice."

The buzz in the courtroom was starting up again. Reporters were leaving their pews, to go to the atrium and use their cell phones to call in their stories. One television news anchorwoman was rushing outside, probably to find her camera crew and position them outside the courthouse, hoping to get an interview with Ross. Mercy was glad her local counsel had shown her the back entrance to the courthouse.

The bailiff called out, "The court is still in session." His tone was sufficient to quiet the buzz.

The judge turned to the defense table. "Please rise, Mr. LeBlanc." Sleepy stood, unwinding for a long time out of the too-small chair. Mercy stood beside him, and local counsel was at his other elbow, both close enough to grab him if he fell. They probably could not hold him up, but they could cushion the fall, and maybe prevent injury to him or to them, she thought.

"Mr. LeBlanc, the State has dismissed the charges against you, with prejudice. That means that this case is over for you. You will be returned to the prison to serve out the remainder of your term. How much longer do you have on your sentence, by the way?"

LeBlanc looked too overcome to speak right away. He breathed deeply, and got his voice back. "Ma'am, I believe I have to serve another five years before I will be eligible for parole."

"Well, I'll leave that to your lawyer. You've got excellent counsel. Maybe they can help you with that."

"Thank you, ma'am."

"I am remanding you to the custody of the Department of Corrections."

With that, the bailiff turned to LeBlanc and said, "Let's go." He escorted him to the lock-up behind the courthouse, where he would stay until the prison bus was ready to return him to the prison.

Mercy waited for the news people to follow Ross from the courtroom, then went to Brenda. "Do you understand what happened?" she asked her.

"I think so. The murder and conspiracy charges have gone away. Sleepy will go back to prison until he can be paroled on the theft charge. Is that right?"

"That's exactly right," Mercy said. "But I think I might be able to do something about this theft charge. I don't want to promise anything, because it won't be easy, but if we can show that he actually was asleep in the dressing room, not hiding and waiting to commit a burglary, we might be able to get the conviction overturned. Last year, the legislature introduced the Innocence Act, which says that if a prisoner can establish that he is actually innocent, he can file a motion for release, even if he's already appealed and filed post-conviction motions. It's a way to see that truly innocent people don't have to stay in jail on some technicality."

Brenda's smile was dazzling. Mercy could surely see why LeBlanc was quick to marry her. She was a real beauty, and she seemed like a good person, in the bargain.

Mercy continued, "I think I'll go this weekend and lay it all out for Sleepy. Give him something to feel hopeful about. What do you think?"

"If you go then, I'll go up next week-end," she said. "I've got some news of my own to make him feel hopeful." This time, the smile was playful, like she had a secret she was not about to share.

"I'll call you when I see him, and let you know how he is."

"Thank you, Ms. Johnson. Thank you for everything." She held her hand out. "If I was able, I would surely pay you for what you've done for Sleepy."

"No need, Ms. LeBlanc. Your husband will pay me when he

can. And if I don't see you again, good luck. When is the wedding date, by the way?"

Brenda looked puzzled. "Oh, the wedding you're speaking of is off. I need to tell Sleepy that. But as for the other wedding date," she emphasized "other" teasingly, "I'd say that depends on you and your legal skills. I surely hope you can get this burglary case taken care of right soon." As she turned to go, she was smiling that dazzling smile again, this time apparently to herself.

Chapter Forty-Six

Sleepy was barely settled back in his quarters when Rosie came to the block. It was free movement time, so Rosie could leave his own block, get a pass, and come to Sleepy's block. He was smiling, a smile that lit up his whole face. He high-fived Sleepy.

"Man, you did it. You got that Nash jerk. I can't believe it. Somebody here finally gets some justice. I'm glad it was you, Sleep. I really am."

Sleepy knew that Rosie meant what he said. Sleepy clapped him on the back. "I'm real glad, too, Rosie. And I'm very grateful to you and your cousin. Ms. Johnson was right on top of things. And Brenda, she was real helpful too. It seemed like the judge really wanted to do the right thing. They had this prosecutor, who didn't seem to care about anything but winning. Winning, and her designer outfits, that is. But Ms. Johnson put her in her place." Then he smiled, "And it's a good thing, too. Brenda was about to go after her. Lord, that prosecutor couldn't know trouble like that."

Rosie laughed. "She's a tough one, huh?"

"Nah," Sleepy replied, "Just the opposite. She's gentle and kind, and wouldn't hurt a fly without a reason. She used to catch any bug that came into the house, and put it outside rather than kill it. Same thing with mice. We lived kind of in the country, down this long road with lots of woods around. Mice would wander into the house when it started to get cold out. Brenda would make me catch them, put them in a paper bag, and take them back outside. No killing of anything that God made, was her rule. I drew the line when it came to snakes, but I tried not to let her know about it."

Rosie nodded. "No wonder you could make a pet out of Be-Bop. He must have known you'd been kind to family members of his." Rosie laughed, a deep rumble from somewhere low in his massive chest. Sleepy laughed, too, and realized that they had not laughed together in months.

Then Sleepy turned serious. "Rosie, man, I still got the rest of this B & E bit to do. But Ms. Johnson thinks there might be a way to get back into court on the case. She says there's something called the Innocence Act, where people who've been convicted but who are really innocent have a chance to prove their innocence. If she can help me, we ought to ask her to help you, too. That is, if you want to."

"Hell, Sleep," Rosie said. "I'd love to have some help. You know I'm innocent, I know I'm innocent, but proving it will take a whole lot of work on somebody's part. You know the governor's aide ain't gonna roll over and play dead. He's got too much at stake. He's afraid if I get any law, it will come out what he did. I don't know, Sleep. I ain't counting on too much."

Sleepy thought about what Rosie said. "I know it will be hard, Rosie. But we have to try. Even if we don't get the result we want, we have to try. You agree?"

"I agree," Rosie said solemnly.

"Good, then we'll try."

They sat quietly for a while, each lost in his own thoughts. Then Sleepy said, "I got an idea. Let's go shoot some baskets, see if we can loosen up these old bones."

"Sure," Rosie agreed. "I'd be happy to show your butt up. Just 'cause you ain't facing no murder beef no more, don't mean you can touch old Rosie out here on this court."

They played for an hour, and Rosie was true to his word. He ran circles around Sleepy, even though he weighed nearly three hundred pounds. They were toweling off, about to go back to their units, when the loudspeaker squawked. "Theodore LeBlanc, please come to the administration building immediately. Theodore LeBlanc, administration building, ASAP."

"What now?" Sleepy wondered aloud.

Rosie was frowning. "I hope it ain't no bad news, Sleep. Let me know soon as you can, okay?"

"Sure, partner." Sleepy made his way to the administration building, not even bothering to stop at his cell and wash up. When he got to the area outside the warden's office, he stopped abruptly. "Nash! Now what does he want?"

Before he could ask the guard on duty in the corridor why he had been called, Nash spoke. "The-oh, I got a little present for you. Got it late this afternoon, from a Superior Court judge. Not that judge that let you off. Another one, who just happened to be on call, after five o'clock. Judge issued this warrant here. Says you get to see the State's psychologist, one who's a specialist in hypnosis. Says you're a material witness for the State in a murder, your memory is blocked by some psychological phenomenon, says hypnosis might free memories that are stored in your brain, says you're to report to the warden's office at 0700 hours next Monday to be taken to the psychologist's office. I'll see you then."

Nash dropped the warrant copy on the desk in front of Sleepy, and was about to leave when he turned and smiled at Sleepy. There was no warmth in the smile.

"And by the way, The-oh. This Ms. Carmichael. I checked her out. Seems she didn't exist before 2010. When I get done looking into why she's a ghost on the information highway, her so-called evaluations won't help you much."

He turned and left.

The warden came out of his office. He had not been present for the meeting with Nash, but apparently he had overheard Nash's comments. The warden looked annoyed. "Now what the hell? LeBlanc, let me see that document."

Sleepy handed him the warrant. He looked it over, then handed it back. "You still in touch with that lawyer who helped you in court?" the warden asked.

"Yes, sir."

"Then call her. Here, you can use my phone. Tell her what just happened. She'll know what you should do."

Sleepy was touched by this gesture on the warden's part. He certainly did not need to put himself out to do anything for Sleepy.

"Thanks, warden, I will call her."

Sleepy dialed Mercy Johnson's office, and in a matter of seconds, was put through to her investigator.

"Sam Lester here."

"Mr. Lester, I need to speak with Ms. Johnson. I just got served with a warrant to see the State's psychologist to be hypnotized.

They say I'm a material witness to a murder and that the hypnosis could jog my memory about what happened."

"She's still down there in your neck of the woods. Let me try her on her cell phone. Sit tight. Try her again in five minutes at this number."

When Sleepy tried again, Mercy was on the line.

Sleepy explained what had happened. She said, "That Nash never sleeps, does he? You don't have to let any hypnotist poke around in your head. This judge was obviously misinformed. I'll go to Judge Keenan. She'll rescind the Order. The motion should not have gone to any judge but her, because it has to do with a case which is still on her calendar. You won't be tried, but the others on the work crew will be. She won't allow her authority to be trumped like this."

Sleepy had time to think, while Ms. Johnson was reasoning out his defense to the warrant. "Ms. Johnson, you know what? I think it wouldn't hurt to have this session. Maybe I really did see or hear something that would help. If not, at least I could get the word out here, and these creeps would leave me alone."

Mercy did not sound convinced. "Theodore, I am not a fan of hypnotism. I'm not sure about these hypnotically-refreshed memories of childhood events that are cropping up everywhere, particularly in sex offense cases. I'm convinced that these so-called memories of long-buried experiences are really the products of over-zealous examiners who plant suggestions during the hypnosis session that the subject believes are actual memories. This is a really dangerous area, in my mind. The possibilities for convictions of innocent people are staggering."

Sleepy was thoughtful. "I hear what you are saying, Ms. Johnson. But remember, I am not trying to dredge up buried memories. I'm trying to see if I really did see and hear things out there that day that could help the police find out what happened. If so, I think I'm bound to let them find it. We can be sure that the process is reliable by getting a psychologist who does not know the details of this case, and by letting you sit in on the session. What do you think about that?"

Mercy was quiet for a moment. "I'm liking the notion better,

Reita Pendry

when we consider those terms. But, I want one other concession from the State. I know you won't think this is important, but I'm a criminal defense attorney. Some things I have to do, just because a good defense attorney does them in every case, regardless of who the client is. And regardless of whether the attorney believes in her client's innocence. That's just my training, and I need you to humor me, okay?"

Sleepy was curious now. "What could you want that I would take offense at?" he asked.

"Theodore, I think you've told me the truth. Based on years of experience with clients in tough situations, I think I've gotten some insight into who is being truthful and who is not. But what I want here is for the State to agree that nothing you say under the influence of hypnosis can be used in any case against you. You could remember a detail that the State could interpret as prior knowledge of the escape on your part, or even as involvement on your part. We can't take that risk. The State agreed not to prosecute you on the current indictment. They did not agree not to prosecute you on any other offenses growing out of the incident. So let's err on the side of caution, alright?"

Sleepy was smiling now. "You're a good lawyer and you've helped me a lot. I will trust you." He couldn't help adding, "But you'll see it wasn't necessary. Just for the record."

Chapter Forty-Seven

The State agreed to Mercy's terms, and she agreed to their choice of psychologist to conduct the hypnosis session. Sam checked him out with the National Association of Criminal Defense Attorneys and Mercy ran her own check among defense attorneys in the area. She told Sleepy that her confidence was boosted by the fact that Dr. Yarborough, the neuropsychologist, knew him and vouched for him.

Two days later, the State's hand-picked psychologist came to the prison, and using a private interviewing room set aside for chaplain visits, conducted a pre-hypnosis interview with Sleepy. "I must have passed," Sleepy said, "since we're going ahead with the session this afternoon."

When 2:00 p.m. came, Sleepy was ready. He was nervous, mostly because this was a new experience. He felt better that Ms. Johnson was sitting in a corner of the room, away from the psychologist but still able to see and hear everything that went on. Sleepy sat across from the psychologist, who held a small device in his hand. The doctor told him to look at the device, and when he did, a soft light came on inside it. Sleepy tried hard to follow the instructions. "Look directly at the light, and listen to my voice," the doctor said softly. The lights in the room had been dimmed to near-darkness, so that the light coming from the doctor's hand was the most powerful light source in the room. Sleepy's eyes were automatically drawn to it. The doctor said, "You are getting sleepy. Your eyelids are heavy. You are relaxing now. You are thinking only about the light." After about a minute, he began, "Nod if you can hear me."

Sleepy nodded.

The doctor then said, "Lift one finger, please. "

Sleepy did so, lazily. "I think we're ready," the doctor said.

"Mr. LeBlanc," he began, "I need your help with something. I need to know what happened out on the road last summer, when the prison guard was shot. Please start at the beginning, and tell me about it."

Sleepy was breathing slowly. He took a deep breath, and began. "I was on the bus. It was a warm day, and I wanted to stay outside and enjoy the fresh air, but Harkness told me to get on the bus. He told me he had a lot to do that day, and didn't have time to watch me. He said if I fell asleep like I do, I could get hurt and he'd have to pay for it. So I got on the bus. I went to the back seat, because it's bigger than the others, and I sat down, kind of stretched out, and went to sleep. After a little while, I heard a truck come up. I knew it was a truck, because it made a lot of noise. I'd guess it was one of those big 4 x 4 pickup trucks. I heard two doors slam. Then I heard voices. 'He must be on the road with the crew,' one voice said. A deeper voice said, 'Yeah, she said he might be. She said we should wait for him to get back, but to try to get him when there weren't inmates around. She wants the road crew to find him. She's pretty sure they'll run off, and when they do, they'll look guilty as hell. That's one smart cookie, Ms. Harkness. Either that, or she's spent a lot of years figuring this out. She wants rid of the guy in the worst way.' The first voice said, 'Yeah, she must. She's paid a pretty penny.'"

Sleepy paused. The doctor coaxed him gently. "Go on. What happened next?"

Sleepy took another deep breath. "Harkness came back to the bus for something. I heard his voice. He'd forgotten something. When he walked up, one of the guys said, 'Hello, Harkness.' Harkness said, "Who the hell are you?' The man said, 'Your worst nightmare.'

Then I heard a gunshot. It was a rifle. It sounded like an explosion it was so loud. I knew there was real bad trouble. I just stayed really quiet. One of the men asked the other, 'What about the other guards?' He said, 'Don't worry. The missus fixed their coffee this morning. There was a little something to make sure they slept through the party. No witnesses, remember?' 'Damn,' the other guy said. 'She sure did think of everything.' It was quiet for a few minutes, then I heard the crew coming back. They were running, because they heard the gunshot, I guess. I heard Hammer first. He said, 'Damn, would you look at this? Somebody killed the S.O.B. Ain't that sweet, boys?' I heard some of the crew laughing. Then Hammer said, 'We better get the hell up out of here. Somebody will think we had something to do with this. I don't know about you all, but I'm willing to pay an extra five years, just to get me a little R & R. That's Rachel and Ruby, in case you can't figure it out.' He was laughing. The other guys laughed, too. Then I heard them talking about who was going where, and warning each other to keep quiet. That's the last I heard. I didn't even hear Strafe and Pockets. Next thing I know the lieutenant is jerking me awake." Sleepy sat very quietly, his hands in his lap. His head was resting partially on his chest now. The room was perfectly quiet.

They sat that way for several minutes. Then the doctor said in a normal tone, "Okay, Mr. LeBlanc, you can wake up now." Sleepy was immediately awake and alert. He felt good, like one of those rare occasions when he'd gotten a very good night's sleep.

"How did I do, doctor?" he asked.

The doctor was smiling. "You did very well, Mr. LeBlanc. At least from my professional point of view. I doubt that the FBI agents will be so thrilled with the results of our session, but that's their problem. I did my job. Now they can do theirs."

Mercy came over to where Sleepy was seated. "I think we'd better get you back to your cell, now, Theodore. I think you're going to want to rest. I'll speak with the prosecutor about today's session, and I'll be back out tomorrow to tell you what will happen next. Meanwhile, you rest, okay?"

Sleepy laughed. "This is the most rested I've been in weeks. I think I'll work today, since it's my usual work day. You can find me tomorrow and fill me in. I can wait 'til then for the news."

When Sleepy was back in his cell, he thought, "The doctor and Ms. Johnson sure seemed surprised. I wonder what it was I said. I hope whatever it was, it will get these goons off my back. I don't want to have to worry about them, and worry about getting this sentence overturned at the same time. If I have to protect myself from one of them, it could make me look bad to the judge."

Sleepy wanted to eat his lunch Rosie had left for him, and then get to the job. Then, when he had finished today's shift, he wanted to use one of his telephone calls to phone Brenda. He needed to let her know that the session went okay, and that he must have said something helpful, given the doctor's reaction.

When Brenda answered the phone, Sleepy's heart moved to his throat. He heard himself squeak, "Brenda?" Then he cleared his throat, and tried again, "Brenda? This is Theodore. How are you?"

"I'm fine. How about you?"

"I think I'm good. I had the session with the hypnotist today. My lawyer and the doctor seemed surprised at whatever I said. But in a good way. I think I helped. If so, maybe they'll be a little easier on me when we go back to the judge to try to get this other case thrown out. I hate to get my hopes up, but I swear, I believe things might be looking up for me."

There was a slight pause on the other end of the line. Then Brenda said, "For us."

He couldn't believe his ears. He didn't know what to say. Then she started laughing. "I got you with that one, didn't I?"

He chuckled. "You sure did. I hope you meant it. Did you mean it, Brenda?"

"Sure I did, Theodore. Otherwise, I wouldn't have said it. Now let's get to this judge, and get you out of there. Time's awasting, as the old folks say."

"Yeah, if we don't get me out of here soon, I'm going to be one of them."

Chapter Forty-Eight

Mercy left the interview with LeBlanc feeling better than she had in weeks. She wanted to do one more thing before she left the prison. She wanted to meet Nancy Carmichael and thank her for her work on LeBlanc's behalf. She went to the officer in charge of the visiting hall and asked if she might use his phone to call Ms. Carmichael. He looked like he didn't want to accommodate the request, but when she said she needed to give some information to the psychologist about her client, he agreed. When Carmichael answered, Mercy identified herself. There was a short pause before Carmichael spoke.

"What can I do for you, Ms. Johnson?"

"I just wanted to stop by and thank you for all your work on Mr. LeBlanc's behalf. I'm here at the prison and I just visited with him. Do you have a few moments ?"

Again, the pause. "Ms. Johnson, you caught me on a very busy day. I'm about to administer a battery of psychological tests to a very cranky inmate. If I delay, I'm afraid he'll change his mind. I really need to get these tests done and make some decisions about his situation."

Something in her tone troubled Mercy, but she certainly understood having a day that was already too crammed with appointments to add one more.

"I'm sorry you're so rushed today. I would like to meet you sometime. Maybe on another visit. I'll continue working on Mr. LeBlanc's behalf."

"That would be fine. Have a safe trip back to D.C."

Mercy thanked her and hung up. Something about Carmichael's voice was familiar, but she was sure they had never met. A thought occurred to Mercy. She had never asked LeBlanc to describe Carmichael. Maybe that would give her a clue as to why she sounded like someone Mercy ought to know.

She turned to the visiting hall officer.

"Can I trouble you to speak with him again, just briefly? I forgot to ask Mr. LeBlanc one question."

The officer grunted and spoke into his walkie-talkie. "Page LeBlanc to come back to the visiting hall."

In a few minutes Mercy heard a steel door slid open. LeBlanc got up from the bench just outside the door. The officer told him that his attorney wanted to see him again.

LeBlanc came back to the interview room, and he and Mercy went to the small attorney interviewing booth. "Theodore, there's something I've been meaning to ask you. I've never met Ms. Carmichael. I want to speak with her, and thank her for all her work with you. But she's busy today, giving tests to an inmate. It occurred to me that I don't really know anything about her. I don't even know what she looks like."

"She's real nice, Ms. Johnson. And she's pretty, too. She's short, and small. She has dark hair and looks Asian to me."

"Do you know where's she's from?"

"No. That's all I know about her. And she said her father died two years ago. She had a picture on her desk of a small boy in some kind of robe. I asked about him. I thought it might be her son. She said it was her dad. She said he died and that she kept the picture to remind her of when times were good for him. I didn't want to pry, so I didn't ask her anything else."

"No problem," Mercy said, getting up to leave the interview area. "It was just something I was curious about."

As she left the interview room she thanked the guard for calling LeBlanc back. As she left the prison, she called Sam. "Sam it's just a question floating around in my mind. Were you able to complete the background check on Nancy Carmichael? I just want to find out more about her. I tried to talk to her today and she said she didn't have time. So I asked Theodore some questions about her. I'd just like to follow up. No rush."

"It's a bit slow around here, with you down the country and me caught up."

Mercy laughed. "Caught up? Does that include the reports?"

Sam ignored the questions. "The State licensing agency needs her full name. Get me her middle name and I'm on it."

Chapter Forty-Nine

Sam walked into Mercy's office, papers in hand. She looked up from her file.

"Good news?"

Sam laughed. "Mercy, that's just like you. You're such a Pollyanna. You always expect good news, and in a business where it's in such short supply."

Mercy held out her hand. "Don't disappoint me, okay? I don't see why I shouldn't hope for the best. Lots of times, I'm right."

"Not this time, I'm afraid." Sam handed her the papers. "I checked every data base I know about. Those we pay subscriptions for, and the free ones. No one has a record for Nancy Carmichael beyond her masters degree at the University, and her state employment. I expanded the searches to include twenty years in each direction of her birth date—nothing. She has absolutely no web presence for most of her life. In this day and age, that is curious. It's also curious that the agency that licenses psychologists has no background information. She has a license, recently issued. That's all they know about her."

Mercy looked over the papers. "It's more than curious. It's downright baffling. Sam, I'm getting one of my warnings. I'm feeling mischief here. Something is just not right, and I don't like it."

"I know what you're thinking. You're thinking Helen. Given Sleepy's description. Small, pretty, Asian. And you thought you caught a hint of something in her voice. Add to that, she wouldn't meet with you. She was sick on the day you were in court with Sleepy. Throw in what that woman at the café told you. I can see why you are suspicious. But we don't have anything to hang those suspicions on. Somehow, I don't see you going to the FBI and talking about mischief."

Sam grinned at her, and she just glowered at him. He knew not to second-guess her intuitions, because she had been right too many times. But that didn't stop him from the occasional tease.

"Right. I wouldn't go to the FBI with that, or anything else. You know how I feel about the FBI. But, I would go to Will if I had enough to go on."

Sergeant William Banks was the head of the District of Columbia Narcotics Task Force. He was her nephew Toby's boss. Two years ago, the Task Force lost twenty kilograms of very pure heroin, labeled for sale on the street as "China White," to a woman named Helen Young. She was the daughter of a major heroin trafficker. He died in police custody. She was working with the police to nab her uncle, the brains behind the heroin operation, but instead she skipped with the drugs, leaving behind twenty freezer bags of flour in its place. Toby was involved in the investigation, and if Mercy's worst fears were right, involved with Helen, too. He was still not the same nearly two years later. Mercy wanted nothing more than that Helen remain as far away from her nephew as the small planet Earth would allow.

Sam was watching her carefully. "I know that look," he said. "You think she's back in the area. You're worried Toby could be mixed up with her again. You're on full tiger mama alert."

Mercy just scowled. "Stay here. I'm calling Banks."

Mercy dialed the office of the Narcotics Task Force. When the secretary answered, she asked for the sergeant. Within seconds, he was on the line.

"Will, how are you? I haven't talked to you in a long time."

"Yeah, I wondered what was up with the city's finest defense attorney."

"You're being facetious, but I'll take it. I'm in an optimistic mood today, as my ace investigator just pointed out."

"Nothing gets by Sam, does it?"

"Not much. Listen, I have something to run by you."

She told him about Nancy Carmichael, and her inability to pin down an identity. When she was finished, Banks was silent. For a minute, she thought they had been disconnected.

"Will? You there?"

"Yeah, Mercy. Just thinking. You know I trust that intuition of yours. I've seen it work too many times to discount it. But you don't have much to go on. Certainly not enough for us to start any kind of investigation. For now, can you just keep your suspicions under your hat? We don't want to cause trouble for the young woman."

"Sure. I wouldn't say anything to anybody but you, anyway. Just let me know if you learn anything more about her, will you? She's still a factor in a case I'm working on. I haven't gotten my client out of jail yet. I may need her help to do that. I don't want to be blindsided by something I should have known about her."

"Sure. I'll do that."

When Mercy ended the call, she felt some better. If her suspicions had any roots, they'd flower with whatever Will did to check out Nancy Carmichael. For now, she'd stop worrying about Toby.

Chapter Fifty

Banks knew why there was no history to be found. Nancy Carmichael was an AKA, also known as. She was using an alias. Banks called the agent in charge at the Washington Field Office of the FBI.

"George, Will Banks. How are things?"

George Ruffing was a former MPD Homicide investigator, one of the best. Will couldn't second-guess his decision to go to the FBI to sit behind a desk all day. The defection was easy enough to understand, given the pay differential between a Washington, D.C. police sergeant and a federal agent.

Ruffing seemed harassed. "Will, good to hear from you. I like to remember that there is an oasis of sanity in this bureaucratic sea of 'can't do' and 'won't do' over here."

Banks laughed. "Man, if you're homesick for the D.C. bureaucracy, the feds must be in worse shape than I figured."

"To put it mildly. What can I do for you?"

"I just got a call from Mercy Johnson. You remember her, from the China White case. Believe it or not, the thing we assumed would never happen, just did. She was retained to represent a prisoner down at Walton Correctional Institute. Turns out the guy had a psychological problem. Guess who was called in to evaluate and treat the guy?"

Ruffing groaned. "No."

"Yep. The subject handled it correctly. She didn't let Mercy see her. She spoke with Mercy on the phone a few times, but with her voice coaching, her voice has changed enough that all Mercy caught was a hint of something familiar. But this was a close call. What do you all want to do now? I don't like hiding the ball from Mercy. We have always had a straight-up relationship. She brought this to me because she knew I wanted to find Helen Young."

"Will, Ms. Johnson has to keep this to herself. Can you trust her to do that?"

"Sure, I trust her. But that isn't how this works. Witness Protection can't work if those few of us in the loop are trusting people outside the loop. That's why I called. I don't think Mercy will do anything to follow up on her suspicions, but I wanted to check with you to see if I should have a heart-to-heart with her, tell her that I can't give her any information, but ask for her commitment to discretion about Nancy Carmichael."

"Do you think that would work?"

"It would, except for two things. Carmichael is a potential witness in a State case where Mercy is trying to get a new trial for the client Carmichael evaluated. If Mercy has information that could reflect on Carmichael's credibility, she might worry that it could undermine her client's case."

"We can fix that. We can get the prosecutor down there just to agree to a new trial, then dismiss against the client. That's a whole lot easier than exposing Carmichael."

"Can you do that?"

"I think so. The woman who heads the DA's office down there has been cooperative in the past. She has a good head on her shoulders. I believe I could persuade her, especially if Mercy's motion is based on solid facts."

"I'm guessing it is."

"Well, then, problem one can go away. What about problem two?"

"That's one of your agents. A guy named Nash."

Ruffing sputtered. "What the hell is that nincompoop doing on a State case?"

"Don't know. I guess it's some kind of Task Force thing. You know how the Task Force likes to get into local business, get more creds for when budget time rolls around."

Ruffing ignored the jab. "I'll talk to the regional director, Jim Messina. Tell him to rein Nash in. If Nash gets his hands on any information about this protection arrangement, he can ruin everything. We can't expose Carmichael like that. The Asian gang that took her mother is still operating. We are trying to shut them down, but without Carmichael's cooperation, we don't have much chance of success."

"You don't trust Nash enough to fill him in on what's going on, and direct him to keep quiet?"

"Nash is a real idiot. He got run out of the New York office because he let a suspect get hold of his service weapon, and the suspect used it to shoot another agent. He was supposed to be put where he couldn't do any harm. Apparently, there is no such place. So the answer is no, I can't trust him with information about this protection arrangement. I'll ask his boss to shut him down. Tell him the investigation into Carmichael is off limits. If he violates the rule, we fire his behind. I heard that is what the Director wanted to do when he screwed up in New York. But someone went to bat for him. I don't think that will happen twice."

"If you hope to keep this thing from blowing up on us, you'd better get to that local DA, and spring Mercy's client. That ought to eliminate any need on her part to investigate Carmichael."

"Done. He's about to be a free man. He'll never know just how lucky he got."

Banks laughed. "That's alright. He'll think Mercy worked a miracle. She has, in fact. Just not this time."

Chapter Fifty-One

Mercy was shaking her head as she walked down the hall to Sam's office. He looked up from his computer. "What's that look for? What did I do, or not do?"

"Sam, it isn't always about you, you know. In fact, it's rarely about you. I'm just puzzled, and I thought you might have some ideas. I just got a call from the DA about LeBlanc's case. The State has reviewed his file from the B & E trial. They are going to concede my motion for new trial. In fact, they are going to concede the motion, and then dismiss the indictment. When the paperwork gets filed, which should be any time, LeBlanc will be a free man."

Sam smiled widely. "Wow. I can't believe it. I figured we could win eventually. I just never figured the State to cave like this."

"Me either. That's why I'm so puzzled. I don't want to sound ungrateful, but why? It's not been my experience that the State is eager to overturn convictions."

Sam nodded. "It's clear, Mercy. They are protecting somebody, or something. There's some piece of information they don't want us to have, something they don't want us to know. I'd bet that's behind what looks like generosity on the State's part."

"I'm betting you are right. And I'm betting it has to do with our Ms. Carmichael. I tell you Sam, that woman worries me. I just don't know what to do next...."

"What did Banks have to say about your worries?"

"He said I should keep them to myself, basically. But then this dismissal falls into our laps. I think you are right that there's a connection. Now I don't need her as a witness, so now I have no reason to poke around in her background."

"So what do we do now?"

"We don't do anything. Our client's case is resolved. I've alerted Banks to my suspicions. As LeBlanc's lawyers, we have accomplished our goal. As a good citizen, I reported to the proper authorities. Unless she shows up somewhere where she can snare Toby, she's history, as far as I am concerned."

"For her sake, she best not come near your nephew. If she is anything like Helen Young, she's smart enough to know that."

"For all our sakes, I surely hope so."

Mercy went back to her office. She picked up the phone to call Walter. Then she put the receiver back in its cradle. Call him and tell him what? That her sense of impending mischief is acting up again? That she has no real facts to support her suspicions? No, she wouldn't worry Walter.

She called Brenda LeBlanc to give her the good news. Then she called Sam. "Sam, can you get Rosie's file and make sure we have all the documents we need? And find out all you can about the governor's aide. Let's plan to meet tomorrow and go over his case."

"You bet."

Mercy let herself out of the office and headed for the subway. On the way, she called Walter. "What's for dinner?"

"Mama's at church. I think she meant for us to fend for ourselves. What were you thinking about dinner?"

"Call that little French place in Adams Morgan we like so much. Get us a reservation for seven thirty. And pour me a glass of wine. I'll be home in twenty minutes. We are celebrating."

"That's always good news. But what are we celebrating?"

"Life, my dear husband. Life."

Chapter Fifty-Two

Agent Nash was pacing his office, staring at a diagram on the wall. He'd placed all the players in the prison escape on the diagram, and charted their probable roles. Hastings was at the center, and coming off from Hastings like spokes on a wheel were the other inmates involved in the escape. He crossed through Theodore LeBlanc's name, but not because he wanted to. He was under orders from higher up. Just the memory of it made him furious all over again. He'd been called to his supervisor's office last week, but the indignation he felt was a fresh as if it was yesterday.

"Agent Nash, this is Jim Messina. How are you?"

Messina was the regional commander of the FBI. He never called to chat. Nash must be in some kind of trouble. Before he could think of what Messina would want with him, Messina continued, "I have been following your investigation of the Harkness killing. I've just spoken with the State prosecutor. He tells me there is evidence that Harkness was shot by a gunman his wife hired. What's the story?"

Nash tried not to stammer when he answered. "Well, sir, that's what this convict said, and he was on the bus. He's the one we got the doc to hypnotize. He claimed to have heard a conversation where the killers mentioned Harkness's wife, and a contract. But you know how that is, sir. These cons say whatever suits them at the time."

Messina's tone was firmer now. "Nash, are you telling me you don't credit what LeBlanc said under hypnosis?"

Nash wondered that Messina knew Sleepy's real name. Why was he taking such an interest in this case, Nash wondered. But he answered with what he hoped was a plausible explanation.

"Sir, I am not sure what I credit here. I arranged the hypnosis session. We used our own doctor, so we know he's someone we can trust. LeBlanc seemed to be recalling events of the shooting. But he might be smart enough to make something up. I'm just not sure."

Messina was sounding frustrated now. "So what would make you sure, Nash? What can happen to this investigation to make you sure that you focused on the wrong suspect, that you ignored credible evidence of his sleep disorder, including evidence from the prison psychologist, that you hounded his aging aunt and his ex-wife, and that you overstepped just about every boundary we use in conducting investigations? Any thoughts on that one, Nash?"

Nash was mad now. He may have messed up, but he wasn't taking the heat for this one. No way. He got approval all up and down the line. Now would be the time to remind Messina of that fact.

"Sir," he began, sounding calmer than he felt. "I spoke to several people who knew LeBlanc and who said he had a sleep problem. I also spoke with the prison psychologist, who thought he had something called narcolepsy. But knowing how some of these guys fake illnesses, and knowing that some of them are academy award performers, I didn't want to accept that without further investigation. Yes, I spoke with his family. I got approval for that. And yes, I spoke with his ex-wife. I got approval for that, too. I believe my investigation was thorough, and I stand by it."

Messina did not respond immediately. When he did, the sarcasm was evident. "Let me get this straight, Nash. You say you spoke with his family. You got approval for that. Did you get approval to threaten an elderly woman with arrest as an accessory to murder? Did you get approval to threaten LeBlanc's ex-wife, and even her fiancé? Did you get approval from any supervising officer in this agency to set in motion a prison war by pitting one suspect against another? I can answer those questions, Nash, because I'm your commanding officer. You never asked me about any of those tactics. You knew damn well not to let me know you were going so far out of bounds in this investigation. Your record reflects a serious lack of judgment, Nash. I want you in my office next Tuesday, prepared to go over every inch of this investigation, and to answer the questions I've put to you today, as well as any others that might arise after I review further the various reports I've received about your conduct."

Messina paused for Nash's response.

"Yes, sir." was all Nash said.

Messina continued, "And, Nash, you may bring an attorney with you to the meeting if you desire to do so. In fact, that might not be a bad idea, all things considered."

Nash was furious. This damn pencil pusher was second-guessing his field work!

How dare he? Messina better believe he'd bring a lawyer. He'd bring whatever he needed to bring, to clear this situation up. He could not afford any more blotches on his record.

Where could they banish him to, that would be worse than this hellhole? Siberia was out of their jurisdiction. Maybe they'd fire him. Maybe he'd lose his pension. Well, he wouldn't allow that to happen. He would fight every inch of the way. He might not win, but he'd tie them up in knots long enough to get to retirement. He was just five years from full retirement. Any yo-yo could prolong a lawsuit for that long. He had been saving his money for a houseboat when he retired. Maybe he'd have to spend it on lawyers, but he was damn sure not going to roll over on this one. Not on a bet. He'd fix that Messina cretin. He hated these agency bureaucrats. Most of them hadn't worked an investigation in years. They forgot what it was like on the streets, but he intended to remind them. He went to his file cabinet, and pulled out a folder. In it he kept all the requests for approval—to use the psychologist, to travel to interview the aunt and ex-wife, to work with the local DA, to work with the corrections staff. He'd covered his butt. That was one thing he knew how to do. Let them come after him. He was ready. His rant was interrupted when Messina shouted his name.

"Nash. Are you still there?"

"Yes, sir. I'm still here. Was there anything else you wanted, sir?"

Messina lowered his voice. "Yes, Nash, there is something more I want you to do. I want you to give up this investigation you started about Ms. Carmichael."

"But sir…." *Nash began.*

"Nash, you listen to me. I want you to forget anything you learned about her. She's the psychologist at the State prison. Nothing more. I won't have her reputation ruined by your poking around about her. Are we clear? You are not authorized to conduct any investigation whatsoever into Nancy Carmichael, via internet, in person, by telephone, by mail. In any way. Are we clear?" *Messina enunciated each word of the question so that a five year old would have answered yes.*

"Yes, sir. We are clear."

"Good. I'll see you next week."

Nash hung up. Then he grabbed the phone off the desk, ripped the cord from the phone jack on the wall, threw the phone in the wastebasket, and stomped out of his office. Why was he being handcuffed in this investigation? Who cares about Carmichael's rights? He longed for the good old days of the Bureau, before a bunch of wusses got all caught up in whose rights were being violated. Nobody worried about any of that when he started at the Bureau. And damned if he'd worry about it. Whatever the boss didn't want him to know about Carmichael, he wanted to know. When he found it, whatever "it" was, he'd go above Messina's head. Messina might give him a dressing down next week. But Nash would be standing, long after that bureaucrat was back on his farm shoveling manure.

Today reviewing last week's meeting stoked Nash's courage. Now he just needed a battle plan.

ABOUT THE AUTHOR

Reita Pendry was born in the mountains of North Carolina and raised in Charlotte, North Carolina. She graduated from the University of North Carolina School of Law and worked for three years in Winston-Salem before moving to the District of Columbia. She practiced law in Washington, D.C. for twenty-five years. For twenty of those years, she was a criminal defense attorney. She now lives and works in Charlotte, where her family resides. Reita is at work on her third novel.

Coming Soon...

Two Wrongs
A Mercy Johnson Novel

When Assistant United States Attorney Laura Moss kills her husband, she believes she is killing an intruder who is attacking her daughter, Anna. Only after the fact does she learn that Anna and Laura's husband, Anna's stepfather, were lovers. Anna, always the problem child, tells the police that Laura knew about the affair and threatened to kill her husband before. Anna becomes the government's primary witness against Laura, and Mercy Johnson must disentangle this complex family relationship before she can defend Laura for first-degree premeditated murder. Her biggest obstacle: Laura's love for her child and her determination to protect Anna, even at the ultimate cost to herself.

Made in the USA
Charleston, SC
30 June 2012